HUDDLED MASSES

BY DEREK CICCONE

OTHER BOOKS BY DEREK CICCONE

Officer Jones (a JP Warner story)

Painless

The Trials of Max Q

The Truant Officer

The Heritage Paper

Kristmas Collins

PART ONE —

AVENGING ANGEL

CHAPTER ONE

Scottsdale, Arizona

December 21

There was blood in the water.

"Xavier Gallegos. Thirty-two, born in Mexico, came to the US when he was three. Had some run-ins with the law in his teens, but clean since joining the military right after high school," the young FBI agent briefed him.

"At least until he gunned down three people in the mall with a sniper rifle," Special Agent Hawkins responded with a sigh, unable to take his eyes off the lifeless shooter floating in the fountain. "You said he was in the military?"

"Served in both Iraq and Afghanistan, but I can't tell you much about his service. He'd been living in Phoenix the last two years, after re-joining civilian life, and made a living cleaning pools."

"What's the holdup on his military record?"

"Most of his file is classified."

Hawkins was first surprised, then annoyed. "I've got three bodies here, and mass hysteria about to break out around the country four days before Christmas, so put in a call to the Director and get it declassified."

"I did—and I was told those decisions were made, to use the Director's words, above his pay grade."

Above the Director of the FBI? Hawkins' face tensed as he continued staring at the dead man. Five hours after the shooting and they still had a lot more questions than answers. He and his team had been flown in from DC this morning, while the Phoenix-based agents interviewed potential witnesses and gathered information.

His partner, Clarisse Johnson, joined him at the edge of the fountain. "What's it say on his shirt?" she asked, pointing at the simple black T-shirt with block lettering. It was soaked with the bloodied water of the fountain, making the words difficult to decipher.

"It reads *Huddled Masses* across the front," the agent replied. "With *Immigrant* on the back."

"The new Arizona immigration laws are controversial, could it be related to that?" Hawkins asked.

"His parents were busted for drugs and sent back to Mexico when Gallegos was seven—he remained here, raised by an aunt in Guadalupe. And while we haven't ruled out any motive, one of his victims, Delores Rodriguez, was of Mexican descent, so that wouldn't be a fit."

"I'd put my money on mental health," Clarisse added. "Which might be why they don't want us to see his military files. If he had previous issues, the quiet crisis of soldiers returning with broken brains just got real loud, real quick."

"Did he say anything when the security guard confronted him?" Hawkins asked.

They instinctively looked up to the third floor where Gallegos had positioned himself—for someone as skilled as him, it was like shooting fish in a barrel. If not for the courageous security guard there was no way to know how many fatalities they'd be talking about.

"She found the janitor tied up and gagged in a third-floor closet. She then did a loop of the area, and came across a roped-off section with signs warning of a wet floor, and not to pass. Further on she found a discarded janitor uniform next to a mop bucket, which Gallegos had used for disguise. At that point, she started hearing the screams. She stepped around the corner to witness a man standing at the railing, aiming at the shoppers below."

The agent pointed at the rifle that lay on the ground near the fountain, in the exact position it had landed. "She rushed him, and was able to shove him over before he could turn the gun on her. He died instantly upon impact— and we left him as is until you arrived. So to answer your question, there wasn't much communication between the two."

"Is there video?" Hawkins asked.

"From multiple cameras. Both the victims and the shooter. We're merging the different angles right now, to provide you the best view."

Clarisse thought for a moment. "I find it interesting that he didn't kill the janitor. And if his goal was to murder as many as possible, he could have taken out another ten or twenty, easily. I think we're talking about targeted hits."

They took a seat on one of the mall benches, usually reserved for tired husbands who couldn't keep up with their shop-till-they-drop wives. Hawkins was growing tired himself … of the senseless killing. In October it was Grady Benson, the serial vigilante killer. November brought the missing child case in Ohio that had a bad ending, which most of them did, and just when he thought he might get a December reprieve, along came Xavier Gallegos.

"We agree that he was targeting his victims, or at least one … Taryn James," the agent said.

He sped through her bio. She was the wife of Walter James III, known to his friends as Wally. He also happened to be one of the richest men in Arizona. Taryn was the owner of an upscale boutique called East of Rodeo— named after the street in Beverly Hills. East of Rodeo had become very trendy within wealthy circles the past couple of years, and had expanded to Manhattan, Chicago, South Beach, and Paris. But the original was located in this Scottsdale mall. This made sense, since Wally James owned the mall. In fact, his grandfather, the first Walter James, was credited with being the originator of the American mall.

The agent displayed a photo of Taryn on a tablet device. She looked like she was purchased straight out of the trophy wife catalog.

"She had a colorful background prior to becoming Mrs. James. She was a dancer at a popular Scottsdale strip club, and was arrested on multiple occasions for robbery. Her M.O. was to bring out-of town businessmen back to her place to do things that wouldn't end up on the expense report. But they would get more than they bargained for, as she would drug and rob them— betting that they'd be too embarrassed or scared to go to the police. But a few of them valued their wallets over their wife's reaction, hence, the arrests."

"Sounds like she landed on her feet ... or on her back," Hawkins said.

"Could you show just a smidgen of respect for the victim?" Clarisse responded with a disapproving look. Their relationship made oil and water look like Romeo and Juliet.

The agent continued, "Once Wally James came into her life that arrest record got cleaned up real quick. But sometimes you can't completely scrub the past, so we are doing a thorough search into her previous life—maybe she rolled the wrong guy, or ruined a marriage, who knows."

Hawkins shook his head. "The husband is the target, not her. Always follow the money, and nobody has more money around here than Wally James."

"Any connection between James and Gallegos?" Clarisse asked.

The agent nodded. "We reviewed security video, and found that Gallegos had been tracking her. Store cameras caught him trailing her last week during one of her many shopping sprees, and he was spotted outside the gate of their home in Paradise Valley. He also made two stops at East of Rodeo the last couple weeks, and he doesn't strike me as an upscale boutique kind of guy.

"Another factor was that he shot Taryn James first, the moment she stepped out of her store, which was his most difficult target. If he'd started with the others, she might have gotten scared and ran back into the store, and out of his scope. It was like he was waiting for her."

"Tell me about the other victims. There's got to be a missing link," Hawkins said.

"Delores Rodriguez was Christmas shopping with her two children. And Elisa Webster was a local designer who was known for her handbags. She had been at the mall to check on stores that carried her line. The only link so far, is that both women were carrying bags from East of Rodeo, as they'd earlier made purchases there."

"Sounds like we've got a lot of work to do," Hawkins said.

"But this might help," Agent Hendrickson, the third member of their team said, as he fast-walked toward them. Tall and thin with an unkempt beard, he looked much like Shaggy from *Scooby Doo*.

He handed Hawkins a piece of paper. "We located the shooter's vehicle in the parking lot. This note was taped to a Yellow Pages book on the passenger's seat."

"Yellow Pages? Was he searching ads for a getaway driver?"

"Based on the letter, I think he planned to die for his cause," Hendrickson said. "So maybe he was pricing funeral homes."

"His cause?"

Hendrickson motioned for him to read.

I was brought to this country as a young boy, believing in the words posted at its entrance. But it was a lie. America is not about freedom and opportunity for all men. It is a place where the Haves enslave the Have Nots, and the chosen elite decide who stays and who goes ... who lives and who dies. The only way to stop this tyranny is to stand up to it, and we have been silent for too long. So let this be a warning that Huddled Masses will no longer have silent lips.

It was about money—just in a different way that Hawkins thought. He flipped the note over, where a portion of the sonnet "New Colossus" was scribbled. The same words that grace the Statue of Liberty.

Give me Your Tired, Your Poor, Your Huddled Masses yearning to breathe free, the wretched refuse of your teeming shore. Send these, the homeless, tempest-tost to me, I lift my lamp beside the golden door!

Hawkins got the sinking feeling that today's shooting wasn't an isolated incident, and there would be a lot more bodies washing up on those teeming shores … or in fountains at the mall.

CHAPTER 2

Rockfield, Connecticut

February 25

As someone who'd spent decades connecting my future to the past, the present wasn't my comfort zone.

To further complicate things, I'd set up camp the last six months in a place where memories were hiding behind each corner. And no place was more infiltrated than the small gymnasium of Samerauk Elementary School.

I took a quick glance to the far end of the gym, which was anchored by a small stage where Gwen and I once starred in the fourth grade play about nutrition, and felt as if I was test-driving a time machine.

In the opposite corner hung the rope we climbed in gym class. I still hadn't figured out the point of that exercise, but it did lead to a still-talked-about moment when Bobby Maloney grew too scared to make his way back down the rope, and the Rockfield Fire Department had to be called. It was a memory that always brought a smile to my face, so whenever I felt J-News trying to rise to the surface, I looked to the rope, and felt a calm wash over me.

The echo of the referee's whistle drew me back to the present. My usually unflappable assistant, Eliot, blew out a frustrated breath as Madison, our point guard, sailed another errant pass out of bounds, returning possession to New Milford Elementary. Despite the optimism leading up to today's game, it wasn't shaping up to be our day.

I peeked at the old scoreboard—the same one that was here when I attended SES, seemingly centuries ago—we were still only down by six points, even if it felt like a hundred.

The most frustrating part of coaching was that I wanted to be out there helping the kids. But all I could do was watch as New Milford's best player took about ten steps without a dribble, and scored another basket to build the lead to eight. "That's traveling," I barked at the referee, and it once again fell on deaf ears.

"Coach Warner—I think it's time to go to our secret weapon," Eliot suggested.

I smiled—I really liked the way this kid thought. But that wasn't to say there was no point of contention between us. "I thought we went over this, I'm JP ... Coach Warner is my brother."

The real Coach Warner was my older brother Ethan, who besides being both a history teacher and head football coach at Rockfield High, was also the Director of Athletics for the region. This meant the Samerauk Elementary girls' basketball team came under his jurisdiction. And he somehow convinced me that to keep busy during my transition from international news correspondent to retired farmer in my hometown, I should coach a basketball team made up of ten-year-old girls, including my niece, Ella. And while at first this seemed to rank with the many other poor choices I've made over the years, it turned out to only be a bad decision for our opponents, as we were one win away from an undefeated season.

We even captured the notice of the local media, who were here to cover the big game. Sure, the local media is made up solely of my girlfriend, Gwen Delaney, and I had to pull every string I could think of to make it happen—

I'm already booked for the ballet next month—but sometimes you got to pay the price to tell a great story.

I glanced up at Gwen, who was sitting up in the rickety, pullout bleachers, and typing away on her laptop. Even in her minimalist look of baggy sweater and little makeup, with her raven hair in a ponytail, she was still the most beautiful creature I'd ever seen.

Next to her sat my mother, who took time away from running the Rockfield Historical Society to watch her granddaughter's final game of the season. And on Gwen's other side was our biggest fan ... literally. My longtime confidant, and former professional wrestler, Jeff "Coldblooded" Carter, who was in town to attend tonight's charity dinner for Byron Jasper's foundation. I almost expected to hear his booming voice echoing through the gym, threatening physical harm to the referee for the missed call. But he'd been rather subdued since his arrival last night, at least for Carter, with his attention focused on his latest girlfriend, Kate.

And while Kate looked like a mousy kindergarten teacher, wearing an outfit that only the Church Lady could love, Carter had proudly informed me that she was better known as Mistress Kate, the world's most renowned dominatrix. I don't know how they determine such things, but I tend not to argue with human brick walls like Carter, so I took his word for it.

The rest of today's crowd was made up of a smattering of mothers and students. One of the few fathers on hand was the rope climber extraordinaire himself, Bobby Maloney, who had resigned his post as Rockfield's first selectman, providing him the free time to attend his daughter's games.

Eliot began tripping over himself apologizing, while still referring to me as Coach Warner, and my patience grew thin. "Are you going to do it or not?"

He leaped to his feet and called out "Z" in his squeaky ten-year-old voice. Z stood for zone, which was a defense that packed our team close to the basket, in theory, forcing our opponents to shoot from the perimeter. And at this exact time in the afternoon, the small gym windows let in the low

February sun at a perfect angle, causing enough distraction to make shooting from the outside near impossible. Home court advantage.

But there was no defense against this incompetent referee. As Ella attempted to drive to the basket for an easy lay-up, an opponent shoved her to the ground. Not only did the referee not call a foul, but had the audacity to call traveling on Ella.

Ella picked herself off the court and jogged back down to the other end of the court, accepting the decision with dignity. It was clear that she'd avoided the JP portion of the Warner family gene pool, which would likely serve her well in life.

Me, on the other hand …

"You've got to be kidding me!" my words ricocheted off the gymnasium walls.

The referee ignored me, adding to my irritation, and I rose to my feet. The slow boil was about to spill over—my six months in Rockfield hadn't solved my internal struggle as well as I'd hoped.

I repeated my complaint, even louder, which this time drew his attention. But all he did was point at the bench. "You need to sit back down, Coach Warner."

I took a step out onto the court … toward the referee. He blew the whistle, but it was going to take a lot more than that to stop me.

When I reached him, I realized that I'd misjudged how large a man he was—about my height, six foot, but double my width. "Why don't you take off the rest of the game? You've already slept through the first half!"

"Watch yourself, Coach Warner," he warned.

"Give him a T, Uncle Greg," one of the New Milford girls shouted out, lobbying for a technical foul.

The comment pushed me over the edge—the *unbiased* referee was related to a member of the other team?—and words began streaming out of my mouth so fast I couldn't keep track of the insults.

His face turned bright red. "You're out of here! Ejected!"

"I'm not going anywhere," I fired back. And to prove I was serious, I took off my designer sports coat and tossed it on the ground.

That's when I felt a tug on my back—someone had grabbed me by the suspenders and was pulling me away from the fracas. It was Eliot. I had instructed him that if I ever lost my mind he was to grab me and save me from myself. I think he thought I was kidding.

He was about ninety pounds, most of it glasses, which were the first things I was able to grab hold of. I'd gotten him a full makeover for the coaching gig—custom fitted suit and stylish hairstyle. The one stumbling block was that his mother said he wasn't old enough for contact lenses. She probably was regretting that decision right now.

I threw the glasses at the referee. "Why don't you try these? Maybe they'll help you see better!"

They bounced off his shoulder and fell to the ground. I felt immediate remorse for bringing Eliot's eyewear into my battle and attempted to retrieve them. That's when I felt a much stronger tug on my shoulder, and I knew it wasn't Eliot.

I turned to see a grinning Carter. "And here I thought I just came for some boring charity dinner."

"They're going to need charity for you if you don't get your hands off of me."

He boomed a laugh. "It's good to see my friend JP Warner back—was wondering if I'd ever see him again."

"Let me go," I said, hopelessly trying to squirm out of his tight grip, as he treated me like one of his challengers in the wrestling ring.

"I got this, Carter," a female voice instructed. "Step back."

I looked to see uniformed officer, Betsy O'Rourke, who was working security at the game.

Carter had gained a respect for the local police during his last visit to town—at least the ones not named Officer Jones—so he obeyed the order, and released me. This gave me the split-second I needed. I made a dash for the glasses, and was able to return them to Eliot before I was escorted away.

"You're in charge," I told him before I was dragged off.

He looked like a frightened squirrel. "You want me to be the head coach?"

"You've been preparing for this all year—you're ready. Just keep in mind that we're only down eight points. So gather the girls around, and make sure everyone is calm and focused on the task at hand."

"Should we play the 'Z'?" he asked, as Officer O'Rourke began to escort me away.

"You're in charge, Eliot … it's up to you."

I looked to the spot near the stage where Ethan had been standing, which was no longer occupied—not a good sign. I then glanced up into the stands, hoping for guidance from my two favorite girls, but there would be none. My mother looked distressed, while Gwen never took her eyes off her computer screen, continuing to type away. I figured she was probably signing up for one of those online dating services, looking for a new boyfriend.

CHAPTER 3

I was led into the hallway, which smelled just as it did when I was a student here. I had always associated the smell with the freshness of youth, but with the wisdom of age I realized it was just industrial cleaner. Carter was right behind me, watching my back as he'd always done.

"He's all yours," Officer O'Rourke told Ethan, as she dropped me off in the coach's office. Ethan sat behind a cluttered desk, wearing a green V-neck sweater with a gold Rockfield High logo on the left breast. I recognized his disapproving look.

The windowless office was mostly used as a changing room for coaches and phys-ed teachers. The thin walls amplified the sounds of the neighboring gymnasium, in which the game had resumed—the bouncing basketball sounding like a snare drum, sneakers squealing, parents yelling. I still had a nervous twitch from my years as a war correspondent when it came to loud noises and confined spaces. And when Carter shut the door behind us, I felt like a trapped rat.

"Did you know he was that girl's uncle?" I went on the offensive.

"I didn't, but I've known Greg Murphy for years, and I truly doubt anything conspiratorial was going on."

"We can watch the tape if you'd like, it was blatant."

"Blatant incompetence, perhaps. I don't know if you're aware of this, JP, but the best referees in the world tend not to work girl's elementary school games on Friday afternoons, for fifty bucks."

"You paid that clown fifty bucks? Mom and Gwen could have done better."

"Maybe, but that doesn't change the fact that your behavior was unacceptable."

A knock on the door was followed by the entrance of a man in a spiffy suit. "You must be kidding me," I muttered, just loud enough for Bobby Maloney to hear.

"What are you doing here, Maloney?" Ethan asked.

"I'm representing the concerned parents, who have great worry over JP Warner's coaching style, and frankly, his mental stability."

You would think that saving him from Officer Jones would have bought me at least a year of goodwill, but I barely got four months. Part of our agreement for keeping his dirty little secret—specifically the truth about the Lamar Thompson case, and the false testimony that had sent Lamar to prison—was that he would step away from Rockfield politics. But I had the feeling he was itching to find a way back, and saw an opportunity to discredit the man standing in the way of his comeback.

Maloney looked to Carter. "What are *you* doing here?"

"I'm JP's legal representative."

"You're not a lawyer."

"If you don't leave, I'm going to show you the law."

When Ethan threatened to call Officer O'Rourke if they *both* didn't leave, they came to a peace accord, or at least an accord, and agreed to exit stage left. When the door slammed behind them, it left me and Ethan, one on one.

"You know what the sad part is, JP? I get daily notes from parents, complimenting you on what a great job you've done with their daughters … how they've seen a positive change in them during the season."

"I'm sorry that things escalated like that, but you knew I was a lunatic when you hired me."

"I don't doubt your mental instability, but that's not what this is about."

"So you're saying I can't plead insanity? Don't make me go get my legal representative ..."

"Joke it off all you want, but I've seen the change in your personality the last couple months, and I know what the problem is."

"The problem is that crooked referee who tried to steal the game from us."

"No, it's that you're happy—for the first time in a long time—and it's scaring the crap out of you."

"Did you actually see what happened in there? Because I can guarantee you that happiness played no role in it."

"You were riding such a whirlwind—held hostage, returning home, Noah's death, and getting him justice—that you didn't have a chance to think. But once the holidays were over, and you were able to take inventory on your life, you got hit with a big dose of reality. And you realized that you had finally achieved your dream, which was to be back together with Gwen. Problem is, it's a lot easier to dream the dream than to live it, JP, and it has you spooked. So I think you're trying to sabotage things—that way you can go back to the safety of dreaming, instead of living."

"What are you talking about? I'm completely happy with Gwen ... and if I didn't want to be here, I'd be gone."

He just shrugged without saying a word. I hated when he did that.

"Is this my punishment ... having to be psych-analyzed by my brother? Because given a choice, I'd much rather be arrested," I said.

"No—you will be suspended for the first three games of next season. That's your punishment."

"Next season? What makes you think I'm going to be coaching here next year?"

"That's what you need to figure out, little brother."

CHAPTER 4

After leaving my sentencing hearing with a three-game suspension, a headache, and a lot to think about, things turned for the better.

I was able to watch through a small window in the gymnasium door, and witness the Samerauk Elementary girls basketball team complete an undefeated season with a furious comeback, capped off by a game-winning shot by Ella.

They leaped into each other's arms with pure joy and sung out like a bunch of mini Taylor Swifts. But the best part was when they raised Eliot up on their shoulders. In a few short months, he'd gone from the kid who almost went into cardiac arrest when a girl spoke to him, to the conquering elementary-school hero.

Watching their jubilation, I wanted to scream out to them, implore them to savor it, as the world would soon steal away that feeling. I would be reminded of this tonight when I attended a dinner to raise money for those who can no longer leap with joy. This included one of my best friends, Byron Jasper, whose paralysis I'm responsible for.

I made my way to the now dark parking lot and found my Jeep—a handed-down Warner mode of transportation for decades. All of us have driven it at one time or another—my youngest brother, Noah, was the last. I could afford a much newer and sleeker vehicle, having once been the highest-paid person in the news industry, but in some strange way it felt like driving the old Jeep was a tribute to Noah.

The drive was less than ten minutes from the school to Skyview Drive. When I ascended the steep, frozen driveway, I noticed the *Rockfield Gazette* van, which belongs to the local newspaper that Gwen edits, writes, sells, and even delivers on Sundays.

The light was on in the cozy A-frame as I stepped out of the Jeep. While I could have used my mother's comfort at this moment, I walked by. I technically don't live with my parents, but to be honest, if you can throw a rock from where you live and break a window in your parents' home, then you live with your parents.

I carefully maneuvered over an icy slate path to the colonial, where I've been residing since my return to Rockfield. It was built when my family outgrew the A-frame after Noah's arrival, but my parents returned to the A-frame after the kids left the nest. I'd looked into buying some farm property last fall, but as Ethan noted, the last six months have been a roller coaster ride, and looking for property in the winter wasn't ideal. I'm sure my critics, those who don't believe I'm long for Rockfield, see my lack of roots as confirmation that I will soon be on my way.

Gwen and I split time between here and the house across town that she shares with her father and younger brother. And while my living situation isn't ideal, it does provide more privacy than hers, so we spend the majority of our time here.

I went upstairs to the bedroom. It had remained untouched during my years away, like a time capsule. The Michael Jordan and Bon Jovi posters still hung on the wall upon my return, and a Rubik's Cube sat just where I'd left it on my desk. But Gwen had recently transformed it into a grownup room—paintings replacing posters, and a canopy bed now in the place of the floor mattress I'd been sleeping on. I am told that I had agreed to this.

I stepped inside an empty room. I could hear Gwen in the connected bathroom, preparing for tonight's event. She had remained eerily calm during my meltdown, which should have been a good sign, but the years have proven that this can be a much more precarious position for me than if she were shouting angrily. There are many differences between the current Gwen Delaney in her late thirties, and the girl I was inseparable from during our youth, but this trait has remained a constant.

"I was thinking about wearing a straitjacket tonight instead of my tux," I said through the bathroom door, testing the waters.

"Oh, good, you're here. I was worried that I'd have to bail you out of jail ... and we're running late as it is."

"So how did the article come out?"

"Let's just say, it wrote itself."

"I was thinking you might want to turn it into a screenplay. Young girls overcome their psycho coach in pursuit of an undefeated season, winning on a dramatic last-second shot. It has Disney movie written all over it."

"From where I was sitting, it more resembled a Stephen King novel."

This was definitely not trending in my favor. I checked my watch, which told me that it was time for an apology. "I'm sorry ... I got a little carried away."

"Ya think?" she said, and stepped out of the bathroom in a floor-length, sparkling purple gown. She accessorized it with white elbow-length gloves, either to give it an old-time, classic feel, or so she wouldn't leave fingerprints when she strangled me. The ponytail was gone—her shoulder-length hair looked like she just walked out of the priciest Manhattan salon.

I smiled at her. "And the screenplay ends with the winning coach getting to take the most beautiful girl in town to the dance."

"Then I guess Eliot has a hot date planned for tonight."

I turned serious, staring intently at her. "Just so you know, I'm not afraid of happiness."

"That's very courageous of you, JP."

"And I'm not going anywhere."

Her face creased with irritation. "If I took the time to put on this dress, you *are* going tonight. I know it's tough to see Byron like this, but you can't always run away from reality."

"That's not what I meant."

She sighed. "JP—we really don't have time for this right now. Your tux is hanging in the bathroom."

The last time I'd worn a tuxedo was a year ago when I was still a GNZ correspondent, and I gave in to Lauren Bowden's insistence that I attend the Cable News Awards with her. I believe we won the prestigious "Best Comedy while Impersonating Journalism" award, but lost out to the heavy competition for the "Most Ridiculous Shouting Match Disguised as a Political Debate" category ... but we were happy to be nominated.

When I came out of the bathroom dressed as James Bond, I didn't receive the same "wow" treatment I gave my date. Gwen greeted me by looking at the clock, and informing, "Carter will be here any minute."

And sure enough, a loud honk of the horn from the Coldblooded Cruiser announced that it had pulled into port. I had no idea how he was able to back his thirty-five-foot luxury bus up the icy driveway, but nobody would ever doubt that the man has unique talents.

Carter wore a similar tuxedo to mine, except his had no sleeves. And Mistress Kate was looking much more mistress-y in a skin-tight cat suit. Her flaming red hair had been unleashed from the winter cap that had covered it at the game. Perhaps those who don't donate enough tonight will receive a trip to the torture dungeon, where she will get them to reconsider, I thought.

My parents came out to meet us, and took photos like we were going to the prom. My father, Peter, was in his typical cheery mood, shaking hands and slapping backs like the longtime politician that he was, while my mother maintained the same concerned look she had at the game. She tended to be more passive-aggressive when it came to her displaying her displeasure with me—she didn't talk to me for weeks when I'd returned from Serbia last year, after I'd almost gotten myself killed ... again.

Once picture-time ended, we boarded the bus. It was only seventy miles from Rockfield to Manhattan, but it seemed galaxies away. Gwen was upbeat during the ride, joking with Carter, and striking up a conversation with Kate, whom she surprisingly had a lot in common with—beyond both of them having crazy boyfriends. But I was thinking back to that school play, and was reminded that Gwen was never the best actor. I could tell something was bothering her.

I stared out the window, watching the rural countryside turn into the concrete jungle of the city. It was a smooth trip—the journey away from Rockfield usually was. It was the return trip that was always a bumpy ride.

CHAPTER 5

The first annual charity dinner for the Byron Jasper Rubber Band Foundation was being held at the NoMad Hotel on 28th Street and Broadway. The neighborhood was once made up of gambling halls and brothels, and Carter appeared disappointed that it had been overtaken by the aristocracy.

Byron was injured last July on our final assignment together, and he wasn't released from the hospital in Germany until late September. So it was amazing that his foundation had come this far in so little time. But I'd learned firsthand that you bet against Byron at your own risk.

The Parisian-inspired hotel was elegant enough to welcome the heavy-walleted upper crust, whose donations would be key in funding spinal cord injury research. But it wasn't stuffy, and was equally accommodating for, let's say, a guy not wearing sleeves and his cat-suited girlfriend.

The main dining room featured a gigantic skylight, which gave an impressive view of the city lights. The event would be spread throughout numerous smaller rooms—a private fireplace alcove, a sitting room, a two-story library, and a bar. It created a more intimate atmosphere to mingle, and get up-close time with potential donors. Byron understood the importance of getting people interested in the cause, and not just writing a check.

When we entered, we were provided inscribed rubber bands to commemorated the occasion. A former teammate of Byron's used to wear a rubber band on his wrist as a reminder of how fragile life was, as it could snap at any time. Byron picked up on the theme for his organization—he now saw his mission in life to re-attach the snapped rubber band of those afflicted with paralysis.

I turned on the charm and worked the rooms like a politician, kissing so much fanny that my lips began to hurt. Gwen followed suit, but she appeared much more interested in talking to the guests than to her boyfriend. I got the feeling that my actions at the game brought back memories of the hard-charging, abrasive reporter who chose the world over her. At least that was her version. My version focused more on her choosing to marry Stephen Dubois.

"I need something to drink," were her first words to me since our arrival, and she started walking in the direction of the bar. She stopped and turned back. "Do you want me to bring you something?"

I knew this was code for 'I want to be alone, do not even think about joining me,' so I declined. I barely finished my response before she was off.

This left me alone in a sea of wealth, and I worked my way through the cavernous atrium, meeting and greeting. I could have used a drink myself, but I decided it was not in my best interests to be within a three-room radius of Gwen, so I chose to enter the library instead. It was impressive with its rich fabrics and floor-to-ceiling bookshelves; a spiral staircase led to a second floor. But when I saw the man coming toward me with a shit-eating grin, I knew I'd made a wrong turn. A library would be the last place I expected to run into Cliff Sutcliffe.

Cliff was in his early thirties, born in a suit, and became the youngest president of a news organization when he was hired by GNZ. He came over from the entertainment world when a ratings-dip made the higher-ups desperate to join the circus. Cliff did his best to try to kill off what was left of the art of journalism, along with playing a central role in expediting my retirement.

"JP Warner ... to what do I owe the pleasure?" he said, flashing a fake smile, and offering his unusually small hand to shake.

"I'm here for Byron's foundation ... there is nothing pleasurable about it," I reminded him.

This triggered a long soliloquy about Byron's bravery, and what an inspirational figure he was, not just to Cliff, but to the entire GNZ family. And once he concluded the prepared speech, he got to the reason for his grin. "So have you seen the ratings?"

"I got the email," I said. Since I was still technically on the GNZ payroll—I do four hour-long specials a year—I receive all company emails, including the ones Cliff sent hourly for a week about the ratings spike. They're still a long way from regaining the top spot, as was commonplace back in GNZ's heyday, but mediocrity was a step in the right direction.

I usually ignored such propaganda, but I felt a certain responsibility in this matter, since I was the one who convinced him to go back to the roots of GNZ and hire the best reporters available, while refocusing on the investigative reporting they were once known for. Cliff had been about to get fired at the time, his 'newsertainment' platform backfiring badly, so he was willing to try anything.

I smiled. "What a novel concept, a news station doing the news. What's next, MTV playing music?"

"I think our coverage of Korea and the Huddled Masses killings has been fantastic, but let's be honest, the reason for the ratings jump is Tino Fernandez, and his chemistry with Lauren."

Since I'd pushed him to hire the best and the brightest, I would be a hypocrite to take issue with the hiring of my onetime arch-rival—often referred to as the 'Spanish JP Warner,' to the chagrin of both of us—and genuine sleazeball, Tino Fernandez.

"Spin it any way you want, Cliff, but when the journalistic integrity of the station went up, so did the ratings. That's a fact."

"C'mon, JP—we both know that watching cable news for the integrity is like reading *Playboy* for the articles. The only thing coincidental here is that when you were sleeping with Lauren last year, ratings were surging, and when you left, they nose-dived. But now she's with a younger ... and no offense ... hotter version of you, who also carries the key Hispanic demographic."

It always amazed me how quickly people return to their DNA after a brief stint of finding religion. Four months ago, Cliff was a desperate man seeking my advice, and Maloney was begging for his life. A few months and one good ratings cycle later, and Cliff was back to being Mr. Newsertainment, while Maloney had returned to his backstabbing political ways. I wondered who exactly I would be when I returned to my DNA.

"I can see it in your eyes, JP," he continued.

"If you did, you wouldn't be standing so close."

He laughed like it was the funniest line he'd ever heard. "I miss that sense of humor." His smile turned salesy. "Just like you miss us. You can try to hide it all you want, but I see it ... you want back in. This hiatus in Sticksville seems to have done wonders for you, recharging your batteries, but eventually you have to be who you are. And once you join Tino in Lauren's bedroom, GNZ will be number one once again."

I felt a sharp pain in my head, like those headaches from eating ice cream too fast. "What did you say?"

"I don't mean that you would actually be sleeping with her, JP. It's about perception. If Lauren's ex-boyfriend comes back, it puts her relationship with Tino into conflict—and every story needs conflict. The key is that we've created a love triangle in the audience's mind."

My mouth hung open. I couldn't believe it, except I could. I also sensed that I was in the middle of another Cliff Sutcliffe orchestration.

And that meant she was right behind—I needed to flee.

But I was too late.

"Hello, John Peter."

CHAPTER 6

Lauren Bowden sauntered toward me in a black evening gown with a plunging neckline. Maybe it was me, but while the world keeps getting smaller, Lauren's breasts seem to keep getting bigger.

"You look stunning," I greeted her.

"You look well yourself, John Peter … at least for a man in your position," she said, flipping her magnetic blonde hair.

"John Peter? I thought JP stood for Just Pathetic," said the fungus named Tino Fernandez, who walked up behind Lauren and put his arm around her.

For the record, it is actually John Pierpont, after JP Morgan. My mother, the Connecticut historian, named all her children after well-known people who were born in the state. But I was never one to get in the way of a juvenile putdown, so I let it go.

Tino looked his usual Rico Suave self, continuing on in his quest to return Miami Vice fashion to the mainstream. He was dressed in an aqua suit, with shirt unbuttoned enough to display a jungle of chest hair. He was also sporting his usual cocky smirk.

Lauren let out a theatrical yawn. "I apologize," she said in her soothing South Carolina twang. "But I'm still a little jet-lagged … Tino took me to Venice for Valentine's Day, and we spent a week there on a well-deserved vacation. Reentry has been a struggle for me, but I guess that's the price one pays for being in love."

Tino took the comment as an opportunity to show off his ability to speak Italian. I understood enough to know that he told her that is was his greatest honor to spend the *day* of love in the *city* of love, with his *one true* love. That's amore ... and a lot of bullshit. Lauren giggled like a schoolgirl, even though she had no idea what he said, and would have had the same reaction if he told her that she almost sunk their gondola because she ate too much spaghetti.

"What did you do for Valentine's Day, John Peter ... are you still with that country girl?" she asked.

"Yes, Farmer Gwen. We had a little dinner, and then spent the night at the tree fort. No jet or lag."

"The Tree Fort, I'm not familiar with it," she said with a look of confusion.

"It's this new hot club," I said.

"Never heard of it," she reiterated, and looked to Tino.

He just shook his head. It was official—if the cool kids didn't know about it then it couldn't exist.

"It's exclusive," I said. "You have to be really famous to even know where it is."

"John Peter, I'm much more famous than you ever ..." She caught herself, knowing I'd hooked her once again. I smiled at her, for old time's sake.

But my gloating would be brief, as the time had arrived for Lauren's big fat 'I told you so' that could sink an entire river of gondolas. "By any chance did you see last month's ratings, John Peter?"

"Was there an email sent out on that?"

"You can try to downplay it all you want, but I hear the regret in your voice ... although, you can't say I didn't warn you about leaving."

"I'm actually thinking about returning—Cliff and I were just talking about a title of Director of Love Triangles. But it's only in the discussion stage."

She flashed a look of pity in my direction. "I know it's hard for you, realizing that you weren't as important to GNZ as you thought. And I'm sure it was difficult seeing Tino and me together, and so in love."

I was in full agreement—seeing her and Tino together ... and so close they could touch me ... was causing me great pain.

I held a long gaze on Lauren, and then raised my voice for all to hear, "I do feel the pain—and it's as if you have stabbed me through the heart! But I will do whatever it takes to win you back. He might have taken you to Venice, but I will take you to the stars," I pointed to the ceiling. It would have played much better if we were in the dining room with the enormous skylight.

Lauren's face flushed, and she began fanning herself. "John Peter—I'm flattered really, but I'm a spoken-for woman."

We could only wish that were true. "If I can't have you, then I don't want to take another breath," I declared, noticing that the entire room had stopped and were staring at us. "So I will throw myself off the second level of this library, and plunge to my end. It will be far less painful than seeing you with him ... farewell, my dear lady."

I took her hand and lightly kissed it on the top. She actually looked impressed by my gesture. So not wanting to let her down, I ran to the spiral staircase, and sprinted upward. It was my stairway to heaven ... or at least an escape hatch from hell.

CHAPTER 7

It seemed like the perfect plan until pain intervened—I was still recovering from a knee injury sustained during my captivity last year. And to make matters worse, upon reaching the top, I plowed right into an attractive fifty-something woman with short blonde hair, almost knocking her over.

"So you're the one causing all this commotion. I thought I taught you to cover the story, not be the story," she said to me.

The woman before me was my former colleague, Katie Barrett, the one who showed me the ropes when I was starting out in the business. And in the smartest move GNZ had made in years, she was recently brought back as News Director. Like me, she had left as part of the Sutcliffe exodus.

"I would congratulate you on the improved ratings, but Cliff just informed me it was due to Lauren and Tino going steady."

She rolled her eyes. "Cliff says a lot of things."

"I think he also just tried to hire me as the office gigolo."

She smiled. "You might be overqualified for that job. And not to rain on Cliff's parade, but I have final say on all news-related hires. Speaking of which, if you're ever looking to return full-time, there is always a place for you here."

"Thanks, appreciate it, but I'm where I need to be."

She nodded with understanding.

Our conversation was interrupted by the words, "So are you an old news guy, or just old news?"

I turned to see Christina Wilkins. If Katie was my guide into this crazy world of TV journalism, then I was Christina's, even if she wouldn't admit it at gunpoint. Since she joined GNZ last fall, she has been traveling the world covering everything from the Korean conflict, which turned out to be not as conflicted as everyone feared, to the latest hysteria to sweep America—the Huddled Masses killings. So the last time I'd seen her in person was last fall in Rockfield, when she assisted me in trying to solve my brother's murder.

Tonight she was dressed in a business suit, and her hair and makeup were professionally done—I barely recognized the grownup version.

The moment seemed to call for a hug, but that wasn't our thing. We were more comfortable tossing zingers at the other.

"We owe you a debt of gratitude, JP, for recommending Christina to us. We threw her right into the fire, and she's done a fabulous job. Reminds me of someone else I know," Katie said.

"I'm very proud of her," I replied.

"Why don't you two just pat me on the head and send me back to the kiddie table," Christina chimed in.

"Funny you should mention that, as I'm on my way to babysit some children myself ... television executives," Katie said with a smile. She then excused herself, and made her way to the next room.

Christina turned her attention to me—I'd forgotten how much her wise-ass grin could annoy me.

"What?"

"I loved your act downstairs—you've still got it."

"Thanks ... I think."

"Although, it was nothing compared to that show you put on this afternoon. I'm curious—who do you think is crazy?"

"How did you know ..." then it hit me. "Carter has a big mouth."

"It wasn't Carter." She held up her phone. "Did you know postal workers call it 'Going JP' when someone loses their mind?"

"What is that?" I asked, as she handed me the phone.

"A website called *Celebrity Meltdown*—and now maybe you'll be the first person to make it twice in one day. I'll bet your mother is proud."

I groaned as I watched the video. It must have been taken by a spectator at the game ... Maloney came to mind. And for what it's worth, I was even more convinced the referee made the wrong call.

"Speaking of Big Ugly, have you seen him? We need to go over the details of our next assignment," Christina said.

As far as I could remember, Byron was the only one Carter would let call him that. But since I'd retired, and Carter had been serving in a similar role for Christina as he'd done for me, I was out of the loop.

I shrugged. "For someone so big, he's really good at sneaking off without anyone noticing. So how are you two getting along?"

"Me and Carter? Great—it's like we know what the other is thinking before we even think it. Have you ever experienced anything like that?"

Yeah, me and Carter, for like fifteen years.

She began to bounce away. "Nice running into you, JP. If you see Big Ugly, let him know I'm looking for him."

Suddenly I was her assistant—it seemed as if the world had been turned upside down. But her "special connection" with Carter must have been a little off tonight, because she didn't look in the most obvious place.

I bellied up to the elegant bar. "I'll have what he's having," I said to the bartender. Words I knew I'd live to regret. Or at least I'd regret.

"I thought you were going to leap to your death?" Carter said, without looking up from his drink.

My drink arrived in a short tumbler glass. I took a sip and my throat felt as if it had caught on fire. "No need to bloody the floor—this stuff will do the trick. What is it?"

"It's an Old Fashioned. Old, as in the past should be left where it is, and fashioned, as in a grown man should never wear an aqua suit."

"When exactly did you start using metaphors to make your points?"

"Don't let Fernandez get under your skin."

I nodded, but it was easier said than done. "Christina is looking for you," I changed the subject.

He sighed, and swigged the remainder of his drink. "She's a great kid, but she doesn't understand the boxes. At this rate, she'll be burned out before she hits twenty-five."

Thanks to a rigid upbringing by his military father, Carter could separate the different aspects of life into boxes. He understood when it was time to work, and when it was time to let down his hair and have fun—or in his case, when to shine his bald dome and style the goatee that hung halfway down the front of his neck.

"I'm getting too old for this shit," he continued. "Maybe it's time to get out while I've still got two functioning legs."

Thoughts of Byron were everywhere tonight, to the point that I think it was making us all say and do things we didn't mean. But I did recall broaching the subject of leaving the business last summer, and Carter responding with something along the lines of, *"What's wrong, sweetheart, too rough being a rich television star?"*

I smiled, pushing my luck. "Maybe you could become Kate's manager, and you could take a, dare I say, more submissive role?"

He shook his head in disbelief. "Last I checked, you're the one who gave up being Batman to be Gwen's Robin. And besides, I've got a few things to take care of before I check out."

After the Officer Jones ordeal, Batman was kind of a bad subject, so I moved on, "Speaking of Gwen, have you seen her? She came here to get a drink some time ago."

"She was, but then she and Kate went to go do some girly stuff or something like that."

A vision of Gwen in full leather, whip in hand, popped into my head. I pushed it out of my mind, somewhat reluctantly.

"Tonight's goal is to raise money, not drink up all the profits," came a familiar, high-pitched voice from behind us.

When I turned, my vision instinctively went to where Byron's face would be if he were standing. It always made me feel like crap when I did it, until my eyes would descend to his chair and see his optimistic smile. Feeling sorry for himself wasn't even in his vocabulary.

"You want a drink?" Carter greeted Byron.

"No—last time I had that stuff you drink, I had to chase it with a fire extinguisher. And besides, I got to give a speech later, and I don't want to be falling-down drunk."

He laughed at what he believed to be a joke, but it really wasn't funny.

"I like this place," I showed off my subject-changing skills once more. "You must be a pretty big deal to be able to book it on short notice."

Byron smiled. "I had to promise them that JP Warner would hold his wedding here. It will be the event of the year."

"You're the one who's engaged," I said. "Not to mention, I think hosting the nuptials of Coldblooded Carter and Mistress Kate is their true motivation. It will be the spectacle of all spectacles."

"I wouldn't book JP's wedding just yet. He seems to be in the doghouse," Carter said, showing off his usual perception.

It didn't sway Byron. "As my college coach used to say, confidence comes from your history, and history tells me that JP and Gwen will always find a way. It will take a lot more than an embarrassing video on *Celebrity Meltdown* to get between them."

Has everyone seen that video?

Two women entered the bar—Byron's fiancée, Tonya, and his mother, affectionately known as Mama Jasper.

When I rose off my barstool to greet them, Mama came at me like a blitzing linebacker. The politically correct term to describe her would be plus-sized, but luckily her heart was equally large, and forgiving. Not only did she not hold me responsible for what happened to her son, but she wrapped her arms around me in full support. And when Mama Jasper wraps you in her arms, breathing becomes a predicament, as it was tonight when she encased me in a big bear hug that squished the air out of my lungs.

Tonya followed with a much softer embrace, as one might expect from a former Miss South Carolina. She and Byron had been dating since college, so the engagement had been a long time coming. It was shaping up to be a big year for the Jasper family—not only would there be a wedding, but Byron had been inducted into the Charleston Hall of Fame. The ceremony was scheduled for April, and we all planned to be there for it. Not that Mama Jasper would allow us to miss it, even if we wanted to.

Mama announced, "I came to inform you that dinner is being served, and they can't start without the guest of honor."

This got Carter to his feet. "My work is never done."

"I think she was referring to Byron," I said.

Mama let out a hearty laugh. "I was actually talking about myself, and I can't be in the dining room if I'm having to chase down you three, now can I?"

She was not a woman to be argued with. I moved behind Byron's chair and began pushing—Carter walked beside the chair like he was Secret Service. The three of us together again on assignment—for a moment it felt like old times.

CHAPTER 8

Through the skylight above the dining room, I viewed the light snow that was still falling. And when I took my seat next to Gwen, I took note that it was also a little frosty inside.

She pulled her attention away from her conversation with Mistress Kate to acknowledge me, "I thought you were planning to off yourself?"

"Why does everyone sound so disappointed?"

"Carter is the one who's upset, he had dibs on your meal."

"For the record, the only woman I would ever leap to my death for is you."

"Is that an offer ... or are you just speaking in hypotheticals?"

"I acted like an ass today ... I get it. If I could take it back I would."

"Don't make this about you, JP—it's Byron's night."

And on that note, our conversation ended ... for now. The awkward silence hovered until the food was served. The meal had been delayed, mostly because the foundation had to hire a taster to check the safety of the food. This was due to the recent Huddled Masses killings, which were targeting the wealthy; a group that made up most of tonight's guest list.

It began with a shooting at a mall in Arizona just before Christmas, followed by a fatal poisoning at the wedding of the richest man in Atlanta. The group claimed they would commit one act a month until their demands were met, and with the days of February dwindling down, there was much uneasiness. It even caused a few possible donors to withdraw from tonight's event.

The basil-ferret water I was drinking wasn't doing the trick, so I attempted another Old Fashioned, which either I was starting to acquire a taste for, or had completely numbed my tongue. After my third, I felt like I could run the New York Marathon in tuxedo shoes, even with my damaged knee.

The lone drawback was that I had the sudden need to make the long journey to the bathroom. I stumbled across the dining room, surprised I didn't fall down. But the way my day had been going, things were bound to take a turn for the worse. And sure enough, primping himself in the bathroom mirror was Aqua Suit Man himself, Tino Fernandez.

"You missed a spot," I said and brushed underneath my nose. "Even a *pathetic* reporter like myself could spot the cocaine residue."

He took a closer look in the mirror, but found nothing. It seemed that my friend Tino was a little paranoid—*gotchya.*

His cocky smile returned. "I guess that's as close as you can come to winning against me these days, Warner. But I understand your desperation— you must be really tired of always losing everything to me."

"No different than you having to take all my hand-me-downs—career, women … well, I take no credit for your wardrobe. That's all you."

"I think the term you're looking for is upgrade. I'm a better reporter than you ever were, and I'm the best Lauren's ever had. At least that's what she screams out in the heat of passion."

He once told me that he would take away any possession of mine that I cared about, no matter how small. I had to stifle a laugh, as I believe he thought Lauren was one of those things. But when I thought of Nora, any humor was swept away.

"It didn't work out so well for the last woman you made those claims about. So is that the plan—get Lauren hooked on that stuff and then ruin her life too?"

"They are both grown women, able to make their own decisions. And if I treated Nora so badly, then how come she still calls me in the middle of the night and begs me to come over."

"Because you're her drug dealer."

He held up his phone and played a voice mail from last night. It was Nora's voice, telling him that they needed to talk, and they should meet up at her place.

Tino smiled again. "She sounds very clear and sober to me. She knew exactly what she wanted … and she got it."

There was part of me that actually felt bad for Lauren at that moment. A small part.

He looked intently at me, his eyes narrowing. "All the excuses in the world can't hide the truth that women tire of you. And I can tell this Gwen is already losing interest."

It took all the serenity I could muster not to send my fist through his nose.

He smiled condescendingly. "It's not even fun anymore … when you just take it like that. You could never beat me, so you have just quit. It's sad, really."

"I would rather quit than embarrass myself by becoming a studio anchor. Reporters report, talking heads talk. You're all talk, no action these days, Fernandez."

I did find it odd that a correspondent of his level would leave the field for a "desk job" in the comforts of the studio. What we did in those dangerous places was not a job, but part of our DNA.

He laughed mockingly. "That's the best you can do? Chide me for being successful? If you saw how much they pay me to be a talking head, I think you'd understand." He moved up as close as he could get, and whispered,

"Say whatever you want about my career, but nobody ended up in a wheelchair because of me."

He patted me lightly on the cheek, gave me one last cocky smile, and left.

I was burning up as I stepped back into the dining hall. And when I heard Byron's familiar voice being amplified throughout the room, my anger further intensified.

I stood in the back and listened to his speech. He started with the grim statistics—over 250,000 living with spinal cord injuries in the US, and 11,000 new SCIs each year. And that most of those afflicted are young and live a normal lifespan, or as Byron put it, "There are too many of us sitting on our butts when we could be contributing more."

He spoke with excitement about new potential breakthroughs—things way over the audience's head like precursor cell implementation, genetic engineering, and embryogenesis. But then took it back to a human story, telling how this once world-class athlete now needs assistance for the simplest of life's tasks. There wasn't a dry eye in the house.

Between seeing Byron in that chair, and Tino's comments still ringing in my ears, I felt like I could explode at any moment. As if Carter sensed this, he made his way back to me.

"When I said I have something to take care of before I leave," he spoke as quietly as he was capable. "It's the same unfinished business you have."

"I'm not sure what you mean. All my business is finished—I'm retired."

"I found him."

"Found who?"

"Uncle Al."

He had my attention—Uncle Al was Carter's pet name for the terrorist groups like Al Qaeda and Al Muttahedah. He says they're like everybody's annoying drunken uncle who always overstays his welcome.

"They're not hard to find—every time there is an act of terror around the world, they're the ones taking credit for it," I said.

"I mean I found Az Zahir. I'm leaving tomorrow, are you in?"

I was completely caught off guard, and now stone cold sober. I looked at Carter, who was as serious as I'd ever seen him. I then viewed Byron, who sat behind a podium in a wheelchair. A chair Az Zahir put him in. "I don't know."

"Sleep on it, and get back to me in the morning."

I nodded, but knew that I wouldn't get any sleep.

CHAPTER 9

Rockfield

I stood frozen in a quandary, watching Gwen fidget with the zipper on the back of her dress.

I was at a dangerous crossroads. If I did the proper boyfriend thing, offering help, I would be swatted away. But if I did nothing, I would be branded uncaring and self-centered. Luckily, she was able to locate the zipper and drag it down her back.

She stepped out of the dress, and removed her heels—now standing only in lacy panties. She folded the dress neatly and placed it on the bed. She then slid her panties to the floor. There would be no slow, seductive striptease like on Valentine's Day.

I stood mesmerized, like a knee-knocking fourteen-year-old. This never got old—Gwen Delaney was standing naked in my bedroom! But the fantasy would be brief. She quickly tossed on a sweatshirt and a pair of boxers.

I walked up behind her, as if in a trance, and lightly wrapped my arms around her waist. She wriggled away. "That's so not happening tonight."

"I hear that make-up sex is the best part of fighting."

"We're not in a fight."

I figured at some point the prosecutor would let me know exactly what I was being charged with. But for now, all I could do was throw myself at the mercy of the judge. "I don't know what's gotten into me lately—it's like I have these out-of-body experiences."

She breathed in the tense air between us, and slowly blew it out. "Listen, JP—you haven't had time to process things. You've had more happen to you in six months than some people have to deal with in a lifetime. You rode in on the white horse, got justice for Noah, and rode off with the girl. It was a happy ending ... and that's the problem."

"You have something against happy endings?"

"In the movies ... no. But in real life there's no such thing. If it was happy it wouldn't end. Real life always has a next chapter, and you need to figure out where this story is going. I think we need some time apart so you can do that."

I felt a punch to the gut. "Are you breaking up with me?"

"I never breakup with anyone while I'm wearing their boxer shorts." She flashed her comforting smile. "Before he left, Carter mentioned that he's going down to Charleston for a few days to spend with Byron, and he thought it would be good for you to go ... and I agree."

I recalled Carter mentioned something about leaving on a trip tomorrow, but nothing about Charleston. Must have been the alcohol.

Gwen turned off the light and slipped under the covers, leaving me with one thought—the last time we decided to spend time apart it lasted for fifteen years.

CHAPTER 10

I didn't even attempt sleep. I threw on a heavy coat and slipped out of the house.

I drove out of Skyview, passed through a sleepy Main Street, and turned onto Zycko Hill Road. I followed the winding, and often treacherous, road to the Samerauk Bridge.

It's amazing how one event can change your entire view of something. The bridge was always one of my favorite spots in town. The picturesque symbol of this fortress of happiness we called Rockfield. But now all I could see was Noah's accident, and the place where Officer Jones, aka Grady Benson, took his life. I remembered coming here as a little boy, my dad holding me up so I could see over the railing and view the rushing river below. But now when I looked down, all I saw was Noah's bloody body lying on the rocks.

I parked the Jeep and got out. I maneuvered down the snow-covered hill. When I reached the river's edge, I took a seat on the cold ground and looked out over the frozen river that was lit only by a pale moonlight. I noticed that Noah's Red Sox cap, which I'd left in tribute, was still there, half embedded in a snowdrift. I figured some creature would have carried it off by now, but it seemed as if even the animals were Yankees fans in these parts.

I'd delivered on my promise to get him justice, but in the whirlwind that followed, I didn't meet my other promise—that I would say a proper goodbye to him when I did. I didn't know exactly what that entailed, so I just talked to him tonight, something we didn't do enough of while he was alive. I first told him about the undefeated season, and how proud he would be of his favorite niece, Ella—those two had a special bond. I told him about his brother's meltdown today, which I'm sure gave him a good laugh. And how Gwen and I had finally gotten back together, but not to get his hopes up, as we were already taking time apart. A sharp wind blew through the river valley, as if it were some kind of response from him, but maybe it was just wind. Nothing was clear to me at the moment.

I told him of the dinner for Byron, and the offer Carter made to get justice, just as I had for Noah. *Didn't I owe Byron the same?* I thought of how both Noah and Byron were felled by different men in different parts of the world, but with the same zealotry in their eyes. I felt the anger cut through me.

I had thought a return to my roots, and reuniting with Gwen, would put an end to the battle that had raged on inside me. But perhaps I would never be at peace until this last piece of unfinished business was taken care of. And when I closed that chapter, and only then, I could write the ending that never ends with Gwen.

But isn't that what gamblers and alcoholics always say? *One last score and then I'll stop forever ... it's just one drink.*

There was no response from Noah, probably because he wasn't here. Why would he spend eternity in the place that caused him the most pain? He was likely off with Lisa, cruising through the pearly gates in his Mustang, laughing at me as I froze my ass off talking to an empty river.

Realizing what a waste of frozen breath this was, I stumbled my way back up the hill. I got in the Jeep and cranked the heat, trying to ease my shivering. I stared out into the darkness, as the monotonous drones of sports talk radio played in the background. The next thing I knew I was woken by a knocking on my window.

Disorientated, I viewed the clock to see that it was quarter to four—I had fallen asleep. Rockfield's police chief, Rich Tolland was tapping on my window, and holding two cups of coffee. I unlatched the door and the large block of a man who we used to call The Toll Booth during our high school football days, climbed in and handed me a hot Styrofoam cup.

"If you're here to arrest me, this coffee is grounds for entrapment."

"The thought crossed my mind, but I couldn't decide whether to charge you with loitering, or almost starting a riot at an elementary school basketball game."

"Shouldn't the chief get to work better hours than this?" I asked

"We're a little short staffed, since you ran off my overnight guy."

This brought a complicated smile to my face. That officer was currently spending his nights in a federal supermax prison in Freemont County, Colorado.

Rich looked out at the bridge, probably regretting that he brought up the subject. "Noah would be really proud of how you had his back. Everyone, me included, took the easy way out and concluded it was suicide."

"Your job is to follow the evidence, and that's where it led."

He nodded, but didn't appear convinced.

"You were right, and I was wrong," I said.

He checked the digital clock on the dashboard. "For the historical record, at 3:52 on what is now Saturday morning, JP Warner has admitted he was wrong about something. And what would that be?"

"You realized what Rockfield was, and never left. I sought something more, not recognizing that I already had everything. It's like that fable about Icarus—the boy who flew too high."

Rich laughed. "I must have slept through that one in class. But I'm here for the same reason you are … a girl. If it wasn't for her, I'd probably be off in Afghanistan or some place like that."

I looked up from my coffee, confused.

"If you remember, I got a partial football scholarship to play at Bryant College," he explained. I did, but that's where the story stopped for me. "Anyway, I hurt my shoulder the first practice of college ball, and my football career was essentially over. I never liked school, and I was close to signing my papers to head off to the army, when I met Cassie."

"She showed me that school could be fun, which it wasn't, but I really liked studying with her. And she convinced me that a degree in criminal justice would help me pursue my dream of getting into the FBI."

"I thought *this* was your dream job—I remember you talking about it all the way back in school."

"It was ... when I was in the seventh grade, and I didn't know anything else. Then we went on that school trip to Washington DC, sophomore year. When we took the tour through the FBI building everything changed for me.

"After graduating, my focus had changed from the FBI to becoming a big city cop, mainly because that way I could remain closer to Cassie. I made final cuts in Boston and Providence, but it seemed as if I was always a bridesmaid. Time went on, and Cassie and I had gotten married, and were living with her parents in Narragansett. She was working toward her teaching degree and I was tending bar, trying to make ends meet.

"Then one day, your dad ran into my dad here in town, and when the subject of me came up, your dad mentioned an opening on Rockfield PD. Thirteen years and three kids later, here I am."

"So I was wrong about being wrong—you did want to leave town."

"I was restless my first couple years back, thinking I'd given up on my dream. But I realized that my real dream was to have a family with Cassie, and this job allowed me to do that."

"You ever get the urge to chase those old dreams?"

He shook his head. "After dealing with our friend Agent Hawkins on the Jones case, I lost any interest in the FBI. And besides, we've made a home here. I guess it comes down to what we can live with, and what we can't live without."

He looked to me. "How about you? I'll bet it wasn't easy to leave the life of adventure behind."

I was momentarily surprised—I was used to asking the questions, not answering them. "It's just that ... I don't know ... sometimes I have voices pulling me in different directions."

He looked bemused. "You're hearing voices? Well, I guess that explains a lot."

I wished it did. "Was I always this big of a mess?"

"I hate to break it to ya, JP, but you're not as different from everyone else as you like to think. Hell, I got a whole team of people in my mind pushing and pulling. Sometimes I'm Rich the husband, sometimes Chief Tolland, and some days when I'm feeling like The Toll Booth, I'll park over by the high school and watch practice, while making it look like I'm doing some police work. If you want my advice, listen to the loudest one—it will take you where you need to go."

"And which one is that for you?"

He smiled wide. "Daddy."

I now understood where I needed to go. I knew who I couldn't live without, but the question was—*could I live with myself?* "Thanks—I think you really helped me find some clarity."

He nodded, and began to step out of the Jeep. "Glad I could be of service. Now I better get back to work before I have to fire myself."

"I need to get going too. I've got an early flight tomorrow."

He looked surprised. "Oh yeah? Where are you off to?"

"To take care of some unfinished business."

CHAPTER 11

Teterboro, New Jersey

Teterboro is a small airport located in New Jersey, twelve miles from Manhattan. It is popular with private aircraft—read: rich dudes with really cool jets—and would be where we would take off from this morning.

Carter didn't reveal where our "unfinished business" would take place, although, I was confident it wouldn't be in Charleston, as he'd told Gwen. This was no different from my days at GNZ, when he would never reveal the location of an assignment until the last moment. He claimed it was to maintain secrecy, since many of our competitors were always tracking our movements. But I got the idea that he enjoyed the spy novel of it.

Waiting for us was a Bombardier Challenger 600-Series jet, price tag twenty-five million. It was owned by an oil sheik, who happened to also be a big wrestling/Coldblooded Carter fan.

The morning was England-gray with an occasional flurry. I stood by my lonesome on the cold runway, as Carter said a long kissy-faced goodbye to his girlfriend. She had shed the leather, and was dressed as plain-old Kate this morning.

I watched as a yellow cab pulled up to the runway, and the third member of our traveling party stepped out. Christina was unaware that I was along for the ride, and I was interested in her reaction.

When she noticed my presence, I didn't receive the same "happy reunion" vibe from last night. She looked to Carter. "What's he doing here?"

He shrugged. "We needed someone with a hard head to test the parachutes in case the engines fail on the plane."

Christina's eyes searched the tarmac. "And where is Flash?"

"This assignment will not require a cameraman," Carter said. "So Flash is on hiatus. JP is taking his place."

Christina's frustration grew. "I'm a television reporter, how can you do a story without video?"

Carter turned to me with a shake of the head. "Kids today."

I smiled. "Tell me about it. If a tree falls in the forest and it's not on YouTube, did the tree really fall?"

"If it fell on your heads, then maybe it would knock some sense into you," Christina was not pleased with the turn of events.

And while part of her did seem a "kid," especially her dress of cammo pants, flip-flops, and a maroon FU sweatshirt—short for Fordham University, the college she attended, and not the sentiment that she had toward Carter and me at the moment. But the seriousness in her eyes, and her new TV hairdo, forced me to think of her as an adult for the first time since she'd barreled her way into my life. It was like she was trapped at sea, somewhere in between child and adult. I would advise her to swim back toward the youth as fast as she could, but she never has listened to me, so there was no point.

I wore a cable-knit sweater and jeans, with my shearling-lamb suede poncho tied around my waist—the same one I'd been wearing when Al Muttahedah captured us last summer. I would be picking things up right where we left off.

As a young reporter, I was nicknamed J-News, because it was said it looked like I'd popped out of the J-Crew catalog, in a time when the industry was conservatively buttoned-up. As time went on, the name became more about the persona I'd become than the clothes I wore—the battle of JP versus J-News symbolized the war that still raged inside me.

Carter wore his standard uniform, whether we were traveling to the stifling jungles of South America or the ice caps of Antarctica—motorcycle boots, jeans, and a sleeveless denim jacket, showing off arms that he claimed were in violation of New Jersey state gun laws. And of course, he had on his wraparound sunglasses, even though I'd yet to see a hint of the sun breaking through the overcast skies.

He informed her, "Here's the deal—you're going to get a story that most reporters would cut off their left nut for. And while you're doing that, JP and I are going to take care of some business. Kill two birds with one leap off the top rope."

She didn't fight back with her normal vigor. It seemed that she'd come to the same realization that I had when I first began working with Carter— that this was his show, and we were just along for the ride.

The flight was delayed over an hour as we waited for the sheik's two twenty-something sons to arrive, which they eventually did in expensive black Mercedes with bulletproof glass. The sons looked like Arabic Justin Biebers, and had with them a group of giggly Lauren Bowdenish-looking women in tight mini dresses. It's good to be born with an oil well in your sandbox, I thought.

But I wasn't complaining, remembering my days at GNZ when we flew commercial. Unless we were trying to remain stealth, and in that case we'd charter a flight with our own personal funds. Christina didn't know how good she had it.

There were parts of the job I'd always miss, but long plane flights were not one of them. As the others congregated in the back of the plane following takeoff, I found a seat near the front where I would attempt to get some rest.

But I didn't even get through the first stages of the sleep cycle, before Carter woke me. "We got a card game going in the back if you want in," he said.

I glanced back at the festive group. "I think I'll pass—I'm on a retirement income these days, and oil sheik money might be a little out of my league."

Carter smiled. "Are you sure? If I win the next hand, I get ownership of their father's soccer team in London."

"What if you lose?"

"What does Gwen think about arranged marriages?"

This time he brought a smile to my face. But it quickly disappeared when he informed me of our destination. It didn't surprise me to learn where Al Muttahedah was hiding. Chaos was their oxygen, and where was it more chaotic than in the middle of a country fighting a war? They were originally formed in Iraq during the most recent conflict there, and this was the logical next move for them.

When Carter returned to the back of the plane, I attempted sleep once more, but if Gwen wasn't enough on my mind, knowledge that I was traveling into the bloodiest place on the planet wasn't the best recipe for rest either.

The loud hijinks coming from the back of the plane, and constant stream of cigar smoke, added to the challenge, so I eventually gave up. Hearing Carter's booming laughter, I couldn't help but think of all the times the three of us would laugh like that on trips like this. It was the only way we stayed sane … if we did. I could almost see Byron struggling down the aisle of the plane, carrying his heavy camera equipment, as he and Carter traded barbs.

For a moment it felt as if we'd gotten the band back together. But if we were a band, our drummer was left paralyzed, and the bass player we hired for our last tour, a baby-faced guide named Milos, was dead. It was a cruel reminder of why I was risking everything to be on this plane.

CHAPTER 12

It was morning when we arrived in one of my favorite cities in the world—Istanbul.

The bond I'd formed with the city was likely due to our similarities when it came to internal tugging and complexities. Istanbul was built on seven hills, and straddled two continents—the Bosphorus River split the European and Asian sides. And besides the cultural pull of the two continents, underlying forces competed between the old world and modern realities.

The sheik's car service dropped us at a five-star hotel. I knew it would be the last comfortable accommodations for the remainder of the trip, so I took advantage to finally get that rest, sleeping the day away. The time where I could fly across the world and be up for 72-straight hours, working only on coffee and Snickers bars, was long gone.

When I woke, I stepped out onto the balcony and viewed the minaret-dotted skyline with the sun setting behind it. It was stunning, and I imagined coming here with Gwen one day. The temperature had dropped about ten degrees into the low 50s, but it was still preferable to the frigid February I'd left in Connecticut.

I returned to my room, grabbed a small bag of essentials, and headed out to meet my traveling partners in the lobby. To no surprise, Carter was being mobbed by tourists and hotel staff, asking for his autograph and taking photos. I'd yet to find the spot on the planet where there were no Coldblooded Carter fans. It was always great theater, but created a challenge when it came to remaining incognito.

We headed out to Leb-i Derya, a restaurant and club in the Beyoglu section of the city. The rooftop terrace, which it was known for, was closed for the winter, but a sea breeze still made its way inside. And it didn't dampen the view of the many ancient monuments and imperial mosques, which sparkled at night.

The city dated back well before it was ruled by the Ottoman Empire, and prior to the Silk Road that brought great riches, but the crowd in Leb-i Derya was young, reminding me of the trendy urban crowds you might find in a club in the Meatpacking District in Manhattan. There were also a lot of foreigners, which besides giving it a cosmopolitan feel, helped us foreigners not stand out like sore thumbs.

We were approached by two attractive, college-age girls. By their accents, I could tell that they were local. Most of the coverage of women in the Middle East, and rightfully so, focused on the places where they're forced to hide themselves behind burkas and such, but these two were decked out in short mini dresses, much like the rest of the crowd. More clashing between the old and modern worlds in Istanbul.

They introduced themselves as Adalet and Muaj, and asked us to dance. We followed them to the crowded dance floor, where we pushed our way to the center. My bad leg was still stiff from the transcontinental flight, and the last thing it needed was a night of dancing. But soon as the next song began, we used the mob of gyrating youth as cover as we slipped out the other side, and continued right out of the club.

They guided us onto the historic red tram at Taksim Square, which we rode along İstiklâl Caddesi, a mile-long street made up of shops, cafes, and pubs. Then without warning, the girls got off the tram and began walking, using the populated streets to meld in. We slipped down a dark side street, and continued until we reached an alleyway where a car was parked. It was a similar Hyundai with two-toned paint job that Milos drove that fateful night in Serbia, adding to the eeriness.

Carter sat in the front seat, as Muaj drove. Adalet was wedged in between Christina and me in the back. We continued out of the city, and the terrain changed to rural landscapes, lit only by the thick moon.

The drop-off point was pretty much what I expected—you can always recognize a border town, whether you're in Texas or Turkey. The girls whisked us into a small cinder-block home, which smelled like animal droppings. We didn't end up spending the night with the attractive women we'd met in the club—they returned to Istanbul, or wherever they were from. We spent it with a trio of heavily-bearded smugglers, who were going to broker a deal to get us into Syria.

CHAPTER 13

For two days we were told, "today will be the day," only to be informed that we'd have to wait another day. All foreign journalists had been banned from entering since the civil war broke out, so we were at their mercy to get us inside.

Carter and I spoke very little Arabic, but Christina had minored in it in college, thinking it would be helpful for a journalist in a post-9/11 world. She became our lead translator.

Besides the frustrations from the delays, and my dislike for hummus, which is all we ate for two days, the time did give me a chance to think things over. And I concluded that the decision that took me from a charity dinner in New York to the Turkish border in just over a day was fueled on emotion, not logic. And the more time I had to analyze it, the more it became clear—this was a bad idea! *What would we do if we actually caught these guys?* The element of surprise might be on our side, but they would surely be more skilled in weaponry than a couple of journalists and a former wrestler. When I broached the subject with Carter, he informed me that all he planned to do was deliver a message from his friend the sheik—to turn themselves in to authorities or face the consequences. It seemed that the sheik didn't like the bad name that Al Muttahedah was giving Muslims, and especially how this bad reputation was starting to hit him where it hurt—in his offshore bank accounts.

I didn't doubt that the sheik was a powerful and influential man, but I had a hard time picturing the Al Muttahedah soldiers dropping their guns and curling up into the fetal position when we delivered the message. As far as I could tell we had no weapons, and while Carter was an intimidating presence, I was sure that even Uncle Al had figured out that pro wrestling was fake by now.

When I ran my concern by Carter, he responded simply, "We have a secret weapon."

"So secret it doesn't exist?"

"Trust me, you'll know it when you see it."

And that was the end of the conversation.

On the third day, we were awoken before sunrise and introduced to the men who were going to get us over the border. Boys might be a more appropriate term, as they didn't look a day over sixteen. They charged us what I thought was a pretty reasonable $300 USD per head, and $500 if motorbikes were used. When factoring in my bad leg, the high elevation, and rocky terrain, it wasn't much of a choice.

The motorbikes were hidden in a nearby olive orchard, alongside a barbed wire fence that separated Turkey and Syria. They did loan us helmets and bulletproof vests, which made me feel a little better. As did the Kalashnikov rifles they had strapped to their backs.

We drove through the orchard, parallel to the fence, for about a mile, until we reached a breach in the barbed wire. We passed through, and just like that we had entered the war torn country. Lucky us.

We bounced over the rough terrain, through dried-out riverbeds, and past fields of rosemary. It was only about sixty degrees, but I was sweating like I'd just taken a shower, making my grip even more precarious.

We were dropped off on the edge of a rocky plateau beside a deserted road, deep in the heart of nowhere. With no further instructions, our guides sped away, leaving us as sitting ducks for the death-squad government militia "Shabiha," and with thoughts of all the other journalists who never made it out of here alive.

With no other options in sight, we began to walk … to where, I had no idea. But we didn't even get a quarter of a mile before we saw a pickup truck barreling in our direction. As it grew closer, I started having Serbia flashbacks.

The truck skidded to a stop in front of us, and a bunch of bandana-wearing men with rifles leaped out and circled us. I wondered if our smugglers got more than $500 from these guys for flipping them a couple of valuable hostages—it wouldn't be the first time we'd been double-crossed.

They proceeded to blindfold us, and all I could do was sigh … here we go again.

CHAPTER 14

New York City

Gwen escaped the wintry bluster, entering the dimly lit Japanese restaurant, Chibi O's. Her first thought—besides it was nice to feel her hands again—was that this place was much nicer than the joints she and Allison used to frequent in their college days.

Through the darkness, which she couldn't decide if it was ambiance or an attempt to lower the electric bill, she spotted Allison Cooper's sophisticated blonde bob. The spotting was mutual, as Allison stood, displaying the power-suit of an ad executive. Gwen made her way to her, and the old friends embraced.

They'd known each other from growing up together in Rockfield, but it wasn't until they both attended college in the big city—Gwen at Columbia, Allison at NYU—that they really became close. And when JP decided he'd rather explore the world than a life with her, Allison was the person who was there for her. She'd never forget that.

Nowadays, they were lucky to pull off these lunches in the city twice a year. But with Gwen's time being sucked away by the small town paper she ran, and Allison trying to balance her two kids and husband, along with her recent return to the work force, it took six months of negotiations to secure this date.

"You look great," Gwen said cheerfully as they took a seat at their table. "I love the hair."

"I had them dim the lights, so I wouldn't look bad sitting next to this twenty-five-year-old supermodel I was having lunch with."

Gwen laughed. "When will she be arriving?"

"Don't play humble with me, Gwendolyn. There's a reason the boys have been chasing you around since we were in third grade. And you certainly don't look like someone who is staring down their twenty-year high school reunion."

Gwen feigned surprise. "Is that this year?"

"Being that I am in charge of the reunion committee, I know for a fact that you have received multiple notices for the past three months."

Gwen smiled. "They must not have arrived yet—you know Rockfield, the mail is still delivered by Pony Express."

A young Asian waitress brought a tray of sake. Gwen flashed a look of surprise. "I thought you were working?" They had picked Chibi O's because it was near Allison's office on East 33rd Street.

She shrugged. "I'm in advertising … haven't you ever seen *Mad Men*?"

"I run a small town newspaper. Studies have confirmed that it's the equivalent of raising thirty-two children. So I don't really have time for television."

"Are we playing top this? Because I believe those same studies proved that raising my two children equated to being a warden at an overpopulated prison. Do you want to see photos of them? I'm obligated by Manhattan law to ask."

"Do they look any different than they did in the Christmas card? If not, not really."

"You're missing out on the two hundred photos I have stored on my phone of Gracie's dance recital. Opportunities like this don't grow on a tree."

"I'll take my chances."

"Your loss. But I'm much more interested in seeing pictures of your child, anyway," Allison said with a sly grin.

"My child? Do you know something I don't?"

Still grinning, she reached into her purse and pulled out a newspaper clipping, and pushed it across the table. It was of Gwen and JP entering Byron's charity dinner at the NoMad, looking happier than she remembered them being that night. Gwen looked at the caption to the photo, which referred to her as "the dashing" JP Warner's "latest gal pal" … how flattering.

"So what do you think of us … being back together?" Gwen asked with hesitation. This was the woman she'd bash JP to on a nightly basis for months after the breakup. She probably thought she'd lost her mind.

"I think it's great. You got the one that got away. What are the odds? It's like winning the lottery … just with better sex."

Gwen didn't know what to do with that one, but was happy for the support.

"By the way you're blushing, I'll take it that you agree with my assessment. So when's the wedding?"

"We're taking it slow this time."

"Uh-oh."

"What's uh-oh?"

"That tone—it's the 'end of the Stephen Era' drone. Right before the divorce."

"We're just taking our time. JP's been through a lot this past year—held hostage, Noah's death …"

Allison's face saddened. "I still can't believe Noah Warner is gone. I used to babysit for him when he was like five."

Gwen nodded—there wasn't anything to add when it came to such a tragedy. "I don't mean to sound negative—for the most part it's been great. Over the holidays, he even worked with my father to build us a tree house on his family's property. It was the one where we once carved our names and *true love forever* when we were kids."

"Oh. My. God! He built you an actual love nest? That's the most romantic thing I've ever heard. I can't even get Marty to wash the dishes."

"It was, but it also highlights our biggest obstacle. Which is that JP's trying to turn back the clock—it's like he wants to pick up where we left off all those years ago. But I want the us of today, with all the baggage of time that comes with it. Sometimes I feel like we're living in different decades."

"Sounds to me like you're over-thinking things. When anyone asks Marty and me how we do it ... like we have a clue! ... I tell them the key is we don't have time to think, and when we do we're too tired. I believe there's something to that."

Gwen felt a wave of regret come over her. "I think I made a big mistake. I convinced JP to go on a trip so that he could 'figure things out.' What if I sent him away for good this time?"

"Oh, please, the guy had fifteen years to think about things, and the only answer he came up with was that he wanted to build his little Gwendolyn a tree fort."

Gwen smiled, as the waitress brought a tray of assorted foods—tempura, chicken teriyaki, salmon yakimono. "Hope you don't mind, I ordered for us. I only have an hour for lunch," Allison said.

"Not a problem," Gwen replied, and dug in to the tempura. "But enough about me and my eternal relationship issues. How are you and Marty doing?"

"He's a new man. Or maybe he's back to being the man from before. Getting laid-off by the firm crushed him—how long was he there, like fourteen or fifteen years? Basically since he graduated from Wharton—and he's always connected his self-esteem to providing for the kids and me. I kept telling him that there is always a silver lining in everything, and you know what, he never would have started his consulting business if he hadn't been let go. So it all worked out in the end."

"So business is good?"

"It was a struggle at first, but things have really picked up lately. He got a couple big clients. Even sent one of them my way for their YP needs, which has got me off to a good start at Whitley."

"Ah … the couple that shares clients stays together. So you're happy to be back in advertising?"

"I'm not sure Yellow Pages advertising is what I had in mind, but it's helped out with the bills while Marty was getting his feet underneath him."

"I had no idea people still used the Yellow Pages."

"Must be the same three people that still read newspapers."

"Touché."

"It's not sexy, but it's an eight billion dollar industry. And is still the top advertising source for services like plumbers, propane, and stuttering lawyers."

"Stuttering lawyers?"

"You know, the sleaze balls that put AAA in front of their name so they can be first alphabetically. A-A-A Ambulance Chasers at Law."

Gwen laughed. "Wow, look at you, all in the business."

She thought back to those days when their canvases were blank, and anything seemed possible. They vowed, and pinky-swore, that they would chase their dreams to the ends of the earth. Gwen would be the editor at the *New York Times,* and Allison was going to be the top ad executive in the city. And suddenly it hit her that their dreams would never come true.

Or maybe they did come true—they just didn't know what their real dreams were back then—and that reaching their dreams wasn't the hard part … holding onto them was.

CHAPTER 15

Allison Cooper entered the building on East 33rd Street. The walk from Chibi O's was just three blocks, but it seemed like fifty on the cold afternoon.

She took the creaky elevator ride to the sixth floor, and entered the offices of Hugo Whitley YPA. When she arrived at her office, she found Dennis Whitley waiting for her—Hugo's son, who now ran the place.

"I'm really worried about General Washington's. Have you been able to get that meeting yet?" he began.

"Hello to you too, Dennis. And you're really worried about an account that has tripled in size in the last six months? One that now bills almost four million, opens new locations seemingly on an hourly basis, and unlike most of your clients, actually takes our advice? That's the client you're worried about?"

She almost laughed at bragging about the four million—that used to be the budgeted bar-tab for some of the accounts she worked on at Dunn & Hill, back when she was a young career-climber.

"It's about diversifying funds. What if you get hit by a bus today, then we're up shit creek without a paddle?"

Only if that bus came through the sixth floor window, because she wasn't getting out of here until way past dinner time tonight. But she understood his point. She was the one who had brought the client in—with Marty's big assist—and David Tully, the head honcho, would only communicate with her. So the only thing keeping her from running off with the account and starting her own business was a flimsy non-compete document she signed, but it likely wouldn't hold up in court. By getting a meeting with the entire staff, theoretically, Tully could become comfortable with working with Hugo Whitley YPA, and not Allison Cooper. But theory and reality rarely intersected in life, which was no different in this case, as he'd refused her requests for months.

Their conversation was interrupted by her intercom, "Allison—I have Mr. Tully on the phone for you."

Speaking of the devil.

"Get that meeting," Dennis said, as he bounced out of her office.

Allison took a deep breath before picking up. She had no idea why she got this case of nerves before they spoke, especially since they'd spoken practically every day during the workweek, and sometimes on weekends, over the last six months. *For goodness sake, he's the owner of a carpet cleaning business, not the actual General Washington, Allison!*

"David—good afternoon," she began. "What can I do for you today?"

"I was going over the February bills, love, and I had a question about three directories in Florida—Pompano Beach, West Palm, and Delray Beach," he replied in his dignified British accent. The accent always threw her off, since his company was headquartered in Valley Forge, Pennsylvania, and was named after George Washington. You couldn't get much more American than that. He was born and raised in the UK, before coming to the States as a young man. "I met a girl, and never left," was the way he explained his staying.

He also spent more time on the tiny details than any CEO she'd ever come across. She couldn't believe he went through each month's bill with a fine tooth comb.

"Those ads are for the West Palm location you opened last summer. All three books are within the fifteen mile radius we determined should be used as part of your advertising strategy."

"I'm aware of my strategy, love. And it's hard not to be familiar with that area of the country these days ... all you need to do is turn on the news."

Sadly, he was right. The third Huddled Masses attack took place yesterday off the coast of West Palm Beach, Florida, and had been covered incessantly by the news media. The latest incident occurred on a yacht, in which a wealthy family was celebrating their daughter's sweet-sixteen party. The one captor chained himself to the daughter, and jumped overboard, the heavy chains dragging them to the bottom. Her parents leaped after them, and perished trying to save their daughter.

"It's just heartbreaking. And misguided. As if murdering that family is going to cure economic inequality," Allison said, unable to shake the thought of someone doing something similar to her children.

"I often think the world has gone mad, and want to lock myself in a cave and never come out. But I didn't mean to get off topic—my question was, these directories didn't come out until last month, February, but they aren't on the bill?"

And Dennis is really worried about a client who thinks we aren't billing him enough? She explained once again that he pays in full on the "close" date, which is the date his ad is locked in the directory, usually three to four months prior to publication. So he had already paid for these three books that closed last October, even if the book didn't hit the street until February.

Once that was cleared up, they moved on to other business. And with the impressive growth of GWCC, there was always much business to cover. New art work proposals, the call data from the individual tracking numbers they placed in each ad, and of course, ad recommendations for his new locations and test markets. There were always new locations. Best. Client. Ever!

He was eager to discuss the progress of the test market directories. GWCC's business plan had been focused on small cities and rural towns. But David was always looking to expand his reach, and willing to take chances, so he'd recently created test markets in New York, Chicago, and San Francisco, among other large metro areas.

They spent a half hour on the test markets, including going through each of the discount codes that he obsessed over, before she segued to the most important part of the call … at least when it came to her standing with her boss. "David—we are so thrilled with your account, and are proud to have done our little part to help in this great expansion of General Washington Carpet Cleaning. We feel like you're our partner, not a client, and Dennis and I would really like to bring our team down to Valley Forge to meet with you, and allow you to get to know the team that's working around the clock to grow your business."

She could hear the sigh coming through the phone line. "Haven't we been over this, love? I hired you to work for me, not meet with me. I believe in doing, not talking about doing."

"I'm sorry to keep bringing it up, but I think it might be beneficial to meet the entire team."

"You mean Dennis Whitley thinks it's the case," he said. "If he's concerned that if you leave the agency, I would follow, he's right. I don't trust many people with my business, but you and your husband have earned that trust. And because of that, I will put in a call to Dennis and explain the situation, if you think that will be helpful."

"I would really appreciate that, thank you."

"It's the least I can do. Without the help from you and your husband, I would never have been able to accomplish all my goals this past year."

CHAPTER 16

Syria

The timeless beauty of Istanbul had been replaced by the horrors of Syria.

Our "captors" who turned out to actually be our "guides," stashed us under a plastic tarp in the back of the pickup and instructed us to keep out of sight. But the journalism in our blood made it an impossible task not to remove our blindfolds and sneak a peek.

Our chauffeurs were members of the Syrian Free Army, better known as the rebels who were fighting the current regime, literally to the death. They knew the landscape intimately and, most importantly, how to avoid the government checkpoints.

We drove through the Orontes River Valley under a cloudless blue sky. It was the rural heartland of Syria, with little hint of the danger we were heading into. But all that would change when we entered the eye of the storm.

Aleppo is the largest city in Syria, about two hundred miles from Damascus, and was one of the oldest continually inhabited cities in the world. It was once a key trading post between the Mediterranean Sea and

Mesopotamia, but now it was an outpost of terror in the heart of the Syrian civil war.

As we entered the city, we were told to get ourselves back under the tarp, as we were sitting ducks for the government snipers. A long ten minutes later, the truck came to a stop on a street in the Salaheddin section of the city. The tarp was ripped away, and we were pulled out of the truck and urged—with guns in our backs—to move in the direction of what looked to be an abandoned bakery. It was the only structure still standing on that side of the street.

I quickly took in the scene before me. But the clanging of the bullet against the metal of the pickup was a sign I'd taken one moment too long. We were shoved toward the bakery entrance, as one of our guides fired back at a building across the street.

Before we could enter, there was one more reminder of where we were. A dead government soldier was propped up in a lawn chair by the front entrance, as if he were a security guard. And by the smell of things, I guessed he'd been on the job for quite a while. It was a rebel trophy. Carter and I covered our noses and looked away, but Christina couldn't take her eyes off the dead soldier.

A few more shots were exchanged before the door was bolted behind us. The room was not filled with bakers in white chef hats removing another tray of hot cinnamon buns from the oven. But rather, a rag-tag looking group of bearded men carrying intimidating guns—much like everyone else we'd met since we left the club in Istanbul. The smell inside was bad, but it was more along the aromas of a sweaty football locker room, which was an upgrade.

The leader introduced himself in broken English, and marched us into what was once the kitchen. It was now a makeshift infirmary, filled with bandaged soldiers sucking on cigarettes like they were their last resort to stifle the pain. Some were missing limbs. Blood and guts were everywhere.

We passed through into a back room that looked to be an office. Standing behind a desk was another gun-toting bearded man with anger in his eyes. When he saw us, he began shouting at the leader. Christina translated—something along the lines of why did you bring those Western pieces of shit here? They don't care about our cause, and are just using us.

Before we could respond to such a friendly greeting, an object appeared seemingly out of nowhere. And the man standing behind the desk was no longer standing.

"You will treat our guests with respect," a woman said to the man who was now heaped in a ball on the floor.

I couldn't take my eyes off her. It was as if a superhero had swooped down from the sky. A real life Lara Croft. She released her boot from the man's chest—the same boot that had just driven into his chest with such speed and veracity that I'm surprised it didn't kill him—and he scrambled to his feet, desperately trying to suck oxygen back into his lungs.

She busted my stare. "You might want to close your mouth. Catching flies in Syria can be deadly."

I was mesmerized. She had dark, exotic features, and her ponytail bounced as she stalked the room like a lion on the prowl. She wore a tank top and faded jeans—she was muscular yet feminine. I now knew what Carter meant when he said we had a secret weapon on our side.

"My name is Jovana," she addressed us in perfect English. "And as long as nobody pisses me off, we can all get what we came here for."

CHAPTER 17

Before we got what we came for, the rebels would get what they wanted.

Which was a PR-type story that described their plight in their struggle against the Syrian government. And that's where Christina came in—preparing a report that would eventually be broadcast worldwide on GNZ. You help us, we'll help you.

The report would include a firsthand look at the city's ruins. We were escorted through the battered streets to a field hospital filled with rebel fighters, and then to what was left of a home—airstrikes had reduced it to rubble just last night. Devastated family members were sifting through the remains, looking for relatives that everyone knew were gone. Christina was provided a Nikon 3D camera, which didn't have incorporated flash that would attract the government planes overhead. She was encouraged to film a dead child, maybe seven or eight years old, who had been pulled from the destruction. I thought she was going to be sick.

They knew only the greatest shock value would gain the attention of the world. I didn't doubt the atrocities they showed us, but I always sought both sides of the story. My experiences told me that sometimes there were no good guys in these types of conflicts.

With each horrible image, Christina appeared to get more emotional, and her usual cool looked shaken. In a strange way, I envied it. These were the situations where I was able to separate the emotionless reporter and the human being. It's a big part of what made me a great reporter, but it came at a cost. This was Christina's first exposure to a war zone, and she was quickly learning that there was nothing romantic about being a war correspondent.

As nightfall approached, we returned to the bakery. Dinner was a falafel served in a stale pita. I could really have gone for a glazed doughnut.

Unlike Carter, who had no problem sleeping through airstrikes, I remained awake and on edge. I found my way to an apartment above the bakery. I strolled out on a small terrace, which was a risk, but I was feeling claustrophobic and needed some fresh air. The temperatures had dropped into the forties, but I felt comfortable as I sat and stared up at the brilliant stars above—I could swear the moon and stars were brighter in this part of the world. When I looked up, I saw Gwen—just as I had in similar circumstances during my past life, and like always, it gave me a feeling of hope.

But when I lowered my eyes from the stars, to the deserted street below, all I could see was Byron. I could hear his piercing screams, waking up the quiet night. I swelled with anger and my throat grew dry, thirsting for revenge.

Lost in thought, I didn't sense my attacker. I felt a strong grip on the back of my collar, and another grabbed my hair. I was powerless as I was dragged back inside. Just as I did, a ceramic pot exploded, struck by gunfire. I had been leaning against it, just seconds ago.

"Do you have a death wish?" Jovana asked angrily.

There were those who thought I did. Before I could respond, she stormed out of the room, leaving me alone with my thoughts once more.

At dawn, Jovana rounded up the three of us. She led us into a tunnel built beneath the bakery, which looked and smelled like a New York City sewer. We returned to the daylight about a block away through a secret entrance in an alley, where a Toyota hatchback was parked. The rebels had gotten their story, and now it was time for unfinished business.

The morning traffic in Aleppo was surprisingly heavy, as if people hadn't got the memo that a civil war was going on around them. For someone who had grown up in a place where they delay school if there is a dusting of snow, I was impressed by their resilience.

"Notice that taxi," Jovana suddenly said, pointing to an American-looking yellow cab that had pulled curbside. Getting in was a man wearing traditional Middle Eastern garb, including a turban.

"That's him," she said.

I looked closer. There are things you remember about someone who held you hostage for weeks—his movements, the way he carries himself—that are impossible to fake. "That's not Az Zahir," I blurted, with the troubling feeling that we were being set up.

Jovana shook her head with mild disgust. "I was referring to the driver."

My eyes refocused on the man behind the wheel, also in disguise, and this time I was looking at the man we'd come all this way to see.

"Let me guess, the man he's picking up isn't a random customer?"

"He works for me. Zahir thinks he's going to direct him to a meeting with the leadership of the Syrian Free Army. Al Muttahedah offers their services—weapons, soldiers, intelligence—to both the government and the rebels in exchange for safe harbor. Then when the two sides are done destroying each other, they can move in and rule the country."

I noticed a detachment in her voice when she discussed the rebels and their cause, which confirmed what I'd thought since our first encounter. "You're not Syrian, are you?"

"I'm from Serbia … a place I'm told you're very familiar with. The rebels hired me for my expertise in these types of domestic disputes—one can learn a lot from monsters like Slobodan Milošević, as my family did."

She seemed to know a lot more about us than we knew about her, which concerned me.

"The rebels are passionate, but not always the smartest," she continued. "When I arrived, they were doing things like using walkie-talkies, whose frequencies were easily detected by government forces. Most of them are chauvinists, so they didn't like the idea of being subordinate to a woman, but they eventually chose living over saving face."

She looked directly at me. "Do you have any more questions, or can I do my job now?"

"One more—where did you learn to speak English so well?"

She smiled. "University of Michigan. Two things I've learned to despise in this world are war and the Ohio State." She turned serious again, and chose her words carefully. "I never completed my degree—I had to return to Serbia when my family needed me. I would do anything for my family."

We followed the taxi out of the city, into an area dominated by farmland and pistachio trees. We kept at a safe distance, and at one point Jovana stopped the car and observed with binoculars—watching the cab pull to a stop in front of a desolate farmhouse. Then Az Zahir and her contact got out and entered the house. Just the sight of Zahir made my blood boil.

Jovana stepped out of our vehicle. She replaced the cartridge in her Glock, before shoving it into the waistband of her jeans. She then outlined how things were going to go down. Carter would come with her—they would approach the farmhouse on foot. Christina and I were ordered to wait exactly five minutes, and then pull the Toyota up to the house. I didn't like being relegated to driving the getaway car, but it was clear there would be no debate.

I moved behind the wheel, and quietly watched as they walked toward the farmhouse.

Christina was anything but quiet. "So this is how things get done? I guess all that rah-rah journalism stuff you drilled into me was nothing but BS."

"What you did yesterday was journalism. This is a lesson about staying one story too long."

"For someone who claimed to do his job without pride or prejudice, you sure made a quick transition to judge, jury, and executioner. That's what this is, right? An execution?"

"It's about sticking up for a friend."

"This has nothing to do with Byron, and you know it! It's all about you and your fragile ego. You can't live with the mistakes you made, so now you have to drag everyone else into them. Why don't we call Byron and see if he wants this … since it's about him, and all?"

She pulled out a phone, and I knocked it out of her hand. "If you stick around this business long enough, you're going to be forced to do things you're not proud of. I guarantee it."

"Nobody's forcing you to do anything."

"If you don't want to be here, why don't you go hitch a ride back to Aleppo? If you do some more PR for your rebel friends, maybe they'll let you live."

"I'll bet Murray would be real proud of you right now."

Bringing my mentor into this was a low blow. But our five minutes were up, and we would have to put our hostilities on hold. I drove the Toyota at an even speed toward the farmhouse, and parked beside the taxicab. Right on cue, Carter burst out of the house with Az Zahir in his clutches. Jovana was right behind, holding a gun at his head. They opened the trunk of the cab and tossed him in. It was straight out of a mob movie.

Jovana pushed me to the side and took over the wheel of the cab, while her contact got into the Toyota. Once Carter was inside the cab we were ready to go … except that Christina pulled the worst possible time to be Christina. She stormed out of the vehicle and trudged off—to where I had no idea, and I doubted she did either.

"Christina—get back here!" I shouted.

"Her funeral," Jovana said, starting the vehicle.

I knew she wouldn't lose a second of sleep about leaving her here. But I would never sleep again. So I got out before she could speed off. I caught up to Christina and grabbed her arm. "Stop acting like a baby—get your ass back in the cab before you get us all killed!"

She pulled her arm away and journeyed on. But she didn't get far before we were hit by a sound so powerful it sucked the air out of the world, and dropped me to my knees. It was the unmistakable sound of a jet fighter, and I knew it was too late.

The Toyota was blown to smithereens, as was the farmhouse. I crawled to Christina and draped myself over her, as if that would somehow shield her from another bomb. It might have been illogical, but it was instinctive. I could feel her whimpering underneath me. Welcome to war.

We then lifted off the ground and began levitating. *Are we dead?*

I must have asked the question out loud, because I received an answer, "If you were, you wouldn't be going up."

It was Carter's voice. He'd slung Christina and me over his shoulders like sacks of potatoes. He also grabbed Jovana, who remained in a trance, staring at the wreckage of the car in which her contact had been blown to bits. Carter knew this was no time for sentimentality—he tossed the three of us into the back of the cab, and sped away.

CHAPTER 18

It didn't take long for Zahir to give up the location of his boss, Qwaui.

If Al Muttahedah was structured like an American corporation, Qwaui would be the president with Az Zahir being middle-management. They both work under the elusive Hakim, the founder and CEO.

We'd pulled to the side of the road, about ten miles from the farmhouse, where Jovana did the honors. Her emerald eyes were on fire, and I thought she was going to pump a round of bullets in him once he gave up the location. I was struck by how emotionally engaged she was—it seemed personal.

According to Zahir, the Syrian headquarters of Al Muttahedah was located in the mountainous region of Jabal al-Zawiya, about fifteen miles from Aleppo. It was a mud-house camouflaged into a hill, which included escape tunnels and secret hiding areas.

Our first obstacle would be the security guarding the entrance. About a mile from the location, Zahir was summoned from the trunk, and ordered to drive us in. The three of us would be stationed in the back seat, and he would claim he'd captured us following him. Jovana would take a different route.

Zahir drove up to the guards, who were posted at the foot of the hill in front of the barbed wire fence. More beards and AK-47s.

I don't think they bought Zahir's story, but it didn't matter. Jovana had come up behind the guards, and dropped them to the ground, and then tied and gagged them with lightning speed and precision.

Zahir spoke into the intercom, asking for entry, adding, "I have a few old friends with me from Serbia." The gates opened, and we drove up the mountainside to the compound. When we arrived, I instructed Christina to remain behind, and stay out of sight. It didn't require a hard sell—she wasn't going anywhere with me at the moment.

Az Zahir acting as our captor, forced us out of the vehicle, jabbing his unloaded gun into our ribs, making it look, or at least feel, a little too real. We were met by armed guards, who took us into the compound.

The moment we entered, I felt the cold metal of a gun pressed to the back of my neck. It jolted me, even though I was expecting it. Carter got the same treatment. The first thing I saw was our old friend, Qwaui, dressed in his fatigues, and calmly playing chess. It was like we were picking up at the exact moment that we'd left off last summer.

"Mr. Warner and Mr. Carter … we've been expecting you," he said in a calm voice. He looked much like his Egyptian mother, but his dialect was that of his British father.

"These stupid infidels thought they could fool us, but who are the fools now!" Zahir exclaimed in his usual bluster, and I detected the Chicago in his voice. Unlike many of these groups that are comprised solely of brainwashed kids from the Middle East, Al Muttahedah had many connections to the Western World, including its leaders, Qwaui and Hakim, who he met in school in England. Az Zahir was originally from the US.

Zahir slammed his fist into Carter's kidney, making him flinch in pain.

Going back to our last encounter, I found Zahir's over-the-top rhetoric a little fugazy. It was the calm zealotry in Qwaui's eyes that had truly scared me. And nothing had changed.

Except this time we had a secret weapon on our side, I thought, as Jovana stepped into the room. But when she did, she sure didn't seem in a hurry to save the day, and I suddenly understood why Qwaui might have been expecting us.

"A job well done," Qwaui addressed her. "May you always be in Allah's loving hand."

"I'm not here for your Jihad nonsense ... I'm here to get paid. And then I'll be on my way," she shot back.

We had been set up ... again.

CHAPTER 19

Carter has a knack for putting things into perspective, and this time was no different, "It seems like Uncle Al brought along his little niece—Benedicta Arnold."

It had become clear that the government airstrike didn't miss us, but provided us cover. It was no coincidence that Jovana and Zahir were spared, in an information-swap between the Syrians and Al Muttahedah, and we would be delivered to them as the payment.

The doors swung open and the guards we'd just tied up—or that Jovana had made to look that way—walked Christina in at gunpoint.

She looked the same way we'd left her—pissed off. And it wasn't directed at the men who were holding her captive. She looked to Jovana, and then me. "You are so easy, Warner—all it takes is some chick to wiggle her cute ass and you're tripping over yourself to follow her to the depths of hell."

I appealed to Qwaui, "She's not part of this—let her go."

Christina glared at me. "I'm not going anywhere ... and you're not my dad!"

Carter's booming voice halted our spat, "If you two don't stop acting like two-year-olds, I'm going to leave you behind when I walk out of here."

The comment piqued Qwaui's interest. "You sound confident you'll be leaving, Mr. Carter, despite the great odds against you. What would spark such bravado?"

Carter shrugged. "I've dealt with turncoats in the ring hundreds of times—Hulk Hogan comes to mind—and I'm always the one standing in the end. Don't see why this time will be any different."

I thought to mention that this wasn't professional wrestling, and the weapons ratio was about twenty to none, not in our favor, but I decided against it.

Qwaui absorbed Carter's words, nodding like he'd made a point. "I think Mr. Carter has hit on an important topic—loyalty."

His gaze moved to Jovana. The guards read the signal, and seized her. After searching her, and removing her weapons, she was forcefully placed alongside us in the infidel conga line.

Qwaui glared at us. "So have the American journalists come to end the civil war in Syria? I find that to be the definition of hypocritical."

Carter and I knew better than to say anything, but Christina had yet to learn that lesson. "You're calling us hypocrites? You've got to be kidding me."

"The United States is an unsustainable cauldron of non-believers. You have created a divisive subculture of secular Haves and Have Nots, who will eventually fight to the death in your own civil war."

"Is that the speech you're going to make me recite this time?" I asked, referring to the propaganda video I was forced to make the last time we had one of these powwows.

"I'm afraid that no further warnings are needed, Mr. Warner. The United States is on course to destroy itself, and nothing you or I say will change that. I plan to just sit back and watch it play out."

"I'm not here to discuss what will or won't happen in my country—I'm here to discuss Byron Jasper."

He remained disturbingly calm, which continued to prick at my uneasiness. "What is your American saying—three strikes and you're out? Well, I'm afraid you've struck out of luck, Mr. Warner. First you exposed our operation, then you tracked us to Serbia, and now here. So when I'm done with your other friends, you're going to think that Mr. Jasper got off easy."

I stepped toward him, knowing, or at least hoping, that they wouldn't kill me until my usefulness had been used up. But I only made it one step before I felt pain shoot through my knee. I fell to the ground in agony. When I looked up, I saw a smiling Zahir, who had kicked out my injured leg.

"As Mr. Warner recuperates, I will use this time to feed my men" Qwaui said. "Unlike the Americans who shun their soldiers and reward them by spitting on their sacrifice, provide them little in jobs and medicine, we take care of those who have risked life and limb for Allah."

Zahir bowed his head to his boss, as if giving thanks.

"Melk al-yamin," Qwaui said with a nod in Jovana's direction.

"Ghanim," Zahir responded back.

"Please don't do this," Jovana said, in full understanding, as she was dragged off at gunpoint. "Kill me! Anything but this!" she screamed out, and for the first time since we'd crossed paths, she didn't seem in control. Considering her double-cross, it was hard to find sympathy, but I wouldn't wish her fate on my worst enemy. I'd seen the end result of Qwaui's work on many occasions, and it was never pretty.

"I thought you clowns were waiting for virgins," Carter belted out. "We all know she's no virgin."

Christina provided an Arabic translation, "Melk al-yamin means non-Muslim sex slave, and ghanim is 'spoils of war.' Basically, they issued a fatwa that gave Islamic fighters permission to rape non-believers during a war of Jihad. That's their penalty for disbelief."

This drew a rare emotional response from Qwaui, "No fatwa was necessary. Allah has provided permission: Marry such women as seem good to you, two and three, and from what your right hand possesses."

"Which you've twisted into a sick rationalization," Christina fired back.

"My right hand is going to possess your nose … when I rip it from your face," Carter backed her up.

A rhythmic squeaking of the bed-frame could be heard from the room they'd taken Jovana into, accompanied by her wails. It was bad enough to know that Zahir was raping her, but I also knew she was just the appetizer—Christina would be the next "spoil of war."

As if reading my mind, Qwaui pointed in her direction, and one of the guards began escorting Christina toward the same room they'd brought Jovana.

"I think Mr. Warner should get the pleasure of watching his protégé in action … the fruits of his teachings on display," Qwaui calmly stated. I felt the tip of a gun lodged in my ribs, as he pushed me behind Christina.

We entered the room in single file. Immediately, the guard at Christina's side dropped to the floor. A second gunshot rang out, and my guard joined his partner.

I looked up to see Jovana bouncing on the bed as if it were a trampoline. She was wailing at the top of her lungs like a wounded animal, but with a smile on her face. She was fully clothed, unlike Zahir, who was tied spread eagle to the bed, naked, and had a bullet hole through his forehead. A bloodstained pillow lay beside him, which Jovana had used as a poor-man's silencer.

Another guard entered the room, responding to the shots, and received the same fate. She was an impressive shot—shooting while bouncing was no easy feat. She hopped off the bed, and her path was now clear.

Qwaui kept a confident posture as she approached him. But just in case, he had Carter in his clutches, standing behind him with a knife to his neck. It was a mistake that I'd seen more times than I could count—never underestimate the skill-set of a professional wrestler. Carter launched a backwards head butt that likely broke Qwaui's nose, and left him momentarily blinded.

Before the last two remaining bodyguards could react, Jovana shot them both dead. Not wasting a second, she then fired two shots into Qwaui's legs and he fell to the floor in agony.

"That's for Byron Jasper," she said, her face pulsating with intensity. "His legs for your legs. A fair trade."

He screamed at her in Arabic, but it fell on deaf ears.

"Where's Hakim? Take us to him and you live," she offered, but everyone in the room knew that even if he gave up the location of the Al Muttahedah leader, Qwaui wasn't leaving this room alive.

He shook his head, his eyes tearing in pain, but not sadness. "Nobody knows. The system is set up that way. He seeks us out when he needs us, not the other way around."

Jovana looked to me. My experiences had left me with sharp instincts on separating the truth from lies. I thought those instincts had betrayed me by trusting her, but it was looking like that might not be the case. I confirmed what she already knew, and Carter and Christina backed it up. He was telling the truth—he didn't know where Hakim was, any more than we did.

Just to be sure, Jovana gave him one last chance. When she got the same answer, she walked up to him and placed her gun directly on his chest. "This is for my brother, Milos ... your men took his life by shooting him through the chest, and now you will get a taste of your own medicine." And then she fired. And fired again. And kept firing.

Carter and I traded a surprised glance. It takes a lot to shock Carter, but this certainly did. Jovana was the sister of our Serbian guide, Milos. It seemed as if she also had unfinished business.

CHAPTER 20

Rockfield

March 13

Home sweet home—the car service dropped me off in front of the dark house.

As expected, getting out of Syria proved more difficult than breaking in. And our motorcycle-driving smugglers appeared much more concerned about being caught by Turkish border patrol without a stamped passport, than anything that befell us on the journey into hell. But three days after the showdown in Jabal al-Zawiya, we had made our way back to Istanbul.

Carter and Christina were called away to their next assignment—I remembered the constant treadmill of "the business," where you hadn't even come down off one high, before you were chasing the next one.

I took my time in the old city, alone, and finally got to indulge in the self-analysis that Gwen suggested. Seeking answers each night, looking at the moon and stars, I thought there was no more perfect place to be at the crossroads than in a city that for centuries had been at this same intersection of past and present.

I was not sorry that men like Qwaui and Az Zahir were dead. But I was left with the hollow feeling that nothing I could do would ever change what happened to Byron. It was a torch I would carry with me for the rest of my life.

I wondered about Jovana's thoughts on the subject, having gotten "justice" for her brother, but she offered none. She did give us a ride to the city of Idlib, where she unceremoniously dropped us off. I doubted she'd be spending much more time in Syria, as she would become enemy number one of Al Muttahedah once word leaked of what she'd done. I knew it was doubtful that I'd ever see her again, yet the reporter in me was filled with curiosity and questions. I couldn't shake her out of my mind.

March had come in like a lion in Connecticut, yet there was no sign of the lamb as it approached mid-month. My teeth chattered from the cold, as I made my way to the colonial. It was dark inside, and it didn't appear that Gwen had spent much time here while I was gone. My stomach was growling, pleading to get some greasy American food into it, but the refrigerator was bare.

So I went to the place where food was always stocked—my parents' house. I knocked, but the place was completely dark inside, and I couldn't detect any movement.

"Hello?" I called out, after using my key to enter, but received no answer. I turned the kitchen light on, and the note on the counter answered my question. Before my mother gave her blessing to my father's return to politics last fall, as interim first selectman, he promised to honor their Myrtle Beach vacation planned for this March. It was the first true vacation they'd taken in a decade.

I found a bag of potato chips and a beer, and plopped on my dad's favorite chair in the living room. There was something about my childhood home that always provided comfort, and after a tumultuous few weeks away, comfort was what I needed.

Just as I began to settle in, I heard the door open, and I sprung to my feet.

But it wasn't Uncle Al dropping by for some good old-fashioned payback—it was Ethan, Pam, and the kids who checked in on the house each day while Mom and Dad were away. The responsible ones. They looked more surprised to see me, than me them.

After warm greetings, and my providing them evasive answers about my mysterious trip, Ethan informed me that our parents were expected to return tonight. We then touched on important topics, such as plans for Easter, Eli's loose tooth, and Ella filled me in on the team pizza party that I had missed.

I offered them to stay for dinner, but potato chips and beer didn't meet the proper nutritional standards of their household, and they headed out in search of the four basic food groups. Alone again, I settled back in, clicking on the Knicks game. But I got the impression that the Samerauk Elementary girls squad could beat the Knicks tonight, so I began the dangerous journey down the television dial. And proving once and for all that I'm a complete masochist, my channel surfing stopped at GNZ.

Lauren Bowden and Tino Fernandez were showing off their disturbingly white teeth on their nightly show. Lauren began with "Breaking News!" about the latest episode of Huddled Masses killings, which had taken place back on the final day of February. It was the third suicide attack—Scottsdale, Atlanta, and now West Palm—targeting wealthy citizens. And like the previous attacks, the killer wore a shirt that displayed his allegiance to the Huddled Masses—this one read "Jobless"—and left behind a note of rhetoric and demands.

But what was different in this case was that two men had boarded the ship, and assisted in the crime. And when the deed was done, they left the scene via speedboat. Unlike the others, they didn't sacrifice themselves for the cause. And the "breaking news" Lauren spoke of, was that a new photo had been released—it was taken by a passenger with his phone as the men sped away. Lauren pleaded with the viewers to call the FBI tip line that flashed on the screen, if they recognized the men.

She looked pleased with herself, until Tino topped her with some "Really Breaking News!"

"It has been confirmed to GNZ that a top Al Muttahedah operative, known as Qwaui, thought to be the second most powerful man within the terrorist organization, has been killed by a US drone attack in the Jabal al-Zawiya section of Syria. Also believed to be dead is Yassad Az Zahir, a Chicago native, best known for his role in the attempted attack on Soldier Field during the NFC Championship game, two years ago."

Their deaths weren't news to me, but the only drone I could recall was named Jovana. Not that I wanted the credit, but I did make a mental note not to believe anything I ever saw on the news, even if I'm the one reporting it. It served as a good refresher course.

Photos were displayed of the Syrian hideout, which was now just a bunch of smoking rocks. It left no doubt it had been hit by the aforementioned drone, even if it was a posthumous attack.

The coverage switched to a pentagon official who was either a great actor or, more likely, wasn't briefed on the truth, as he was able to keep a straight face while patting himself on the back for bringing Qwaui and Az Zahir "to justice."

Tino did the honors of reading the president's response—to summarize: world a safer place, his policies rock, drones are cool, bad people still out there, need to remain diligent—before passing the baton to Lauren, who segued, "And speaking of Syria, coming up in the next hour will be an exclusive report from our own Christina Wilkins, who had been embedded within the Syrian Rebels, and she will tell their harrowing story as they fight for freedom."

Tino added, "I've been to the most horrific war zones, Lauren, and I can say with great certainty that Syria is the worst I've seen."

I didn't know if it was the greasy chips or just the sight of Tino Fernandez, but I began to feel a pain in my stomach. So just to be safe, I turned off the television.

But I couldn't escape the "Breaking News!" as I noticed the headlights coming up the driveway.

CHAPTER 21

I watched as she stepped out of the van and walked toward the A-frame. The front door was unlocked, and she stepped inside.

Gwen stood in the doorway, her raven hair streaming out of the knit winter cap. We just stared at each other from across the room. It felt like I'd gone another fifteen years without seeing her.

"I was going to call you tomorrow," I said. "I didn't know if you had plans tonight, or something."

"I just saw Ethan and the kids in the Village Store, and he told me that he'd run into you here. So I thought I'd come over and say hello ... so hello, JP Warner. Welcome home."

"It's good to be home, Gwen Delaney."

Gwen closed the door, cutting off the cold draft. But I really didn't feel anything at the moment.

"So how was your trip?"

"It was a little hectic at first, but it calmed down towards the end, and I was able to do some thinking."

"About that, JP—I was being stupid. If we're going to be together, then we have to figure out things together, not apart."

"It wasn't stupid. I think it's what I needed, and you were able to read that. You're always much better at reading me than I am at reading myself."

"Did this thinking result in any conclusions?"

"That I'd already done this before, and I was wasting my time ... and yours."

Gwen's face sunk, and there was an edge in her voice, "So you're saying coming back here, and us, was just a waste of time?"

"No—I mean spending time away from you was."

Right answer. She walked over to me, and wrapped her arms around my neck. We kissed ... and kissed ... and kept kissing. It could have gone on forever, but a voice stopped us.

It was my father, "Don't let us interrupt anything."

My mother trailed him into the house. She looked tanned and rested, but also annoyed by her spouse. She hit my father on the shoulder. "Will you give them some space ... for goodness' sake, Peter."

Gwen put an end to the awkward moment by going to them and hugging them home. "How was your trip?" It was the question of the night.

My father went on to describe each meal they ate along the way, and the results of every hole of golf he played. If you give a politician the floor, expect a filibuster.

My mother's summary was much more concise. "We had such a nice time ... and your friends Byron and Tonya had us down to Charleston one night, which was fantastic. The history in that city is just amazing, I could have spent weeks there."

Last time I'd returned home after an overseas hostage situation, my mother refused to talk to me—I was sort of missing that right now. She continued, "And Mama Jasper's—let me tell you, I don't think I've ever eaten food that good ... it practically melted in my mouth. They said you've never been there, JP, which is hard to believe. Anyhow ... they both say hello, and look forward to seeing you for the Hall of Fame ceremonies next month."

Gwen sent a suspicious look my way, as if to say, *why would they need to say hello if you and Carter were down there visiting?* This is where I could have brought up Syria and unfinished business and how hollow revenge can feel, but I chose not to further incriminate myself.

"I was actually there once, but I had to leave before I ate. Something came up," I said.

"Something always seems to come up," Gwen said, while examining me closely.

"And you should see that Byron play golf. He's better in a wheelchair than most people are on two legs," my father exclaimed, and then detailed each hole they played together.

As he talked ... and kept talking ... my mother performed the Warner family ritual, which occurs after returning to the homestead from any vacation or long road trip. She cooked up fried egg sandwiches for everyone. It really was good to be home.

After the impromptu meal, Gwen and I retired to the colonial, and made our way up to the bedroom. I decided to get out in front of this, "I've been an idiot plenty over the years, but I've never lied to you before and I don't plan to start now."

"You didn't lie, JP—I didn't really think you went to Charleston, and you never said you did. Carter cares about you, and I think he thought you needed to go wherever he took you, and that it was best I didn't know where that was. I was fully aware of this when I encouraged you to go."

"Ask me anything about my trip and I'll tell you every detail."

"I don't want to know. That's the past, and I'm only interested in right here, right now."

"Right now can wait. Tonight we're going back in time."

I took her hand and led her outside and into the woods. I'd made my way over this terrain so many times since I was a child that it didn't matter that it was steeped in darkness.

I found the tree where we once carved *JP and Gwen. True Love Forever,* pulled down the attic-like staircase, and helped her climb into the tree house. I followed her in and closed the hatch behind us.

The tree house was my idea, but Gwen's carpenter father made it come to life, including all the modern amenities. And it took quite a bit of cloak and dagger to make sure she didn't find out, as it was her Christmas gift. It looks like a college dorm room, including bunk beds. If our bedroom had grown into an adult, the tree house was a reminder of our childhood.

Her breath was visible, and she stuck her hands in the pockets of her pea coat, seeking warmth. I turned on the heater, but it would take a few minutes to kick in. I put on some mood music with the iPod docking station. Our song: "Never Say Goodbye" by Bon Jovi.

We picked up the kissing right where we'd left off. I began unbuttoning her coat. "Why don't you take off your coat and stay awhile?"

She grew frustrated with my clumsiness, and undid the buttons herself. She tossed it on the couch, and then pushed me down on the bottom bunk. She climbed on top of me, and we wrapped tightly around each other.

I looked upward, and no longer had to search for her in the moon and stars. My angel was right above me, and she whispered, "Welcome home, JP."

PART TWO –

OLD NEWZ

CHAPTER 22

New York City

March 15

Two weeks ago to the day, Nora Reign passed through this same lobby of her modest Upper West Side apartment building.

She'd approached Luca Rebazzo, the security guard at the front desk. The short, balding man didn't exactly strike comparisons to Hercules, but it always made her feel safer that he was here. The neighborhood was a long way off from the luxury apartment on Central Park West where she used to live. And lifetime away from her formative years in South Africa.

When he saw her approaching, he spread his arms. "Ah, the beautiful Nora comes to warm my heart on such a cold day. What can I do for you?"

She smiled—a rarity for her the last few years, and even more so in her current predicament. "Hello, Luca—I'm looking for the new Yellow Pages book. It was supposed to be delivered yesterday."

He looked incredulous—he wore all his emotions so comfortably on his face. "You gotta be kidding me, Nora."

"Why is that?"

"Because I just broke my back hauling them outside."

"I don't understand."

"I've been working buildings in this city for ten years, and in that time, no resident, guest, or even a homeless guy off the street, has ever taken one. They're a big shrink-wrapped pain in my rear, and the sooner I get rid of them the less I have to look at them."

"Well, I guess you just missed out on witnessing a first then."

"What do ya need, a plumber? I got a pinup board of recommendations by the residents—restaurants, carpet cleaning, plumbers, you name it." He pointed to the cork bulletin board behind him that looked like it had been attacked by a swarm of business cards.

"Thanks for the offer, but I don't want to look up a business—I want to stack them so I can reach up to clean my roof. I've got this spider web the size of a small automobile."

Luca looked quizzically at her. "We've got a ladder in the storage room."

"Sorry, I'm deathly afraid of ladders. Fell off once as a child and knocked my two front teeth out." As if standing on a stack of phone books would be safer.

"But why would you need this year's version? Wouldn't last year's do the trick?"

He sure was an inquisitive one. Just like Nora was when she first got into journalism, but he wasn't making things easier for either of them. "When Tino and I broke up, after I found out that he'd cheated on me with half the city, I threw it out the window at him as he walked out of my life. It was the first thing I could find, and the damn thing was heavy—think I cracked the sidewalk."

He got a chuckle out of that. "I wish you'd hit that rat. I still can't believe he got you hooked on that garbage, but you're the one who got fired, and he's still on the air."

She shrugged. "My reward is I've been sober for nine months now … and he'll get his one day. You know, Karma, she can be a bitch."

"I thought payback was?"

"And when they're working together, it's not going to end well for Tino," she said with a smile.

He nodded with a grin. "They're in the dumpster out back. Take 'em all if you want."

Today, Nora walked through the same lobby. She could see the car headlights out the front door of the building as darkness was beginning to settle. Most people were coming home from work, but Nora was headed out looking for a job.

Her hair was now brunette—the way she wore it during her first jobs at Reuters and the BBC, when she wanted to be taken seriously as a journalist. But then she joined a network for the American cable news, which didn't seem to take the profession as seriously, and she returned to being a blonde, much like the woman she'd encounter tonight—Lauren Bowden.

What she was about to do was very serious business, so it seemed appropriate to call on those serious journalism days, and darken the hair. She also wore her most professional combo of blazer, skirt, and heels. She felt alive for the first time in a long time, which was ironic, since the plan called for her to not be in a few hours.

Luca did a double take when he saw her, a wide grin exploding across his face. "I thought I needed to turn the heat down in here, then I realized it was you, Nora. You got a date tonight?"

She took in his smile, as it would be the last time she saw it. "Even better—I've got a job interview."

"Congratulations! Let me know how it goes," he said, with genuine happiness for her.

She forced one final smile back at him as she made her way to the entrance. There would be no need to fill him in on "how it goes" … the whole world would soon know exactly how it went.

CHAPTER 23

Rockfield

The bell rang.

I grabbed the books out of my locker, but before I headed to class, I took a look at my fellow classmates—Cervino, Herbie, and Rich Tolland. I then made eye contact with Gwen, who was strolling down the hall with her friends Allison and Kristi, holding their notebooks by their side. It was the good old days at Rockfield High.

But when Gwen smiled back at me, I snapped back to reality. The bell was actually coming from the front door, and this wasn't high school. Much worse ... it was a meeting for the high school reunion committee, hosted at the Delaney's house.

Gwen hurried to let in the guest. I braced, knowing what stood behind that door. But because the host had threatened me—I was to be on my best behavior tonight, or else—I held back my groan when Bobby Maloney entered.

But the others present hadn't taken that pledge.

"Look who's here ... Bobby Baloney," Vic Cervino said with a laugh, and the others joined in. I could feel Gwen's eyes on me, and I didn't even risk a smile.

Apparently while I was out of the country, Gwen had lunch in the city with her old friend, Allison Stankiewicz, now Allison Cooper, who was in charge of our class reunion. And at some point during this lunch, Gwen agreed to host this high-powered meeting of the reunion committee. This was all fine and dandy with me, until I found out that my attendance was mandatory. I had tried to sneak away with Gwen's father, who had taken her much, much younger brother, Tommy, to the latest animated Disney movie, but no such luck.

Like a seventh-grade dance, the committee had separated by gender. On one side of the room, we males were discussing our brackets for the "March Madness" college basketball tournament, and plotting ways to sneak away to watch the games. On the female side of the ledger, Gwen appeared sincerely interested as she listened to Allison, Kristi Randolph, and Sarah Aronson describe in great detail the fascinating exploits of their children.

At one point, I observed Allison picked up a copy of today's *Rockfield Gazette* off the kitchen table, which featured a headline about recent sightings of dangerous fisher cats in Rockfield. Her look turned melancholy—reunions have a way of reminding us of the things we hadn't accomplished, which was one of the reasons I don't care for them.

"Fisher cats ... Yellow Pages ... just how we drew it up in college, huh Gwen? Not exactly the *New York Times* and Dunn & Hill."

"Since you took my journalism class, Ms. Stankiewicz, you should know full well that local issues always hold the most importance. The presence of fisher cats possibly threatening the town's children, should be held with much higher priority than something that happened in some embassy in some country you'll never step foot in," said the familiar voice.

Murray Brown, my mentor, the founder of the *Rockfield Gazette*, and our high school English teacher back in the day, had quietly entered during the commotion. He was also our class adviser, which explained his presence at the meeting.

Murray might have been in his eighties, but he still was the most youthful one in the room, as inquisitive and energetic as ever. Along with being the most dapper—wearing his trademark red suspenders and matching bow tie.

"I wish I could say that about my profession, but I don't think it applies to advertising," Allison replied.

"Poppycock—the Yellow Pages remains the most important local search engine. If your furnace went out this winter, it would be the first place you'd turn. Not to a sleek advertisement for an automobile you can't afford."

Now that Murray had arrived, the meeting could officially begin. And it began by going through the list of those who'd been contacted, and how many had responded. Even by small town standards, the fifty-three people in our graduating class was a miniscule number—forty-six had been reached, and of those, thirty-five had committed to attending.

We then went over the details, including the rental of the Hastings Inn in town, which would include discounted rooms for travelers, and the securing of Lefebvre Park, for a family picnic the following day.

Kristi Randolph, who had the same bubbly energy and blonde curls from when she sat next to me in kindergarten, had set up a Facebook page to post information about the reunion for class members. I thought this was a good idea ... until I found out that she had posted numerous embarrassing photos from our high school days. It was the early 90s, so fluorescent colors were the rage. As were the regrettable fashion choices of acid wash jeans, spandex leggings, and slap bracelets. Gwen seemed to have an affinity for hot pink, hair scrunchies, and hoop earrings the size of a Ferris wheel. Seeing myself in my baggy overalls with one hook undone, it was hard to imagine that one day I'd grace the cover of *GQ*.

There were photos of us hamming it up in the school hallways, parties at The Natty, and even a few classics from the beach trip we made the day following graduation. There were plenty from the prom, including one of me and Gwen slow dancing like we were the only ones in the room. It was like we were hanging on for dear life in the photo, as if we knew a storm was heading our way.

When pictures were revealed of Cervino performing his infamous "Cervy Shuffle" at a school dance, it inspired Sarah Aronson to flatter him with imitation. The group urged her on *"Go Sarah ... Go Sarah!"* But someone should have reminded her to first set down her wine glass. The sound of breaking glass ended the dance, and turned the rug the color of Merlot.

She began apologizing profusely, but Gwen wouldn't hear it. "Don't worry about it—I'm just glad you didn't pull a hamstring. And besides, Allison owes me some free carpet cleaning—we'll see if they're as good as she claims."

"General Washington's Carpet Cleaning ... my top client."

"I love them!" Kristi chimed in. "I used the one out of Ridgefield—they got out a stain I never thought anyone could get out in a million years."

During my teenage years, in the few times I had pondered where I might be in twenty years, not once did I think I'd be standing around with my fellow classmates discussing carpet stains. Murray must have been equally distressed, as he let out a yawn and declared that he must be going.

He smiled as he made his rounds of goodbyes, while mentioning that he looked forward to the next meeting. *There would be more?* When he got to me, I said, "You're making a fast getaway. Hot date?"

He grinned as he whispered, "To quote the real George Washington, I can never tell a lie—I want to catch the second half of the games. A little birdie told me that Kentucky is tied with Villanova at the half."

I smiled back. I knew I should have been suspicious of the multiple trips he'd made to the bathroom, when he was really just checking the scores.

The meeting was adjourned, but that didn't mean the party was over. We returned to segregation—the women remained upstairs to continue their quest to determine who has the cutest children, while the men ventured down into Mr. Delaney's man cave to watch the basketball games.

I had to admit, that even though I approached the meeting with cynicism, I actually had an enjoyable time strolling down Memory Lane. It was an overall nice evening, and even Maloney stayed off my nerves—with an assist from Rich Tolland, who served as buffer between us most of the night.

Just as I stepped into the man cave, my phone began beeping like something was wrong with it. I pulled it out of my pocket to find that it was overloading with messages—I didn't even know this many people had my number. I read the first one from Byron. *Are you watching GNZ!? OMG!*

Moments later, I realized I had been a little premature in declaring it a good night.

CHAPTER 24

The last time I'd seen Nora Reign was in a hotel room in Brussels. It was a room she was sharing with Tino Fernandez. Ironically, she was now sitting in the seat Tino normally occupied on their nightly show.

And she was pointing a gun at Lauren Bowden.

Nora and I had come up through the ranks together—I never saw her as a competitor, but as a member of the small, isolated fraternity of war correspondents. The stories we covered were often emotional, and that led to those emotions sometimes spilling over. We were never in love—Nora referred to our time together as "keeping each other warm"—but our bond was deep. Or at least I thought it was. I never saw her again after that night, but the drug rumors soon began to spread throughout the fraternity, and it wasn't really surprising when she was let go by her network. As far as I knew, she hadn't worked since.

I wondered what events had sent Nora down this path. Was it that Tino was just so irresistible? Or maybe it was the lasting scars from when she'd been taken captive in Samawah, while covering a story? I knew the feeling all too well—I still occasionally woke up thinking I was back in that dilapidated house in Serbia with a knife to my neck. The removal of Qwaui and Az Zahir didn't change that.

But whatever it was, it didn't look as though it would have a happy ending.

Nora looked directly into the camera. "I am here to deliver a message from Huddled Masses. I do so because our previous warnings were not heeded.

"Whenever a society—especially one that is supposed to be of the people and by the people—becomes run by an all-powerful minority, which enslaves the masses, a revolution is inevitable. We represent the enslaved— your tired, your poor, your racial minorities, your homosexuals, your sick, your unemployed, your addicted … your Huddled Masses. We had hoped that this could be done without any further bloodshed." Her South African accent always made her words sound sophisticated, even the crazed lunacy she was selling at the moment.

She handed a piece of paper to Lauren, who looked remarkably calm, considering. With a point of the gun, she was urged to read. Lauren kept looking back at the floor behind her, and I wondered if that's where Tino had been displaced to.

The cynic in me thought we might be witnessing Cliff Sutcliffe's ultimate ratings dream. But while some might insist pulling the plug would be the proper move here—before they encourage every wacko to take to the airwaves to spread their crazy ideas—in this case, it was the last thing Cliff should do. This was a crime scene that had millions of witnesses.

Lauren read, "If meaningful steps are not taken to return America to its people, the events that you've witnessed over the last few months— Scottsdale, Atlanta, West Palm … and tonight in New York—will not only continue, but will become a daily occurrence. A new normal for America. The elites will not be able to hide from us, whether that be in a shopping mall, at a wedding, on a yacht, and numerous ways not yet seen, but already feared."

When Lauren finished reading the statement, Nora forced her to her feet, "You have done your duty, and now you will die with honor. You will be remembered as a hero of this revolution."

Lauren scoffed, "It's your own fault that your life is what it is. Nobody made you do those drugs. These elite people you talk of didn't shove that needle into your arm."

The words didn't sway Nora. But just before she pulled the trigger, a monster rose up, like a scene out of a horror movie. Except this monster was wearing a mauve colored suit.

Tino Fernandez made a noble attempt to save the day, but he was limited, with his hands still tied behind his back and his mouth gagged. Nora turned and fired a shot into his chest, and he fell back to the floor behind the anchor desk. Lauren screamed as Nora continued to fire shots at him.

Nora turned back toward Lauren and fired. But nothing happened. She had used up all her shots on Tino, and she began to do a quick change of the clip. It gave Lauren a moment to act, but she remained frozen, blubbering.

If she was going to make it out alive, she needed some sort of intervention, and perhaps the divine type. *Where were the police? The SWAT team? Anybody?* The place must have been surrounded by this point. If now wasn't the time to act, then when? "Somebody help her!" I shouted at the TV screen.

And then somebody did.

The last person I'd ever suspect. Cliff Sutcliffe dashed in as Nora attempted to reload, and tackled her to the ground. Maybe not exactly a tackle, but he was able to grab hold of her, and hold on until the hostage team could move in.

CHAPTER 25

I stared out my bedroom window at a world I wasn't sure I recognized anymore.

In the reflection of the dark glass, I noticed Gwen step out of the bathroom. She was wearing one of the T-shirts that Kristi had given us at the meeting—green and gold school colors with the standard "Class of" followed by the year across the front. Except mine, in which they conveniently left off the CL. It got a lot of laughs at the time, but then everything stopped being funny.

"You were right, you know," I said, staring out at the darkness.

"Did you think I was making up the fisher cat epidemic?"

"I meant about how I was trying to pick up where we left off, and remove anything that happened in between."

"That's a pretty big chunk of your life to just toss aside like it never happened."

"I was just a kid when I started at GNZ. I didn't always like the direction, and the last few years were a constant battle between the reporters in the field and management back in New York. We were a big dysfunctional family, but a family nevertheless, and I feel like someone broke into the family home tonight."

"And it wasn't just some random burglar who broke in, was it?"

I kept eye contact with her in the reflection, as she stood behind me. "When you're out there with the bombs going off around you, and you don't know if you'll make it out alive, you form a certain bond with people."

"But this bond was stronger than the usual one, wasn't it? I could see it in your eyes while you were watching her."

"You're the only one I truly ever cared about, Gwen."

She sighed. "That's a sweet story, but we both know it's not true."

"You think I was in love with her?"

"What I think is that there's been a lot of talk lately about who we are today, and how we have changed. But certain things about us remain a constant, and your constant, JP Warner, is that you care ... maybe too much sometimes. So it's alright that you cared about this Nora Reign, or some other woman who wasn't me—I'd be disappointed to find out that you didn't."

"She's not a killer," I said, which was an odd thing to say, having just watched her shoot someone in cold blood on national TV.

"We never really know people."

"We know them, we just don't know what they're really capable of ... or what might set them off. I'm sure Grady Benson didn't set out to become a serial killer, but something changed inside him. Something changed inside of her."

Gwen wrapped her arms around me from behind, and together we stared out the window. One thing that would never change was how safe I felt in her arms.

My phone broke up the soft moment, and I reluctantly answered. As I listened to the voice on the other end, my calm evaporated, and I could feel my pulse racing.

When the call ended, Gwen asked with concern, "Who was that?"

"It was Nora's lawyer—he told me she is refusing to talk to anyone ... except JP Warner."

CHAPTER 26

I met with Nora in an airless room in the bowels of the Metropolitan Correctional Center in lower Manhattan.

She entered the room, accompanied by armed guards, who chained her to a metal table. She wore a blue, prison-issued jumpsuit. The makeup had been scrubbed from her face, and she looked like she hadn't slept in weeks, but she still didn't look like a cold-blooded killer.

The guards left the room, but were still nearby, and just a suspicious wink could send them into action. Nora's lawyer—a thin, nondescript man with silver hair—remained. The only conversations in this place that weren't taped were the ones solely between attorney and client, so I didn't expect some grand confession from her, but her motives for bringing me here had roused my curiosity.

I took a seat across from her, and met her tired eyes. Apart from the weariness, they looked as they often did—a vulnerability frosted over by a stubborn fire. "It's been a long time," I said.

"Brussels, I believe," she responded in a soft voice.

"Like I said … a long time ago. Why am I here, Nora?"

"To tell my story. Who better to do that than the best reporter in the business? I don't expect you to go soft on me because of our relationship. So dig away."

"I think that's exactly why you brought me here. Hoping you could manipulate me like you always have—put out a propaganda piece for you and your new Huddled Masses friends."

"And what would that accomplish at this point?" she said, viewing the chains wrapped around her wrists.

"To influence potential jurors—the ones who will decide your fate at trial."

"Trial? That's a good one, JP. But I'll be lucky to see my arraignment. I wasn't able to complete my mission, and now they're going to finish it for me."

"And by not finish, you mean you didn't take one for the team. All the other Huddled Masses killers took their own lives ... except those cowards in West Palm who fled the scene."

"Unfortunately, I ran out of bullets."

"If I recall, you wasted them on Tino's already dead body. Was that part of the plan, or was that personal for what he did to you?"

She shook her head, suddenly animated. "If you're talking about the drugs, I'd started on that path long before I had met him. Just a few pills to get me through a bomb-filled night, smoking a joint to make the empty life a little less empty, easing my hop from one war zone to the next. And if I was going to shoot him for revenge, I certainly wouldn't do it on television, and turn him into an even bigger hero."

"How did you get mixed up with this Huddled Masses group?"

"I went to many dark places, but I've been sober for nine months now. It's amazing how different things look when you're sober."

"So you're going to use drugs as an excuse?" I turned to her lawyer. "I hope you can come up with something better than that." He didn't appear amused.

This time an ugly resolve came over her face. "Just so we're clear, I don't regret what I did last night. And I will never apologize for protecting those I care about."

"So if you were protecting someone, then you were threatened. They forced you to do this, didn't they, Nora?"

"I know this must be hard for you to comprehend, JP, but the facts are that I am a full-fledged member of Huddled Masses, and as I said, I have no regrets about what I did last night."

"Not even that you didn't finish the job?"

"I have a feeling I will be made to regret that very soon, but your focus on me is too narrow. You should be concentrating on the bigger picture of what is Huddled Masses."

"Then tell me how it works—who is behind it? Are there clandestine meetings in dark alleys, or is it like some big Amway conference where you all get together?"

She shook her head like I just wasn't getting it. "The revolution is happening right before our eyes, for all the world to see. Maybe the world has just chosen not to see it."

"Very well, but every revolution needs leadership. The American Revolution wouldn't have survived without George Washington and the signers of the Declaration. Average citizens didn't just start randomly shooting British soldiers because 'the revolution was happening right before their eyes'."

"And your point is?"

"That someone gave you specific orders to go to GNZ and do what you did, and they were the ones who targeted Tino and Lauren. And based on the fact that you'd set up a job interview weeks in advance, the timing was not coincidental. Who's behind the curtain, Nora?"

"I just looked in the Good Book. The plan is laid out everywhere you look—in homes, in hotel rooms, I found mine in the dumpster."

"The Good Book? You never struck me as the religious type."

She smiled coyly. "I'm a reporter—I'm wired to get to the most direct source. So for me to buy into religion, I needed to talk directly to God to get the true story. His messengers were always suspect to me."

"So are you saying you found God?"

"I came close, but I ran out of time."

"So what's the name of the holy creator of Huddled Masses?"

"They call him New Colossus," she said, which was also the name of the sonnet behind their namesake. "But as I got closer, I realized that it wasn't a new religion—just a paint job on an old one."

I took a deep breath—if she was preparing for an insanity defense, this conversation could only be helpful.

She looked intently at me. "I think it's important that you find the message of God before it's too late, JP. You've cheated death for so long—I worry you won't find Him before death comes looking for you."

"Is that a threat?"

"Just a friendly warning."

We were going around in circles, but there was one aspect of the shooting that continued to puzzle me, and I needed to get to the bottom of it. "Who brought the gun into the studio? Someone on the inside was helping you."

She shrugged. "That's what makes Huddled Masses such a threat—your neighbor, your co-worker, your spouse. Nobody has ever seen New Colossus, or any tangible proof that he truly exists ... yet like all gods throughout history, there has never been a shortage of those willing to act in their name."

The armed guards re-entered the room, informing us that we were out of time. I grew annoyed. "You basically told me nothing, Nora. So what was the point of all of this?"

She looked at me with an intensity that burned through me, and for a brief moment I recognized the old Nora. "I knew this would be the last opportunity to see you. And I just wanted to apologize for the way things went down with us, and let you know that I'll always care about you ... no matter what you think of me."

CHAPTER 27

Tino Fernandez's funeral took place on St. Patrick's Day in the cathedral of the same name.

You had to be a pretty big deal to have your final sendoff in this venue, and Tino was all that and more. So much so that another service would be held in his hometown of Miami the following day.

I took my seat in the back, and watched somber speaker after somber speaker remember a Tino Fernandez that I'd never met.

When the powerful pipe organ signified that the service was over, I went to say my goodbyes to my GNZ colleagues, including the suddenly single Lauren Bowden. She was dressed in black, with hat and veil covering her blonde tresses. I don't know if it was the dress, or maybe she'd been drowning her sorrows in food the last few days, but she looked like she'd gained significant weight in her midsection.

Before we could make our way out, Cliff Sutcliffe approached me with an offer, as was his way, "What do you say I take you out to eat, JP? To show my appreciation for how you supported a fallen colleague."

I almost laughed, but this didn't seem like the proper venue for that. "I don't think so, Cliff."

"It would really mean a lot to Lauren," he said, as if that might actually help his cause.

"What I meant to say, Cliff, is that I'm the one who's going to take you and Lauren out. I think you both deserve it, for the heroism you showed the other night. It made me proud to be a member of the GNZ family."

"It was nothing, really."

"It was a lot more than nothing, and we both know it. Gwen and I will feel much safer dining out with you by our side."

When Lauren learned of my gesture, she appeared touched. Gwen, on the other hand, looked like she wanted to touch me in the most painful of places. "You do know this is all about getting information from you about your interview with Nora Reign, right?" she whispered.

"The information superhighway is a two lane road, my dear," I replied with a grin, before addressing the group, "I took the liberty of booking a table at Norvell's." A near impossible task on one of New York's most popular holidays, I thought to add.

This led to more tears from Lauren. "Our restaurant, John Peter … you remembered after all this time."

"How could I forget? Our time together was unforgettable."

Gwen looked like she wanted to burst out in laughter, but was confined by the same church/funeral constrictions that held me back earlier.

It was eight months ago during patio lunch with Lauren at Norvell's, when I decided to give up the crazy circus. And when Carter literally carried me out, it also effectively ended my relationship with Lauren. But to prove there were no hard feelings, I was going to take her to a pricey restaurant tonight and extract information about a murder she'd witnessed. One that just didn't add up.

We made the short walk from St. Patrick's Cathedral to Norvell's. Tino's funeral didn't seem to dampen the enthusiasm of the St. Patty's Day revelry in Manhattan. I'm normally in favor of all holidays that are created solely as an excuse for drinking—St. Patty's, Cinco de Mayo, Arbor Day— but that was before I moved to the city and realized that there was a one in three chance that some drunken idiot would puke on you before the night was over. And if you ride the train, the odds go up to fifty-fifty.

We moved through the patio area where Lauren and I had eaten our final meal, and into the warm restaurant. I'd requested a table in the back for privacy.

I recognized our waitress as Bridget, who often waited on Lauren and me when we used to frequent the place. I think she received a medal of honor for her bravery, or should have, anyway.

She looked happily surprised to see me. I'd like to think it was because she missed my lovable charm, but it was likely because I was a really good tipper. But when she saw that I was with Lauren, it was like she'd seen a ghost.

When I introduced Gwen as my girlfriend, Bridget's look turned to pleasant confusion. Perhaps she wasn't an avid tabloid reader, and was unaware that Lauren and I had broken up. Or maybe she did read them, so she was wondering what would compel me to invite my girlfriend and ex to dinner together. I was starting to wonder the same thing.

But being the professional she was, Bridget kept to the basics, "It's good to see you again, and thank you for choosing Norvell's. Our St. Patrick's Day special is corned beef and steamed vegetables. It comes with turnips, boiled potatoes, and a slice of our homemade soda bread. Would you like to order … or maybe start with something to drink?"

The question caused Lauren to burst into tears. And once she had all eyes upon her, she whimpered, "Tino would always order for me … and now I don't know what to do."

"We are so sorry for your loss," Bridget said in an empathetic voice. "And he was very brave to try to save you."

Bridget's eyes moved to the man sitting beside her, and a light bulb went on. "Oh my gosh … you're Cliff Sutcliffe—the one who saved the day!"

"It was really nothing," Cliff tried to play humble.

"Nothing? If it wasn't for you, there's no telling how many lives might have been lost."

Lauren found her resolve. "To be fair and accurate, which is what we in the field of journalism strive for, the assailant's gun had run out of ammunition, so anyone really could have stopped her at that point. As a news organization, I think it's important to get the details right."

Her words didn't seem to dampen Bridget's enthusiasm. I would have loved to see how this played out, but there was more important business to get to tonight. "I think we're ready to order," I interrupted.

Bridget took out her pad, and looked at me, "Will you have your usual, Mr. Warner—our greasiest cheeseburger and bottle of our cheapest beer?"

"Yes, and Ms. Bowden would like an order of hosomaki and a glass of cabernet."

Lauren looked glowingly to me. "John Peter ... you remembered."

Bridget inquired what Gwen would like, and she replied, "I think I've lost my appetite."

"Why don't you bring two bottles of that cheap beer, and we'll share the cheeseburger," I said.

"Two beers, two forks," she said with an "aw so sweet" look.

Last but never least, Cliff ordered the special.

"And that will be on the house. American heroes eat free at Norvell's," Bridget replied.

Cliff ate it up, to the point he didn't really need a meal, while Lauren seethed.

The appetizers were now complete, and it was time for the main course. Good thing, because J-News was hungry for the truth.

CHAPTER 28

I couldn't shake the feeling that there was more to what we'd witnessed. That it was real, but like the way Reality TV is real.

And following my interview with Nora, my suspicion grew. She took the time to plot out this event in cold and calculated style, yet when the moment of truth came, she was overcome by emotion and rage, causing her to not complete the job, letting Lauren live? I was convinced that Lauren was the key to unlocking the truth, even if she didn't know it.

I stared across the table at her like we were the only two people in the room. "Do you know how amazing you are?"

"John Peter? You're embarrassing me," she said, but her blush was urging me to go on.

"You were so courageous in the face of death. Tell me how you did it."

I knew it wouldn't take much for Lauren to tell her heroic tale, and recapture some of the thunder Cliff had stolen from her.

"I was just doing my usual nightly recap of the day's top stories, when all of a sudden I heard someone scream out. When I looked, it was already too late. Nora was behind Tino, and had pulled his tie back, and was strangling him with it. She dragged him off the chair, and his face was the color of his suit. But before I could react, she was pointing her gun right at me."

It made sense that Nora was able to blend in, I thought. She was a known person in the industry, and she was dressed professionally from the job interview, which had gotten her in the door. It wasn't out of the question that she'd convinced an impressionable staffer that she was to be a guest on one of the shows. "Where did she get the gun?"

"I have no idea, my total focus was on Tino. She'd tied his hands with his own belt, then removed his tie and used it to gag his mouth so he couldn't speak ... it was just so horrible."

Another burst of tears came. "I can talk all night, but you just can't understand what it's like to be held captive, unless you experience it."

I had ... on multiple occasions. As had Gwen, when she was held hostage in Grady Benson's beach house and left to die. Probably because of that, she looked empathetic toward Lauren.

"We do know how hard it can be," Gwen said, things suddenly taking a strange turn. "And it wasn't your fault."

"Thank you for your words, it's very kind of you, but you really can't compare our situations. The loss of an international television star would have had much greater effect on people's psyche than the loss of someone who aspired to an anonymous life in a small town."

And just like that, the universe had returned to normalcy. I grabbed Gwen's hand under the table, partly out of support, but mostly to keep her from grabbing a sharp utensil. I didn't like the odds of Cliff saving two lives in one week.

With tragedy temporarily averted, it was time for the old 'divide and conquer.' "Nobody can understand what you felt in that moment, Lauren," I said, feeling that I was losing my grip on Gwen's hand, as she tried to squirm away. "But thank goodness that Cliff was there to save you."

Her face clenched. "The only reason Nora Reign was allowed to get so close to me in the first place was because of Cliff's incompetence. He's the one who invited her in ... he's the one who should be in jail."

I looked to Cliff, seeking an explanation, which he provided, "It is true that I had Nora come in for an interview. But I was just doing what you instructed me to do, JP, which was bring in the top reporters in the business. Nora was one of the best, and you had always spoken highly of her."

And suddenly I was the reason that a crazed woman killed a man on live television. "What was she like in the interview?" I asked Cliff.

"If you're asking me if she seemed like someone who was about to commit murder, absolutely not. And as far as her relationship with Tino, she was very open about it during the interview, and didn't think it would be a problem working with him."

"What about the gun? How did she get it past security?" If she did. I had my doubts.

"Security had emptied her bag, patted her down, and she had to go through a metal detector. A more thorough search than you get at the airport. It was captured on video, and the FBI already went over it in detail."

Appearing overwhelmed by emotion, Lauren excused herself, and made her way to the ladies' room. Gwen glared at her as she walked away from the table. I felt like I should say something supportive, so I said, "I really think she's gained some weight."

"She's gonna gain some more when I fatten her lip."

This was going well—*where's that cheeseburger?*

Without his cohort in tow—and by cohort, I mean the woman who just blamed him for a murder—Cliff moved on to his agenda. My questions would have to be put on hold.

"Okay, JP, you win … I blink."

"Do I get a trophy?"

"No, but my offer is a million dollars."

"It is a little on the expensive side here, but I don't think the cheeseburger and corned beef will be that much. Maybe like five hundred grand."

"I mean the jailhouse interview you did with Nora Reign. I'd hoped that being an employee of GNZ you'd be willing to come forward freely with it, but I understand capitalism, and my lawyers have informed me that you own the rights to the interview, not GNZ. There are no hard feelings."

"It wasn't an interview—it was a private conversation between two old friends."

"That woman gave up privacy when she came onto my set and murdered the anchor of my top rated show. If a 'friend' had a 'private' conversation with Oswald after he shot Kennedy, wouldn't the public have the right to know what was said in that conversation?"

"Tino Fernandez wasn't the president of the United States."

"The president wishes he had Tino's popularity numbers! I'm willing to go to 1.5 million, and offer you the vacated co-host position."

Vacated? "I'm flattered, Cliff, really, but just like the last time you offered, and the time before that, and the time … anyway, I'm not interested in returning to television." And to try to get back into Gwen's good graces, I added, "And if I was, I certainly wouldn't share a screen with Lauren."

"Two million, Lauren's out, and that's as far as I can go. You can do the show solo, or," he looked to Gwen, and I didn't like that look, "maybe you two can do it together."

"You want Gwen to be a TV host?"

"Why not? She's gorgeous, intelligent, and your chemistry is off the charts. And unlike Lauren, she actually has a journalism background."

Gwen thought about it a little longer than I'd hoped, before saying, "That's nice of you to offer, but I've made a commitment to my newspaper." It wasn't exactly a 'hell no, that's the dumbest idea I ever heard,' but it was a no.

"Don't you think it's a little too soon to be talking about Tino's replacement?" I asked.

"All the more reason—we need to stabilize the ship. Our sponsors are nervous and our competitors are ready to pounce. There's no time to waste."

Lauren returned from her scripted trip to the ladies' room, and recited her lines, "So what is it, John Peter … did you make the right decision this time?"

"Oh, I definitely did."

She looked to Cliff, who delivered the bad news with a tilt of the head. There would be no exclusive jailhouse interview to be revealed on her show by its new co-host, JP Warner.

Lauren stood by her chair, her disgusted stare locked on me—perhaps she was waiting for me to pull it out for her, like the good old days. But upon further inspection, she wasn't looking at me—Gwen was the one in her sights. *Uh-oh.*

"I feel sorry for you, I really do," Lauren said to her.

"Excuse me?"

"I mean, I understand why you'd try to hold John Peter back, but it still saddens me."

"I'm not holding anyone back. And who the hell is John Peter?"

"You're a desperate divorcee who lives in a nowhere town and works at a nothing newspaper. That's why you hold on so tight, and convince him not to take this opportunity to get his career back on track."

If you looked close enough, you could see the fire coming out of Gwen's nostrils with each breath. "JP makes his own decisions, and if he wants to go back to TV, he's free to do whatever he wishes."

"Perhaps you're unaware that I'm a professional journalist, and I can see right through your spin. We both know the idea of John Peter spending so much time next to me scares you, especially now that I'm a single woman again. And if he remembers my favorite meals, then surely he also recalls what I would give him for dessert."

Gwen turned to me with a look, as if to say if I didn't do something about this she was going to take that job out of spite, just to make Lauren's life miserable … and mine. So I turned to Lauren, and did what I do best—turning all the anger in my direction.

"Have you gained weight?"

CHAPTER 29

The walk from Norvell's to Grand Central was a short one, but it seemed much longer due to Cliff and Lauren accompanying us. I figured it had more to do with Cliff making his final sales pitch, than making sure we made it safely to our train.

I didn't extract the type of information I'd hoped for during dinner, and I came away thinking the whole thing was fishier than ever. But all was not lost—Cliff received adoration from a cute waitress, and a free meal, Gwen got a job offer, and Lauren likely earned a SAG card for her performance.

The Manhattan streets were quieter than usual, as most of the city was tucked away in festive bars, chugging their green beer. I strategically stationed myself between Lauren and Gwen. My ego wanted me to believe that they were fighting over me, but that would grossly overrate my role in this. Gwen was finding out what I already knew—Lauren's ability to irritate was legendary. It was the one thing we had in common during our relationship.

We turned off Fifth Avenue onto 42nd Street. We passed Bryant Park and the New York Public Library, then stepped under a "sidewalk shed." The tunnel-like structures were set up alongside building construction to protect pedestrians from falling debris and scaffolding. But tonight it just provided a little relief from the stiff March wind.

"Stop! Freeze!" a voice rang out.

We turned to see a police officer fast approaching. When he realized that he'd startled us, he smiled, and said, "I'm just messing with you, J-News. I was patrolling the park when I saw you pass by. I figured it was my only chance to meet you."

He was Hispanic, a wiry six foot, and athletic looking. He stuck out his hand and we shook, even though something was telling me that running away would have been a smarter move.

"Can I help you?" I asked. I noticed his partner remained back by the entrance to the sidewalk shed, maybe twenty feet away.

"Sorry—I didn't mean to scare you and your friends. I'm just a big fan. Man, I was hanging on every second with you when they had you hostage last summer. I don't even watch the news anymore since you hung it up."

Lauren took exception, "That would put you in a minority. Ratings are up greatly since John Peter left."

He shot her a dirty look. "I know all about being in a minority, Blondie. And I said I don't watch the *news* anymore—I wasn't talking about that staged sideshow you put on the other night."

While I couldn't disagree with his assessment, there was something about the tone. When I glanced back at the other cop, I noticed that he was sealing off the entrance with yellow police tape. A squad car had blocked off the other end of the tunnel. The wall facing the street was lined with razor wire. We were trapped

"What's he doing?" I pointed back to his partner.

"His job," the cop responded, no longer sounding like a fan. "This is now a crime scene, so he's walling it off. We don't want any civilians wandering in here while we're taking care of police business."

As he spoke, I focused closely on his face. And I recognized it. "You mean finishing business."

All pretense was over. His gun came out and was pointed directly at me. His partner had made his way to us and held his gun on the others. "Keep your pot holes shut or I'll shut them for you," the partner said in a British accent. Not something you hear every day coming from NYPD.

"I'm going to need to see some identification," I said, trying to remain calm.

The lead cop took out a badge, and jammed it in my face so hard it felt like a punch. He also delivered an actual punch to my midsection, which bent me in half, gasping for air.

The natural reaction would be to scream out for help, but that was the brilliance of the police cover. How many times do you see the suspect calling out bloody murder as the police arrest them? So they could hold us hostage on 42nd Street in New York City and nobody would even give it a second look. Also working in their favor was that the "city that never sleeps" was passed out drunk in an alley this night.

Lauren remained defiant. "Don't you know who we are? I am going to talk to the mayor—he'll have your badge for this."

Not only did they know, but this was a planned meeting. Gwen looked at me for answers. I had none, but my return glance said to play along for now. We must have something they want—if we didn't, we'd already be dead.

"We need to talk," the cop imposter said to me. "We can do it one of two ways. Talk here, or take you down to the station for questioning."

And by station, I got the idea he meant a deserted place where nobody could hear our screams. And I'd seen enough mob movies to know you never get in the car with the bad guy. I would take my chances here. Maybe a real cop would show up, or a drunk might stumble in.

"Then talk," I said.

"I don't know why you continue to try to stop the revolution, Warner—once it began, there was no way to stop it."

"Good to know. But I can guarantee you I have no interest in stopping your revolution, or even slowing it down. Now that we've cleared that up, we have a train to catch."

"Then why were you talking to Nora Reign?"

"She gave me exclusive rights to her interview. I'm a reporter, that's not something you turn down."

"We both know that your relationship with Nora Reign runs much deeper. So time to come clean—what did she tell you in that interview?"

"If you guys are as advertised, then you already know what was said."

"We heard the tape, but we're not interested in Nora's words—we want to know what she told you."

"I have no idea what you're talking about."

The punch to my kidney dropped me to my knees. But I wasn't going to let these guys win, so I struggled through the pain back to my feet.

"She was giving you clues—it's no accident that she chose you to do the interview."

If she had, I wasn't sure what they were. But I didn't think that answer would go over well, so I thought it might be time to make something up. To buy time, I found my inner-Carter, "The code was—if she wore the orange jumpsuit, it meant you were the one who liked to wear women's underwear. But if she wore the blue one, it was Prince William over there."

He looked bemused. Probably because he already knew how this was going to end. "What about the meetings you had with her in Rockfield?"

This one surprised me. But judging by the look on Gwen's face, not as much as her.

"I haven't seen Nora in years."

This time the punch smashed across my lip, drawing blood. Gwen looked like she was contemplating coming to my rescue. My eyes begged her to stand down—these guys weren't playing around.

"Maybe he needs a little incentive," British said. "From what I've heard, JP Warner doesn't do anything for free."

The cop nodded to his partner, and then looked to Gwen. When he pointed his gun at her, my stomach hit the pavement.

"Time to start talking, or your girl is gonna die with a broken heart … as in, I'm going to shoot a hole right through it."

They had to know that shooting her would be a deal killer in getting any information from me, whether I had it or not. They must be bluffing, but I wasn't willing to risk it.

"Last chance, Warner."

"Fine—I'll tell you whatever you want. Just let her go."

"This isn't a negotiation."

I blurted the first thing that came into my mind, "Nora was my everything—my heart, my soul, my life. And then Tino came and ripped her away from me, like some sick game he was playing, and then he threw her away like a piece of garbage. But not before he got her hooked on drugs, and ruined her career. Nora wanted revenge, and that's why she came to Rockfield, seeking my help."

"Now we're making progress—seems a little incentive goes a long way."

"The plan was for Huddled Masses to use GNZ as a vehicle to get their message out, and Nora was the one to deliver that message. But all she wanted was to take down Tino, and she knew I was the one who could help her do it. Because I was still connected to GNZ, I was able to convince them to interview her, which got her in the building, and I was able to plant the gun during a recent visit. All I asked in return was that Nora didn't harm Lauren, as Huddled Masses planned … I couldn't bear to see her harmed.

"It's why she used up all the bullets on Tino, and was unable to 'finish' the job. You're right about the jailhouse interview, we were speaking in code, but it was just about getting our story straight, nothing else."

The only person present gullible enough to buy my story was Lauren. She looked lovingly at me. "You saved my life, John Peter … I'm forever grateful."

"Is this some sort of joke to you," the fake cop said, and re-established the point of his gun at Gwen's head. With his free hand, he shoved me to the ground.

"Seems as if Warner's girlfriends always have bad endings," British added with a cocky laugh.

The gunman nodded, his finger clutching the trigger, and he began to slowly pull it back. Gwen looked to me, urging me to do something.

Someone beat me to it. I'd underestimated Cliff's new love for the heroic. He stepped in front of Gwen. "If you shoot her, you're going to have to shoot me first."

It was honorable, and anything to delay things was a positive. But the bullet would rip right through both Cliff and Gwen at this distance.

"You should have stopped while you were ahead," British said.

And with that, Cliff fell hard to the ground.

But it wasn't a bullet that sent him there. Lauren had shoved him out of the way—a fierce competitiveness on her face. "There's no way I'm letting you take all the credit again, Clifford."

I couldn't believe she was willing to trade her life for some good PR. Well ... actually ...

The moment the words left her mouth, the gunman pulled the trigger. A shot fired directly into her chest, knocking her over like a speeding motorcycle had hit her.

Gwen and I screamed out simultaneously, "No!"

Things then turned from bad to worse, as the gunman now had a clear shot at Gwen. His finger returned to the trigger.

There was no way Cliff was going back for more, as he was curled up on the ground, his superhero days essentially over. I didn't know what to do, but knew I only had a split second to come up with something. My most primal instincts came out, and from my position on the cold ground, I bit into the gunman's leg like a dog.

And then everything went black.

CHAPTER 30

I'd always thought the most spectacular sight to wake up to was the sunrise at Mount Batur in Bali. But I was wrong.

My head was ringing like a fire alarm was going off inside of it, but that couldn't dampen the sight before me.

It was Gwen.

And she was alive!

She set down her novel and slowly made her way to my bed. She had changed out of her "funeral dress" into jeans and a turtleneck sweater. Her eyes were tired, but full of life ... just the way I liked them.

"Are you okay?" we both said at the same time.

Since I was the one lying in a hospital bed, I got to go first. "I am now," I said with a spacey smile. I continued staring at her, before adding, "I can't remember you ever looking more beautiful."

She smiled back at me. "You're on heavy medication."

"What am I on medication for?"

"You have a severe concussion, which is why it probably feels like someone is hammering a nail into your brain at the moment."

I looked at her intently. "I thought they were going to shoot you."

"Dr. Clarkin said that you might suffer from delusional episodes, and short term memory loss, it's to be expected." She leaned in close, right by my ear—my sense of smell was still intact as her perfume was intoxicating. She whispered, "Your nurse slipped this to me on the way in."

She handed me a note, which read; *Don't let the bedbugs bite.*

When I nodded that I understood, she slowly mouthed, *F ... B ... I.*

The FBI was bugging my room? I'd burned some bridges there, especially with an Agent Hawkins on the Officer Jones case, but last I checked I was the victim here.

She pulled back, and smiled again at me. "Now that I know you're going to live, I'm going to have a cup of coffee with Allison."

"I guess it depends on your definition of live," I replied.

She took my hand in hers, and I felt goosebumps run up my arm—my sense of touch was still working. She kissed me softly on the lips. It was good to be alive.

But when she left me alone, the euphoria faded. I had some work I needed to do. If Gwen was unable to fill me in on what had happened after I was clocked over the head, then I'd have to find out myself.

The suit I'd worn to the funeral—and almost to my own funeral—was neatly hanging on a door. Next to it was the chair where Gwen had been patiently waiting for me to come to. Resting on it was a clear plastic bag, which contained the other items I'd been carrying. I needed to get there.

It was only five feet away, but there were a couple of obstacles. The first was the IV in my arm. But the stand was mobile, and I thought I would be able to take it along for the ride. The more pressing issue was that every time I tried to sit up it felt like my head was being bounced like a basketball on the floor.

I'd always been a believer in the "tear off the Band-Aid" method—endure short-term pain for the long-term results. So I forced myself up to my feet, and in my fashionable, backless hospital gown, I made my way across the room, dragging the IV stand.

Pins and needles stabbed my insides and the room began to spin. I somehow made it to the chair, and searched through the bag. Everything was present—wallet, phone, watch, cuff links—except what I needed. *Where was it?* I frantically searched once more—nothing. Son of a ...

I checked the pockets of my suit, still nothing. Did the fake cops take it at the scene? Did the FBI get their hands on it? I heard a stirring in the hallway outside my room.

I hurried—relative term—back toward the bed. I was almost there, and was two movements from being safely tucked in, when my body betrayed me. The spinning increased, first making me dizzy, and then nauseous. I collapsed to the cold, linoleum floor, dragging the IV unit with me. It detached from my arm upon the crash landing, and blood began spilling across the floor.

The cavalry rushed in. A combination of nurses, orderlies, and security, rescued me, and got me into bed. Nurse Graziano, who looked like the stereotypical Italian grandmother, stayed behind to clean up my bloody mess.

"Thank you for your note," I said to her as she continued to wipe the floor. "About the bed bugs."

She looked up at me like I had two heads. She had no idea what I was talking about.

When she left, a man in a suit entered. We had met before, and I could tell by the look on his face that he wasn't here to help me.

CHAPTER 31

The great philosopher, my mother, once said, "Things can always get worse."

I thought of that as I watched FBI agent Scott Hawkins enter my room. His usual partner, Clarisse Johnson, was the one with the sense, which was why she likely made a career decision to avoid JP Warner for the rest of her life.

"It's been too long, Mr. Warner," he greeted me, while pacing my room.

Since we'd crossed paths just back in October, it seemed as if we had a different definition of "too long."

"It's been a busy few months for me, so I apologize that I haven't called," I said. "But I hope you got my Christmas card."

"I spent Christmas investigating the first of the Huddled Masses killings … I'm the lead investigator on the case."

"Congratulations—you're doing a fantastic job. Did you come here so I can reel in the bad guy for you, like I did with Officer Jones?" It appeared that both my sarcasm and my smart-ass were both still intact.

He smiled, or maybe it was a grimace. "I think you mean when I saved the lives of you and your friends."

Not exactly how I remembered things going down, but then again, my memory was a little cloudy at the moment.

Hawkins stopped his pacing beside the chair. He picked up the bag that contained my personal belongings and began rummaging through it, which was probably against some sort of constitutional right. He didn't find what he was looking for, and appeared frustrated.

He resumed his pacing. "So what happened?" he asked.

"I was trying to get to the bathroom, and on my way back ..."

"Cut the crap, Warner—I'm talking about last night."

He paused, before adding, "And before you open your mouth, it's my duty to inform you that I've already talked to the others in this case, and lying to a federal agent comes with a long prison sentence. And you're too pretty for prison."

"Well, in that case, perhaps you can tell me what they said, so I don't perjure myself. Nobody will know ... it's not like anybody is taping us."

He didn't acknowledge my thinly veiled accusation, and continued onward and downward.

"If it helps me get to the truth, then sure, I'll tell you. Obviously, Lauren Bowden isn't talking to anyone," my stomach sank as he confirmed my fears. "But I was able to speak to both Cliff Sutcliffe and Gwen Delaney."

"My former boss, and my current one."

"Mr. Sutcliffe told me an interesting story about the gunman, and how they were annoyed with you for sticking your nose into their business, or revolution, as they called it. He believed that the men were connected to Huddled Masses. Of course, he was able to thwart them by sacrificing his own body to save your current boss from getting shot."

"Seems like Cliff always shows up at the right time to save the day. Come to think of it, he kind of looks like Clark Kent. Has anyone checked his closet for a cape?"

"We'll get right on that. But sticking with the theme, your Lois Lane had a completely different view of events. Or at least a much less descriptive one—in fact, she didn't have much to say at all. Claimed the four of you were approached by police, turned out to be muggers, things escalated, Lauren Bowden got shot. No mention of revolutions."

"Perhaps she didn't trust the man who played fast and loose with her life when she was being held captive in that beach house."

"Question my methods all you want, but she ended up safe, and Grady Benson is going to spend the rest of his life in prison. And whether she trusts me or not, if she stonewalls my investigation, I'll be forced to consider her an accomplice of Huddled Masses, because we all know that's who we're dealing with here."

"So you're taking the word of the 'king of sensationalism,' over Gwen, who happens to be a respected journalist?"

"I haven't chosen sides—I'm going to let you do that. You can break the tie."

"That is very kind of you." I scrunched my face like I was straining to remember. "I recall that we'd eaten dinner at Norvell's, and were walking to Grand Central to catch a train back to Connecticut. Two cops approached, who turned out not to be cops, and trapped us in one of those sidewalk shelters along 42nd Street. They never identified themselves as Huddled Masses, or any group, but they were focused on the interview I did with Nora Reign, and accused me and Nora of using secret codes to relay some hidden messages between us."

"And did you?"

"I had no idea what they were talking about, but when I told them that, they threatened to kill Gwen. So I made up some story, which they obviously didn't buy, because the guy took a shot at her, anyway. That's when Lauren jumped in front, and took the bullet."

I cringed as I re-lived the moment in my head—the bullet ripping into Lauren's chest, knocking her backwards.

"And you're sure they didn't identify themselves as members of Huddled Masses?"

"Only in Cliff's imagination."

He held up the now-famous photo of the men leaving the scene of the West Palm yacht killing. The media was now referring to them as the 'pirates.' "Were these the men?"

"It's hard to tell. It was dark, and they were disguised in police uniforms. Not to mention, the West Palm photo is at a long distance and isn't exactly in HD. All I know is one guy was Hispanic, and the other spoke with a British accent. I don't know if that helps."

"But it would be fair for a reasonable thinking man to make a connection between the events of last night and Huddled Masses, wouldn't it?"

"I'm not a reasonable thinking man."

He nodded his agreement. "What happened next?"

"I have no idea. After the Hispanic one shot Lauren, he aimed at Gwen. I did whatever I could to hold him off, which was to bite the shooter's leg. Next thing I know I woke up here."

I was performing a high-wire balancing act, all with clouded senses. Lying would end up with me in a prison cell, which I got the idea Hawkins would enjoy mightily. But at the same time, I was going to remain in control of my safety, and figure out why these Huddled Masses guys were so interested in me, and what Nora may or may not have told or signaled me. I'd learned from the Officer Jones case that I couldn't trust my life, or Gwen's, to Agent Hawkins.

He looked skeptical. "Tell me more about these meetings you had with Nora Reign in Rockfield."

Did Cliff leave anything out? It's like he taped the entire encounter and played it back for Hawkins. "I don't know where they came up with that—I hadn't seen Nora in years, prior to our jailhouse interview."

"Are you sure?"

"I think I would remember something like that."

He pulled out a tablet device from his bag. A click of a button and a video played. It was of a basketball game. A game I recognized. *"Celebrity Meltdown?* Now you're playing dirty, Hawkins."

"Keep watching."

I did, re-living the moment when I marched toward the referee. Finding out that his niece was on the other team. There went Eliot's glasses. Officer O'Rourke escorts me out. Hawkins hit a button, freezing the screen. "Look closely."

I didn't see anything of note, and wasn't sure what I was even looking for. He switched to a screen-shot made from the video. The still-photo had been edited—a red circle had been drawn around a spectator in the bleachers, directly across from our bench, wearing sunglasses and a baseball cap.

When he enlarged it, I couldn't hold back my surprise. "Holy crap—that's Nora."

Even though I didn't ask, he explained his brilliance to me. Following the shooting, the FBI looked into all of Nora's movements over the last few months. She'd gotten a parking ticket during her visit, and they couldn't understand what Nora Reign was doing in Rockfield, Connecticut on a Friday afternoon, obviously underestimating the historical importance of our game against New Milford Elementary. But she did have one connection to one of the town's residents. So when they checked what JP Warner was doing that afternoon, with an assist from the website *Celebrity Meltdown*, they were able to locate her in the video.

"I never met with her."

"That would go against what we were told by Mr. Sutcliffe. According to his statement, you admitted to not only meeting with Nora, but conspiring with her to murder Tino Fernandez."

"I already told you—I made that up because they threatened to shoot Gwen. And like I said, they obviously didn't believe my story, which is why you weren't able to interview Lauren about it."

"Unless you were in on it together."

"Excuse me?"

"Sounds like a clean up job to me—Lauren knew too much, and had to go, which is why you pushed to take them to dinner."

"You must be kidding."

"And to come up with such an intricate tale in the heat of the moment … it just doesn't sound very plausible."

"I told you, I was trying to save us, or at least buy some time."

"I'm telling the truth, unless it benefits me to lie … is that what you're going with? And frankly, your *impromptu* story adds up—you did have a relationship with Nora, and you both had motive to want Tino eliminated. You did have connections to GNZ to get her in for that interview, and to get a weapon inside."

"So your theory, based on the combination of Cliff Sutcliffe's word, and a video of an elementary school basketball game, is that I'm working in concert with Huddled Masses?"

If Hawkins were capable of laughing at himself, this would have been a good moment to do so. But I also thought he might be starting high, purposely throwing out ridiculous claims, and would eventually work his way down to getting the information he really sought. We were negotiating, and he was creating leverage.

"No, but you know a hell of a lot more than you're telling me, and without further information, people's imaginations might run wild. And if that turns out to be a federal prosecutor trying to make a name for himself, this might not be such a cute game for you."

I was wondering when he would get to the threats. "What do you really want to know, Hawkins?"

"Many things. But you can start by telling me where the murder weapon is."

"We've been over this—I blacked out after he hit me over the head. I assume they took the gun with them when they left the scene."

"I'm referring to the gun that Nora Reign used to shoot Fernandez. She indicated to you the location of it during that interview, didn't she? That's what all this code stuff was about, and it's what you were looking for just now. It was in your bag, wasn't it?"

I began to laugh, but it felt like someone was stabbing me in the eye. "You lost the murder weapon? The one she shot Tino Fernandez with on national TV? How is that even possible?"

"It wasn't lost, it was taken from evidence. Huddled Masses has friends everywhere ... and it seems that you're the friend Nora Reign trusts most. I'll be back to visit tonight, Warner, and I better have it back in my possession by then. And if your girlfriend is hiding it for you, you need to explain the consequences to her. Conjugal visits are not all they're cracked up to be."

When Hawkins finally left, I tried to make sense of things. Meetings that never took place, weapons I didn't have, revolutions I was somehow getting in the way of. None of it made sense. And there was only one person in this world who could make sense of things to me when nothing else added up—I needed to get to Gwen.

CHAPTER 32

Gwen hadn't been inside Nellie's in fifteen years, but the Upper West Side sports bar looked and smelled the same.

Allison made a mad dash for her and wrapped her in a hug. "Oh my God, Gwen! Are you okay?"

"Just happy to still be breathing."

"Even if you have to breathe in the smell of testosterone mixed with Buffalo wings?" She took a dramatic whiff of Nellie's. "You must be feeling pretty nostalgic today to bring me here?"

Since Gwen and Allison had worked here during college, Gwen knew that it would be crowded, even in the afternoon, to watch the college basketball tournament. So it would be a good place to talk without anyone listening in on their conversation.

Allison had snatched the table in the back corner, up against the wall, just as Gwen requested. When they worked here, it was the nightly table of a professional baseball player who used to set up shop and scope the place, picking out the girl he planned to take home that night. And his batting average was much better in Nellie's than it was on the field, or so Gwen was told.

When they took a seat, Allison gave her a long look. "It's amazing—even when you look like crap, you look great."

"Thanks—I hear puffy eyes with dark circles are totally in this year."

Allison then took the place in. "Looks exactly the same. But I must say I'm a little surprised there's no plaque on the wall to honor us. Best. Waitresses. Ever!"

"If it makes you feel any better, I hear your name is still prominently displayed on the men's room wall."

Allison smiled. "Glad to see your sense of humor is still working." But the light moment was fleeting, and she turned serious. "How's JP?"

"He took a pretty nasty hit to the head. Has a concussion—the doctor wants to keep him in the hospital for a few days for observation. I'm sure that will go over well."

"He deserved worse."

"Excuse me?"

"C'mon, Gwen—taking his girlfriend out with his ex, to their 'special' restaurant?"

Gwen shrugged. "I have to give him some credit—most men wouldn't be brazen enough to even attempt that. But I do think there was some method to his madness."

A waitress briefly interrupted their conversation to take their drink order. When she moved on to the next table, Allison said, "Okay, I need details. The news said you were cornered in one of those construction thingies by muggers, who were posing as policemen. But I read a report this morning that the FBI believes it was related to Huddled Masses, and that they shot Lauren Bowden as retaliation for foiling their television hijacking the other night."

"Maybe you can ask my FBI bodyguard," Gwen said, nodding in the direction of a stiff-looking man in a suit. He was sitting at the bar, pretending he was engrossed in a basketball game.

"They assigned you a bodyguard? They must really think you're in danger."

"Can you keep it down? He's not really my bodyguard, but he is an FBI agent, and he's following me."

"If the FBI is involved, then it must be connected to Huddled Masses."

"You can't believe everything you read on the Internet, Allison."

"So you're saying it wasn't Huddled Masses?"

"No—it was them. But you still shouldn't believe everything you read on the Internet."

"Oh. My God! Spill it, Gwendolyn. Why are these crazy people after you?"

"I really shouldn't say anything else. If they think I'm passing information to you, then you could be in danger."

"So we can never have lunch ever again, because someone might think we're passing notes in class? That's ridiculous. And besides, you know I would never give up the secrets—I have everyone's deepest and darkest stored in the vault. How do you think I got such a good turnout for the reunion?"

Gwen gave in—she really did need to tell someone. She stepped her through the story, from JP receiving the call from Nora's lawyer until their trip to the hospital. But it just led to more questions from Allison.

"What I don't get is how you're so sure it was Huddled Masses. You said they never identified themselves as such, and in all the other cases, they were hardly shy about promoting their brand."

"Because I recognized the two guys as the ones from West Palm—the pirates."

"And what about this meeting between JP and Nora Reign?"

"Her lawyer called him—said he was the only one she'd talk to. They had worked together in the past, and he was one of the few people she trusted."

"And from what I've been reading they used to trust each other *a lot.*"

Gwen winced. She didn't think she'd ever get used to JP's past relationships being splashed across the news.

"And what about these secret meetings you mentioned—the ones they supposedly had in Rockfield? Meeting some psycho-ex behind your back is way worse than the dinner with Lauren Bowden, and that was pretty bad."

"I don't think there was any meeting—the look on JP's face said he had no idea what they were talking about, and he's a horrible liar. Besides, if he had the information they wanted, I'd like to think he'd come clean when they threatened to shoot me."

"They were going to shoot you!?"

"They actually *did* shoot at me."

Allison gasped, but tried to cover it with humor, "I always knew you were Wonder Woman. You used your indestructible bracelets to ward off the bullets, right?"

"Not exactly—Lauren jumped in front of me, and she took the bullet. Good thing she had all that protection."

"I knew those weren't real."

Gwen smiled. "Those might have helped to cushion the blow, but it was the bulletproof vest that saved her life." The smile fell off her face. "Whatever the reason, she got to live another day, which I didn't think I would be doing when he pointed the gun at me the second time."

CHAPTER 33

As Gwen continued to describe the events from the night before, the reality started to sink in, and a pit began to form in her stomach.

"The strange thing is, the first time he aimed I was sure he wouldn't shoot me. Almost as if he was waiting for Lauren to step in front. I'm convinced she was the target all along. But when he pointed it at me again, I thought I was a goner."

"Oh my God, Gwen ... I would have totally peed in my pants."

"It happened so fast there wasn't really any time to be scared. There was nothing we could do. Although, JP did try to bite the shooter's leg."

"And they say chivalry is dead."

"He didn't exactly stop him, but caused enough of a distraction to throw things off kilter. So much so that the shooter pistol-whipped him unconscious. And that's when the shots started firing."

"So he did shoot at you the second time."

"No, it wasn't the Huddled Masses guys. I have no idea where it was coming from. I dove to the ground, and covered myself the best I could. When the shooting stopped the fake cops were gone—I assumed they'd been scared off."

"I can't believe this all happened on 42nd Street on St. Patrick's night. Was it the real police?"

She shook her head. "They were as confused as I was when they arrived. It seemed as if we had a guardian angel on our side."

Allison looked out at Gwen's "bodyguard." "Did the FBI have a theory when you told them this?"

"If they did, they didn't share it with me. But to be fair, I didn't share much with them, either."

"Why wouldn't you tell them everything you knew? You're supposed to be on the same team."

"We dealt with the agent in charge, Hawkins, during the Officer Jones case. We learned firsthand that he'd use us as bait if it meant getting his man, and we all know what happens to bait. He was already willing to trade my life once, when Carter and I were held hostage in that beach house."

Allison looked befuddled. "What are you talking about—hostages? And who is Carter?"

Gwen had forgotten that part never made the final draft of the Officer Jones story. She didn't want to get into it—discussing one near-death situation per day was her limit—and luckily Allison's phone rang, so she wouldn't have to.

She looked at it with exasperation. "It's Tully—my carpet cleaner client—I gotta take this."

The call featured a lot of technical terminology that Gwen didn't understand—close dates, pub dates, DQCs and TQCs—so she took a moment to look around the bar and reminisce about her days working here. She wondered if she realized at the time how truly carefree those days were, and if she properly savored them. Probably not, nobody realizes how good they have it at the time.

She felt Allison tapping her on the arm, as she continued to talk into the phone, "Hey, David, since I've done all this work for you, do you think you could do me a favor?"

She smiled at Gwen like she was up to something.

"We held a reunion committee meeting at my friend's house the other day in Connecticut, and someone spilled a glass of red wine on her carpet. So I was thinking that it would be really cool if I could get one of your guys to come out and surprise clean it for her."

Allison waited a moment, struggling to hear over the bar crowd, before saying, "That would be fantastic, David ... and will really get me off the hook. Listen, I'm out at a lunch meeting right now, but let me give you a call when I get back to the office."

After the phone conversation ended, Allison let out an extended breath. "He thinks I'm on call 24/7, like I'm his doctor. He's all freaked out about the Pittsburgh directory for his test market. But since it hits the street in April, I can't tell him anything until then. It's not like the publisher is calling me up to give updates on the printing."

Gwen smiled. "I have no idea what any of that means, but I do understand free carpet cleaning ... so thank you."

Allison seemed still stuck on David Tully. "He's so weird. He calls me anywhere and everywhere, but whenever I try to set up a meeting with him, he refuses. Maybe I should bring you along, and head down to Valley Forge unannounced."

"And you think my presence will get him to meet with you?"

"Not at all, but that way my boss will think I'm going the extra mile for his best client, and you and I can go to the King of Prussia Mall."

"I do love the King of Prussia Mall," Gwen said. "But it's not as easy to drop everything and take off on a road-trip these days," she said, looking directly at her FBI babysitter.

"Tell me about it," Allison replied, checking her watch. Gwen noticed that her demeanor had completely changed since the call—so much of her and Marty's economics hinged on this Tully guy. "I must be getting back to the office—are you going to be okay?"

"I'll be fine—I got the FBI watching over me, how could I not be?" Gwen said with a smile.

"What do you do now?"

"I'm going to head back to the hospital and check on JP. And when he's released we'll go back to Rockfield and live our lives. I don't know what else we could do at this point."

"What if they come after you?"

"I figure if Rich Tolland has been able to keep the paparazzi away since JP returned, then these Huddled Masses guys should be no sweat."

Allison didn't see the humor. "With all due respect to Rich, who does a great job, this is a little beyond his resources. Maybe you should reconsider, and work with the feds."

"JP is doing that as we speak. And besides, he's the one they think is standing in the way of their revolution, not me."

"Yeah, but they know that you're his weak spot."

Gwen thought of the comment the gunman had made about things never working out well for JP's girlfriends.

When they got up to leave, the FBI agent followed. Gwen figured he would have to follow them all the way back to Rockfield. Because if Huddled Masses came after them again, their best chance would be to fight them on their home turf.

CHAPTER 34

My alone time didn't last very long, as I soon received a visit from Dr. Clarkin. He stressed the seriousness of concussions, and I could tell from his tone that many of his patients don't take them seriously enough.

But he was preaching to the choir, as I was well versed in their severity. I once did an investigative report on soldiers who were being sent back to the front lines of war while suffering from concussion-like symptoms, which had devastating effects.

That didn't mean I would completely follow doctor's orders—it just meant that I was aware of the consequences. His plan was for me to stay overnight for observation, and then receive a CT Scan in the morning. In the interim, he suggested rest.

I had a healthy dislike for hospitals, even before my lengthy stay in Landstuhl last summer. And when you add in that I was in the cross-hairs of a group that could get to anyone at any time, I felt the urge to get out of here ASAP. But I knew arguing with Dr. Clarkin wouldn't speed up the process, so I took his advice ... for now ... and drifted off to sleep.

I was woken by my nurse taking my temperature. She then strapped a blood pressure cuff around my right bicep. I'm not sure the harm of waiting until I was awake, but they had a job to do and I respected that. Or at least I'd learned from Landstuhl that my yelling and screaming never accomplished much of anything.

This was a different nurse. And if Nurse Graziano was the Italian grandmother, then this new nurse looked more like a late night cable movie—*Hot Nurses Part Gazillion.* Her white uniform looked about two sizes too small, showing off her many curves. Her dark hair was tied up, highlighting the exotic beauty of her features.

"Sorry to wake you," she said in a soft voice, with a slight hint of an accent I couldn't place. She noted my temperature on the chart, and then pumped the blood pressure cuff.

"Am I going to live?" I asked, forcing a smile.

"As long as you don't make any more trips across the room, you might. It's a very dangerous journey for a man in your situation."

"Because I might faint and hit my head?"

"No, because if I have to clean up your blood, I'm going to kill you with my bare hands."

I chuckled lightly, causing a pot-banging sound in my head, but it didn't seem as if she was kidding.

"Was your journey worth the spill of blood? We must always ask ourselves if the sacrifice is worth the bloodshed?"

I tensed. I don't remember any nurse ever speaking like that—and I'd spent six weeks in a military hospital. "I just needed to use the bathroom."

"Are you sure you weren't looking for this?"

She held up my key chain that contained the automatic car starter. She swung it slowly like a hypnotist to tantalize me.

It was what I was looking for. "How did you …"

"I thought it was odd that you had an object like this in your personal items, especially when you and your girlfriend took the train into the city. And that Jeep you drive is too old to have an automatic starter like this."

My instincts were to sit up to attention, but my head vetoed it. "Who are you?"

She walked up to me and placed her strong hand over my mouth. "You don't want to wake up the bed bugs."

I looked into her steely eyes, and shock waves went through me.

"Jovana?" I said, but it sounded like nothing but muffled gibberish with her hand firmly over my mouth.

"We need to move. I'm going to slowly remove my hand, and I need you to remain quiet. Understand?"

The last time I followed her I was delivered to a terrorist leader like a pig to slaughter, but anything was better than being a sitting duck in this hospital room.

She handed me the clipboard on which she'd allegedly been charting my vitals. It did contain notes, but nothing about blood pressure or body temperature. Across the top was a reminder not to talk, which I would do my best with, but couldn't guarantee. And further instructions included putting on my suit from the previous day. Without time for modesty, I changed right in front of her. She handed me a bathrobe to put on over the suit. She then pointed me to a wheelchair that was ready for takeoff.

"What about the security guards outside my door? They entered when I fell," I asked quietly, breaking the first rule.

"I took care of them," she said. Then reading my horrified look, she added, "I mean I sent them away. I only kill serial murderers and terrorists, but if you keep opening your mouth, I'm going to make an exception for you."

With that settled, she pushed me out into the hallway. There were no guards, just as she said, but with the amount of law enforcement officials in the hall, I doubted they would be needed. It was like the place was in lockdown.

"Is this for me?"

"You certainly live up to your reputation of being completely full of yourself, Warner. Nora Reign went into a diabetic coma in prison last night—supposedly didn't take her insulin, and never informed the prison that she was diabetic."

I didn't remember Nora ever mentioning anything about being diabetic, but it was pretty clear that I didn't know her as well as I'd thought. But her words from the interview hung over me—*I'll be lucky to see my arraignment.*

"She told me that they'd kill her," I said softly, as Jovana pushed me along the hallway.

"She isn't dead. She was transferred here, and they walled off the entire top floor for her, and she's being guarded by presidential-level security. Only in America do murderers get the best medical care."

The heavy police presence increased the possibility that we'd be stopped and questioned, but Nora's arrival had caused enough higher-priority and confusion to allow us to travel freely. We arrived at an elevator that was being guarded by an NYPD cop. Jovana provided him her nurse ID, and he let us proceed.

Once in the elevator, she pushed the button and the elevator began to move. But not in the direction I expected.

"If we're leaving the hospital, why are we going up?"

"First we need to stop off and see an old friend of yours."

CHAPTER 35

She couldn't possibly be taking me to see Nora, could she? I knew from my brief history with Jovana that anything was possible, but even for her that would be a suicide mission.

We got off on the fifth floor. Since Nora was supposedly on the top floor, which this wasn't, it answered my question. But if not Nora, then who?

Jovana wheeled me along the hallway, until we came to a room guarded by another burly cop. She explained that she'd brought her patient, JP Warner, to visit a friend. And when he checked his list of potential visitors, sure enough, I was on it. At this point, I thought the only fitting conclusion to this would be if Jovana was actually a nurse.

She pushed me through the door, where I was staring straight at a woman in a hospital bed. She didn't look like her usual pretentious self, hooked to a series of machines, but she still glowed.

I never thought I'd be so excited to see Lauren Bowden ... alive.

I looked to Jovana in stunned silence.

"Feel free to talk in here, Warner ... the room's been debugged."

"What about the guard?"

"Don't worry about him—he's one of ours."

"Ours?"

"I don't have time for your questions—I have work to do, and then we need to get out of here. Got it?"

"She got hit pointblank in the chest—how did she survive?" I asked anyway.

"Thanks to the bulletproof vest she was wearing. It still hit her good enough to crack her sternum, and collapse a lung. She had surgery last night, but should make a full recovery."

The vest explained the appearance of weight gain in her midsection, but like everything else in this case, led to more questions. "What was she doing wearing a vest?"

"You'll have to ask her when she wakes up, but usually people wear them because they're concerned about getting shot. And since she'd been threatened at gunpoint on television, just days earlier, it seems like the prudent thing to do. But my concern is to find out if the bullets lodged in the vest match the type of weapon that was used in the Fernandez murder."

"So you're the one who stole the gun from the FBI. They think it's me."

She laughed. "Like you could possibly pull that off."

"Who are you working for? If you don't tell me, I'm going to find Hawkins, and then you can explain all of this to him."

"All you need to know is that I'm on your team. But if you're uncomfortable with me getting you out of here, I'll wheel you right back to your room and you can sleep up for your CT Scan tomorrow. Just a friendly warning—sleep with one eye open, because these people you're dealing with are big on cleaning up their messes."

"I get the point—what now?"

"I need to get that vest Lauren was wearing."

"Wouldn't they have cut it off her before surgery?"

"They did, and your buddy Hawkins took it into evidence. But luckily, I was able to get the real one off her prior to that, and replace it with a lookalike, before they were able to screw with my evidence."

She walked to the window and opened it outward. Then seemingly out of nowhere, Spiderman appeared. I'd become so used to the bizarre that this didn't even faze me.

It was actually one of the window washers, who dress up as superheroes to entertain the kids in the children's ward one floor above us. Spidey handed the vest through the window to Jovana, and scaled back up the wall. Seems he was holding onto it for safekeeping. She handed the vest directly to me, with instructions to put it on.

I had a lot of experience with vests from my years spent in war zones, so I was able to hook it on quickly, pleasing Jovana. I placed my suit coat on over it, which was a little tight. Jovana took my bathrobe and tossed it into the hamper.

I took one last look at Lauren as we left the room. Man, was she going to be tough to live with as a heroic shooting survivor, on the heels of the on-air hostage situation. But I smiled—it sure beat the alternative.

We returned to the elevator, and this time made our way to the ground floor. As we rolled into the lobby, Jovana handed me my release papers, which to my surprise, and likely Dr. Clarkin's, we both had signed.

More security and hospital officials met us, and I handed them my papers for review. One of them asked me for an autograph, which I happily obliged.

As Jovana pushed me toward the front entrance, a couple, who looked to be in their late sixties, made their way toward me. "It's your Uncle Fred and Aunt Marie, they came to pick you up—why don't you go give them a hug."

I looked quizzically at her, and received an annoyed "go on" nod. So I did. I stood and walked gingerly—my head feeling like a punching bag. My steps were slow, but steady, no dizziness.

"Aunt Marie" greeted me for the first time with a big hug, wrapping tightly around my bulletproof vest.

"The car is waiting outside," Uncle Fred said, after we shook hands. They led me out the front entrance of the hospital. As we exited, I looked back to Jovana, but she was already gone.

CHAPTER 36

The cab dropped me off in front of my brownstone in Upper Manhattan.

There were no tearful goodbyes exchanged with Uncle Fred and Aunt Marie—just a direction to go inside and await further instructions. I had a lot of instructions at this point, but very little answers.

I entered through the ground floor entrance, and savored the smell of home, even if I'd rarely been here since relocating to Rockfield. And with Christina now traveling the world for GNZ, she no longer was my unofficial house-sitter. On the rare occasions she was in town, she shared an apartment in Hoboken with her friend Daman.

I have a cleaning service come in twice a week to keep the place up. Now that I was retired, I no longer housed sensitive information here that my rivals desired to get their hands on, so I was less paranoid about letting strangers inside. I had to admit, the place never looked better. But it also felt colder, and less homey.

I closed the front door behind me, and strolled to the French doors that led to the outside garden. It had always been my favorite part of the place—an oasis within the concrete jungle of Manhattan that always reminded me of home. The garden was still dormant in March, yet I could visualize Gwen and me planting it this spring, working in the yard like an old married couple.

But for that to happen, we would have to make it through the next few months alive, which wasn't a given.

I started to make my way up the spiral staircase when I heard a noise. Someone was upstairs, and the cleaning service wasn't scheduled for today. This is the part where Carter would whip the gun out of the waistband of his jeans, and almost look happy about the sudden turn of events. I didn't own a gun, but I was wearing a bulletproof vest, which might come in equally handy. It certainly did for Lauren.

I reached the second floor Great Room. With its high ceilings and natural light shining through its oversized windows, it was my favorite room in the place, and where I spent most of my time when I was here. For the most part, it looked its normal minimalist self—a desk, flat screen television, and a leather couch. A couple of paintings on the walls. The one main difference was the woman sitting on the couch with her legs tucked underneath her, and sipping on a bottled water like she didn't have a care in the world.

An uncomfortable feeling came over me. And not just because Jovana had broken into my home.

She looked up at me. "How's your head?"

"It has a lot of questions in it at the moment."

"Can I get you anything for the pain?"

"They haven't invented the drug to stop this pain, but thanks."

"Good—it's better you don't take anything. I need your mind as clear as possible. Do you understand?"

"It still feels a little cloudy, but once I got my bearings, and began moving around, I started to feel sharper."

I knew my brief resurgence was being fueled by adrenaline. I also knew it would soon wear off, resulting in a crash.

"You deserved what you got, you know," she said.

"Because I attempted to stop the revolution?"

"No, because you were stupid enough to take your girlfriend out with your ex. You're going to need to be smarter if you plan to get out of this alive."

Speaking of my girlfriend, and the main reason for my discomfort. "What are you doing in that dress?"

It was the back-less, shoulder-less, generally less-is-more dress that Gwen had worn when we spent New Year's in the city. She'd left it here that night, and we hadn't been back to pick it up. The vision of me and Gwen in the garden was replaced by a less happy one—Gwen walking in to discover Jovana lounging on my couch and wearing her dress.

"The nurse's uniform wasn't the most functional attire, and about three sizes too small."

"Plenty of my clothes were available, and they're quite functional—jeans, T-shirts ..."

"If you haven't noticed, JP, I'm very much a woman."

Oh, I had noticed. And I got the idea she was aware that I had. As much as she claimed to want my mind clear, it was in her best interests to keep me under her spell.

"It seems your reporter skills have eroded in retirement. The JP Warner I studied wouldn't be asking me about fashion—he'd want to know what the hell I was doing in his home."

"No—a good reporter would know that you must first return to the beginning to get the true story. So how about starting from the top?"

"Will you settle for the ending?" she said, and clicked my key chain. There was a recorder set up in the plastic car starter. I had used it to tape Lauren's answers at dinner, but now I hoped it would tell me what happened after everything went dark.

When she played that portion that the media was now calling the '42nd Street Shootout', all I could make out is what sounded like gunfire, pinging off the scaffolding, and a lot of shouting and commotion. "I take it that you were responsible for this. Who are you, and who are you working for?"

"I'm just the girl who keeps saving your ass. Now come over here so I can explain our next move."

She patted the couch beside her. I knew getting that close would not be wise, but my legs were starting to wobble, and my head was feeling heavier by the second. And since there was no other furniture in the room, I took a seat next to her.

This did not mean I would completely cave in. "There isn't going to be any next move until I start getting answers."

"You're a pain in the ass, do you know that?"

"So I've been told. Now tell me who you are, or get out of my house."

Jovana sighed. "Since you're so keen on going back to the beginning, I grew up in Serbia during the atrocities. My parents had a certain level of influence, and contacts within the United States. That allowed me to come here and study at the University of Michigan. While in college, I was approached by members of the CIA. They were short on agents in the region, who could get inside the Milošević government, and thought I would be a perfect choice."

"So you're CIA? That's who 'ours' are—the guards, the window washer, my loving aunt and uncle?"

"I turned them down on numerous occasions. But after my parents were killed, and I returned to Serbia, things changed. I now saw it as an opportunity to get close to those who killed them."

"And did you?"

"They won't be harming anyone else," she said coldly.

"Was anything you told us in Syria true? Was Milos even your brother?"

It looked like I'd set her face on fire. "Of course he was! After the civil war ended, and post 9/11, my duties shifted to the Arab world. My looks could pass for Middle Eastern, and my Arabic was strong. I'd been tracking Qwaui and Az Zahir for more than a year—I was the one who convinced them to hide out in Serbia, and proved my worth with them by setting up the deal that freed Az Zahir.

"The plan was for them to lead us to Hakim. But when there was no contact, and doubts rose that Hakim was even alive, we decided to take them out last July. That was, until a reporter named JP Warner showed up looking to do an interview, and ended up becoming front page news when he was taken hostage."

"Was Milos CIA, also?"

"No—he worked only for me. And his mission that night was to get you and your team as far away from Qwaui as possible. He was supposed to drive you on a wild goose chase to nowhere, but Al Muttahedah was one step ahead of us."

She grew emotional, and I gave her a moment to recover. I needed a break myself. Reliving my capture was taxing my remaining strength.

When the passion returned to her face, I said, "You used us to get your revenge on them. We were your stooges."

"Willing stooges—you wanted them as badly as I did. I admit I took advantage of Al Muttahedah's unhealthy obsession with you—I knew if I could get Carter to bring you along, Qwaui would open his doors to us, and give me the opportunity I needed. You were easy marks."

"You toyed with our lives. And you brought innocent people into it—Christina had nothing to do with this."

"Christina Wilkins can take care of herself just fine, but I understand your protectiveness. I was the same way with Milos, as were my other siblings—he was the baby of the family. And don't act like your trip to Syria didn't turn out well for you—you got your revenge without having the responsibility of pulling the trigger. I did all the dirty work ... so a simple thank you would be appreciated."

She wasn't getting that anytime soon. "I'll bet your bosses weren't thrilled about your dirty work?"

"They would have preferred Qwaui taken alive, yes. But we got all we could out of him—you saw it with your own eyes—and we were able to recover a treasure trove of documents and computers that has set their organization back years. And my bosses got to clean everything up with the drones ... they love playing with their drones. So all's well that ends well."

"If things ended so well, why the demotion?"

"What are you talking about?"

"One day you're taking down Al Muttahedah's number two man, and now you're playing nurse for a retired reporter."

Her confusion turned to laughter. "You really don't see it, do you? It's like you're in the center of a storm and you still think it's a sunny day."

"What's that supposed to mean?"

"I wasn't demoted. I'm working on the same case I've been on for years ... Huddled Masses *is* Al Muttahedah."

CHAPTER 37

For once I was speechless. So Jovana did all the talking, "Do you remember a few years back when a group of contractors from Heathcott Security were taken hostage in Iraq, in the city of Basra? The company was based out of London, and the hostages were made up of Americans and British."

I thought for a second, trying to fight through the ringing in my head, but had no recollection

"How about a caravan of civil engineers captured on the same day in southern Muthanna, near the Saudi Arabia border? They were attacked by uniformed men, posing as Iraqi police ... sound familiar?"

"There were so many of those type situations that it was hard to keep track of."

"Yes, there were a lot of hostages taken, but very little coverage by the Western media. By that time, the US had stopped caring about the war they started and tried to shove it into the back of the closet with the out-of-style shirts."

"So you're blaming the media for these people being kidnapped?"

"Partially. But you weren't alone—the politicians were facing an election year and they wanted no part of hostages being paraded on the news every night. Most people were very comfortable with the story being buried."

"And this is somehow connected to this Huddled Masses group?"

"Both groups of hostages were taken to the same place. An abandoned Education Department building in Samawah."

My memory was jarred, just as Jovana thought it might. "Nora."

She nodded. "Nobody much cared about the hostages until a well-known reporter got too close, and was taken captive herself. Suddenly the headlines were on the front page, which got my bosses involved. The situation in Samawah became a top priority, and we sent in some of our best men to get them out."

She held up a photo of a man I recognized. "Xavier Gallegos was a sharpshooter on our elite, and most secretive rescue team. He was the best we had."

"He was also the guy who shot up the Scottsdale Mall last Christmas in the name of Huddled Masses."

She held up another photo. "Timothy Wade was also part of this team."

"The wedding in Atlanta—the one who poisoned the food, before taking his own life."

"Now that's the reporter I remember."

"So you're saying that the Huddled Masses are composed of a secret CIA-sponsored special forces unit? No wonder you don't want the FBI, or anyone else to know."

"I didn't say that. We do know that Gallegos and Wade were Huddled Masses members, and they were the ones who gained access to the building where the hostages were being held, and were given the most credit for their release. It wasn't an accident, and they weren't releasing the hostages to safety … they were unleashing them upon an unsuspecting world."

She reached for a folder that sat on the coffee table, and removed another photo, which she handed to me. This one of a burly, bearded man on a boat. "Jimbo Thompson—he worked for Heathcott Security, and was one of the hostages. If you haven't figured it out by now, Heathcott was a dummy company set up by Al Muttahedah."

"He was also the captain of that yacht in West Palm."

"Jimbo went missing after his release, as did all the other thirty-two men and women who were held hostage in Samawah. The only time they pop up on the radar is to murder innocent people."

The reason these people could disappear was obvious—nobody was looking for them. And these types of contractors and security officials in Iraq, and places like it, lived transient lives, going from country to country, willing to work for the highest bidder. It had been a years since their capture, and the killings in the US didn't begin until a few months ago. They were completely off the radar, and the CIA wanted to keep it that way.

"How did you make the connection?"

"The files I told you about in Qwaui's hideout. Liam Scott and Manny Ontiveros were prominently featured, and identified as high-level Al Muttahedah operatives. We were able to match them to the photo of the 'pirates' of West Palm. Up until that point, we thought Gallegos and Wade were just rogue agents hired by Huddled Masses, but hadn't connected it."

I knew them better as the two goons who were aiming guns at my girl, and responsible for this nasty headache.

"Are you trying to tell me that Al Muttahedah took these hostages, brainwashed them, and turned them into suicide killers? Seems farfetched."

She looked incredulous. "No, Warner—the indoctrination was already complete by that time. What I'm telling you is that this was a meeting. A Huddled Masses convention, if you will, made to look like a hostage situation. This was a convenient way to meet."

I tried to wrap my throbbing head around what she told me. "I guess it *was* like an Amway meeting. Nora said they called the leader New Colossus—have you figured out his identity?"

"The man who is ultimately in charge of Al Muttahedah is Hakim. But that makes things even murkier. Many believe Hakim is dead, or hidden away so deep in a cave that he might as well be. But his ghost is being kept alive to act as the boogieman, so nobody is completely sure who is running Al Muttahedah these days."

They had operated more erratically this past year, and had drawn more attention to themselves, which was in contrast to Hakim's style. "Could Qwaui be New Colossus? He was second in command."

"If the killings suddenly stop now that he's dead, or take on a different signature, then we can assume he was the orchestrator."

"But don't these terror cells have plans years in advance?"

"That's the thing about Huddled Masses. They are current and agile. You can plan an attack on a building years in advance, but not a wedding or a party. There is real-time communication going on. Yet there is almost no related chatter—we have no idea how they're doing it."

"Nora said they got their marching orders from the Good Book."

"From what I know about Nora Reign, she spent a lot of time on her knees, but it was rarely to pray."

I grew irritated. "Watch what you say about her."

"You still care for her … that's cute."

"She's not here to defend herself."

"She cares about you too, you know."

"You don't know her."

"When she told you that they threatened someone she 'cares about,' who exactly did you think she was referring?"

"How would I know that?"

"According to the documents we found, when she sobered up last summer and balked at going through with her mission—the response was to threaten her by taking someone close to her hostage. Anything interesting happen to you last summer?"

"Serbia was about Nora?"

"And here you thought the world was all about you."

I refused to let her under my skin, and moved on, "So why not go public with what you know—work with the FBI instead of against them to stop the next attack? Maybe someone out there has seen these missing contractors."

"It's important that we keep this contained, which is why we confiscated the evidence, such as the gun and vest. And you trust Agent Hawkins as much as I do when it comes to being a team player."

"Or you don't want it to get out that many of those involved can be traced back to the CIA and their affiliates. It would be quite embarrassing, especially after all the praise you received for the hostages' release. The same hostages who turned out to be Huddled Masses."

"No, because if the American public finds out, the country will likely end up under martial law. You know how it is here—killing is just the cost of freedom, until a turban is involved, and then you trip over each other to feed your constitution through the shredder."

"You do know my *American* taxpayer dollars pay your salary, right? So maybe a little respect."

"I'm the best use of your tax dollars in a long time … and while you're busy waving your flag, I'll be the one making sure it's still flying."

I blew out a deep breath, and tried to process everything she'd told me. And then something hit me. "The one reporter who beat all of us to the scoops on the Samawah hostages was Tino Fernandez. Did he get too close … is that why they killed him?"

Her eyes pierced me. "You've got to be kidding me, Warner. It's right in front of your face."

When I remained myopic, she exclaimed, "Tino was one of them! He's the one who got Nora involved. He was the one who got the gun inside the studio. Nora was supposed to shoot Lauren, but she went off script, and turned on Huddled Masses, killing one of their key members instead. It also meant her actions left them with three threats they needed to clean up—Nora, Lauren, and you. Nora is obvious, but they also couldn't ignore what Tino might have told Lauren during their relationship. And you, because of what they believed Nora might have signaled you during your meeting."

I needed to sit down, but realized I was already sitting. Nora was actually fighting back against Huddled Masses. She was far from a hero, and was involved in this up to her neck, but I was starting to recognize the woman I once knew.

Jovana stretched like a cat and yawned. "Saving your ass has tired me out, so how about you giving me a shoulder rub?"

I could see where this could go very wrong for me. "I really shouldn't."

"C'mon, Warner ... it's the least you can do for me getting you out of that hospital. Those places are germ factories. You'd probably be dead by morning."

More likely from a gun than germs. "I really can't. I don't think my girlfriend would approve."

"Last I checked, she's not here. Just a shoulder rub ... I'm not asking you to take me to bed."

"Don't stop on my account."

I snapped my head around, which hurt like hell, to see Gwen, which was going to hurt much more.

She stared down at Jovana. "Nice dress," she said, before turning her attention to me. It wasn't the same loving look from earlier. "I went back to the hospital to look for you, and I was told you checked out, which was not only news to me, but also to your doctor."

I pointed to Jovana. "She's my nurse, and said it was okay."

"I know ... we met at the hospital. Thanks for the note about the bedbugs, but you failed to mention the other insects I needed to look out for."

The room grew awkwardly quiet, so much so that all I could do was hear the ringing in my head. I clicked on the TV, attempting a distraction. It turned on to GNZ—just my luck.

The anchor was previewing an interview they planned to do tonight with Lauren Bowden, who had just woken from surgery. He added that Lauren had gained access to a tape that proved that Huddled Masses was connected to an international terrorist group. "And much more!" he teased

Jovana began ripping off my shirt, which I didn't think would help things with Gwen. When she exposed the bulletproof vest, she searched it until she located the recording device hidden deep within it. "Son of a bitch," she shouted out. Lauren did have a source on this information—she had been recording our every word since we took possession of the vest.

PART THREE –

WHISKEY SOUR

CHAPTER 38

Upper East Side, New York

April 10

It was past eleven when Marty Cooper returned home. And despite another sixteen-hour workday, he felt invigorated the moment he stepped through the door.

He smiled, remembering back to when he first came to the city, right out of Wharton. At the time, the idea that a high-rise apartment could ever be considered a home seemed as crazy an idea as aliens landing on the Empire State Building. But that's exactly what Allison and the kids had done—they'd turned it into a home.

He tiptoed through the foyer, trying not to wake the sleeping household. When he entered the living room area, he heard a monotonous electronic drone.

Allison had fallen asleep at her computer, using her keyboard as a pillow. He was convinced that his wife could sleep through anything. At their first apartment in Brooklyn, the elevated G and F trains ran right by their bedroom window and she didn't miss a wink.

He gently lifted her head off the keyboard, stopping the terrible sound. Her eyes fluttered open and she smiled. It made the entire day worth it.

He took note of the papers and binders surrounding her workstation—David Tully tying them to the grindstone once again. But after almost losing the life they'd built, he realized that work, even at these crazy hours, was easy. It was not working that sucked the life out of him.

"Hey, sweetie," Allison said in a groggy voice. "There's some leftover pizza in the fridge if you're hungry."

"Thanks, but I had a sandwich at the office. It should hold me until morning," he replied. He took her into his arms and carried her to the couch. He gave her a kiss on the forehead and watched her fall back into a deep sleep.

He kicked off his shoes, and stretched his tired legs out on the coffee table. He then clicked on the TV.

He turned to the news, hoping to catch up on the world he'd missed out on all day. The top story was another attack on innocent citizens. This one took place in Pittsburgh, at an encampment on the South Side, an area frequented by the city's homeless. It was retaliation against the Huddled Masses group, which had declared war on the wealthiest segment of the population.

This group, which called itself Whiskey Tax, had fired numerous shots from a cannon—*a cannon?*—into a group of homeless, killing three, and injuring many others. Nobody was arrested or charged, but a written message had been left behind. In short, the group would continue to target the poor and minorities, until Huddled Masses ceased their war against them. It went on to say they were forced to take this route, since the US government had not lived up to their obligation to protect them.

At a press conference, an FBI agent named Hawkins described the actions as "vigilante justice." He held up a sketch of a man seen behaving suspiciously in the park prior to the attack, who they wanted to bring in for questioning. A phone number for the FBI tip line was provided, and he promised anonymity to anyone with information.

Marty turned it off. The amount of crazy in the world really bothered him, even more so since the kids were born. *They shot a cannon at homeless people ... really? Who does that?* He wondered if the world had always been this nuts, or whether you just hear about it more with all the Internet and social media.

The report prompted him to look in on his sleeping children. His first stop was Gracie, the ten year old. *Where had the time gone?* While she more resembled him physically, especially the dark hair, she was all her mother when it came to personality. Both his kids were, which made him proud—he couldn't think of anyone he'd rather them take after than Allison.

He kissed Gracie goodnight, softly wishing her sweet dreams, and then ventured into the room of eight-year-old Chase. He tucked him under the covers that he'd kicked off onto the floor, and tousled his mop of blond hair.

On his return to the living room, he passed by Allison's workstation, and something caught his eye. It was a printout with the heading *Test Markets.* Marty Cooper Consulting LLC had been hired by General Washington Carpet Cleaning to be in charge of their rapid expansion across the country, and he knew all their markets backwards and forwards. He used a complex formula to pinpoint what they called "Red Wine, White Carpet" clusters. They usually ranged from small cities to upper-crust towns like Ridgefield, Connecticut and Lake Zurich, Illinois.

Large metro areas didn't fit their demographic. Yet according to this printout, these "test markets" were in major cities like Atlanta, Phoenix, and even Manhattan. *What the hell?*

He went to Allison, and lightly shook her awake.

When her eyes focused on the sheet, she said, "Those are markets that David has been testing advertising in."

"I realize that, but he never cleared them with me. He's doing it all on his own."

"Well, sweetie, it is his company. All you can do is make recommendations … if they fail, then he can't blame you."

"But why do all this analysis, and work—radius studies, street level mapping, yada, yada—if he's just going to do whatever he wants?" Marty replied, his irritation building.

"You know David—he needs to feel he's in charge. That's why he calls me twenty times a day."

"I think he does that because he has a crush on you."

"Could you blame him?" she said with a sleepy smile. "You're probably doing too good of a job, and he feels left out of the success. And for the record, next time you tell me I shouldn't bring my work home with me, I will reference this conversation," she made her point, and drifted back off to sleep.

Marty knew she was right—he took the list back and stuck it in the folder. But when he did, another sheet caught his eye—a list of directories and their publish dates.

The news report of the Pittsburgh attack was still fresh in his mind, otherwise he wouldn't have given it a second thought. The Phoenix/Scottsdale directory came out last December, the same month as the mall shooting. When he looked down the list, he noticed that Atlanta was published in January, West Palm in February, Manhattan in March, and now Pittsburgh in April.

He found a stack of proofs for the test market ads. Allison would proofread all ads methodically before releasing them to the publisher—even the smallest error would be caught by Tully.

Marty scanned down to the discount code. Basic stuff—call the listed number, provide this code, and you get 15% off your next carpet cleaning. He studied the Manhattan ad, and then the Atlanta one. But what caught his attention were the numbers used in the code—he recognized them.

He retrieved his laptop, opened the software, and began punching in the discount codes. First he focused on the ads related to the cities where attacks

took place, and then compared it to ones where no attack occurred. *What the*
...

He thought of waking Allison again, but she would just laugh at him. So he got a pad and paper out and began writing. And when he connected all the dots, a sick feeling came over him.

It had to be a coincidence, he told himself. It made no sense. These long hours were causing him to lose his mind. He would sleep on it, and things would make sense in the morning.

But one of those commercials popped into his head. The ones incessantly shown in New York since 9/11—*If you see something, say something!*

Sounds simple enough, until what you saw earns you a lengthy psych-evaluation at Bellevue. And what if *saying something* would bite the hand that literally fed you? It would be easy to let it go, see how things play out ... until you factor in that if you're right, more innocent people could die.

The FBI tip line popped into Marty's head. That's what he would do—he knew he wouldn't be able to sleep if he didn't. So he found the number, and thought of the best way to do this. Should he use the home phone? Should he disguise his voice?

But logic overtook his paranoia. If they "outed" those who use these tip lines, nobody would ever use them. He still didn't want to wake Allison, so he used the phone in their bedroom. And it wasn't a person who answered, but a voice message. So he laid out his theory the best he could without sounding like a total nut—adding a little voice disguise, just to be safe.

He felt better. At least for a few minutes, until the phone rang. This time there was a voice at the other end of the line. A man's voice, telling him that he was an agent for the FBI. That they believed there was credence to his theory, and it was important that they meet right away.

"Can't this wait until morning?" Marty asked.

"Lives are at stake, Mr. Cooper," said the voice on the other end.

CHAPTER 39

Allison Cooper woke up to the sounds of her little ones scurrying around the apartment. She reached over to Marty's side of the bed out of habit, but all she got was a big handful of couch cushion.

She pulled herself to her feet, realizing she'd never made it to bed. It started to come back to her—she'd fallen asleep at the computer and Marty carried her to the couch. *Her middle-aged, white-collar Hercules!* He kept waking her up to talk about work … test markets, or something like that.

She peeked into Gracie's room, and found her and Chase engrossed in a video game, already dressed in their school uniforms. "You guys getting ready?" she asked.

Gracie looked at her, and with her beautiful sarcasm, replied, "Are *you,* Mom?"

She looked down at her sweats, and ran her hands through her messy hair. Good point. She took a quickie shower, and dressed in her battle gear—a blue pantsuit—for another crazy day of following her favorite band, David Tully & the Yellow Pages.

She made her way to the kitchen, to find that the greatest kids in the world had made breakfast. Toast, slightly burned, which was overcompensated with gobs of strawberry jam. Not exactly Eggs Benedict, but better than anything she would have been able to whip up with so little time to spare. What she really could have used was a cup—more like a whole pot—of coffee, but she would pick one up en route.

As they were getting ready to leave, Allison noticed a folder sitting on a table near the front entrance. It was where Marty would often leave one of his quirky notes when he left for work at some God-awful hour, always guaranteed to make her laugh. But there was nothing funny about what was written on a sticky note attached to it—a number for the FBI tip line. *Why would Marty be calling the FBI?*

Allison did a quick search through the folder, and at first glance it looked business related—which meant Tully related. She shrugged, and decided to take it with her—maybe she'd make a trip downtown at lunch and drop it off to him. *What a great wife!* And get the scoop on the FBI number. *What a sneaky wife!*

The Dunning School was within walking distance, and what a pleasant walk it was; the morning giving off the first hints of spring. The school was a little Upper East Sidey pretentious, but the kids loved it, and with Marty's business taking off this year, they could actually afford it again. *All hail General Washington Carpet Cleaning, the father of their bank account!*

She walked them right to the door, and as always, they were met by the no-nonsense security guards who would usher her children inside. The ritual always made Allison feel safe about dropping her kids here for the day. She wished Gracie luck with her science project presentation, and she nodded back her thanks for the support—her first-born was too cool for a hug from Mom. Chase ran by, barely scraping her cheek with the kiss.

Allison would hail a cab to the office, but her first priority was coffee. And she found her favorite street vendor, Merton, who sold only straight black coffee that would straighten your posture. Not the cappuccino double latte nonsense that the Upper East Side mothers tried to impress each other with.

She reached the curb, and was about to flag a cab, when two men in dark suits approached her. One was Spanish looking, the other pasty white.

"Are you Allison Cooper?" the Spanish one asked.

"Actually I'm late for work."

"I'm FBI Agent Nunez, and this is Agent Lillibridge," he pointed to his buddy, who faked a smile back at her. "Could we speak to you for a moment?"

They both shoved badges in her direction. She looked them over meticulously, as if she knew what she was looking for.

"And what would you like to speak to me about?"

"Your husband ... Marty Cooper."

Her stomach dropped. "Is he okay?"

Agent Nunez flashed a comforting smile. "Oh, he's fine ... sorry if I alarmed you. We had a meeting with him this morning, and he has some information for us. He said he might have left it in a folder at your apartment."

"Why would my husband be meeting with the FBI?"

"We are not at liberty to go into detail, other than to say we're investigating one of his clients, and he has been very cooperative." He held out a cell phone. "You can call him to confirm if you'd like."

She remembered the sticky note about the FBI tip line, which was attached to the folder containing information on Tully ... their meal ticket. She knew he was too good to be true. What business grows like that without doing something illegal?

She composed herself. It was probably nothing. And even if it was, all she could do was cooperate and hope for the best.

"That won't be necessary. And it's your lucky day, because I have it right here." She searched through her bag, but found nothing. That's weird— she swore she stuffed it in her bag at the school, because she didn't really want the security guards to see a folder that read *FBI Tip Line*.

"Well, I thought I did," she said, coming up empty. But now she began to second-guess herself—did she actually bring it with her? Had she set it down momentarily when she helped Gracie with her backpack?

"I'm sorry—I must have left it behind in my rush."

"Then perhaps we can stop by and get it. It shouldn't take long, and we can vouch for you at your place of business," Nunez said.

As if Dennis wasn't paranoid enough. She could picture her face when she showed up late with a couple of federal agents on her arm.

"If I said no, you guys could go in and get it anyway, right?"

The agents looked confused. "Yes, we could get a warrant, but we're hoping not to have to go that route."

"What I'm saying, is I'm late for work, and you need this folder, which I can't stop you from getting. So why don't you just go there and get it without me?"

They looked surprised, and caught off guard. "I guess we could, but would need written permission," the Spanish one said.

"I'll do you one better," she said and called ahead to their doorman, Booker, who would arrange for the building security to supervise their visit. They would know more about what they could legally touch or not touch, anyway. A deal had been struck. Just doing her civic duty … and expediting their journey to the unemployment line.

She wanted to discuss her FBI encounter with Marty, but she wasn't able to reach him all morning. She did remember him telling her that he had a meeting with a prospective client today—one they might really need if Tully ended up sharing a cell with Madoff.

Just before noon, she got her first Tully call of the day. She did her best acting, not wanting to sound like anything was amiss.

The only thing unusual from their conversation was that Tully voiced frustration about not being able to get hold of Marty all morning. *That must be some important meeting not to return the Tully calls,* she thought.

Just before she left for lunch, she got a call from Booker. He informed her that the FBI was unable to find what they were looking for at their apartment, and they tore the place up pretty good in the search. Booker also had the impression that they were headed to her office to discuss things.

Great … that's the last thing she needed. She grabbed her coat—time to get out of Dodge before the cavalry arrived. But before she could escape, her phone buzzed. "Allison—you got a call on line three … says it's urgent."

She groaned—it had to be either Tully or the FBI. But she was pleasantly surprised to find that it was Gracie. At least until she realized that Gracie had never called her from school before … *and urgent?*

"Is something wrong, honey?"

"No—I had to say it was urgent for them to let me call you. They have a strict policy about personal calls here unless you're sick."

"Did you just want to talk to your Mommy before your big presentation?" she tried to keep it light.

"I already finished … totally killed it," which Allison had learned is a good thing. "I'm calling because I must have accidentally taken Dad's work folder when I grabbed my backpack this morning. I thought he might need it for his meeting today … I tried to get him, but got no answer."

She had momentarily held Gracie's backpack before she entered the school, so she could straighten her uniform. Allison must have placed the folder in there, instead of her own bag.

"Thank you so much for calling, Gracie. It *is* important. I'm just about to head out for lunch—I'll drop by the school and pick it up."

"Sounds good … I'll leave it in the office for you."

"No," Allison said with a little too much intensity. "You hold onto it, and I'll have them call you down to the office when I get there."

She was almost out the door when her phone buzzed again. "Allison—there's two FBI agents here to see you in the conference room."

Crap! She was so close.

But when she entered the conference room, it wasn't Nunez and the pasty guy. It was Agent Hawkins, whom she recalled seeing on TV from the Huddled Masses investigation. She also remembered that Gwen wasn't a fan.

His partner was a black woman who introduced herself as Clarisse Johnson. Allison was struck by the seriousness in her eyes.

"Where is Agent Nunez?"

The woman agent looked confused. "Who is Nunez?"

"The FBI agent who I talked to this morning. Isn't that what this is about ... the missing folder?"

"No, this isn't about a folder. It's about your husband."

CHAPTER 40

I don't know what the official first day of spring is, but for me, it's marked by that initial whiff of springy smell in the air. Today was that day.

I drove along Blueberry Bush Road with the top down on the Jeep. It was a beautiful morning … at least until I clicked on the radio. The story of the day was the retaliation against Huddled Masses by a group called Whiskey Tax. Americans had officially hit the panic button, and were now starting to take up arms against each other.

It had been over three weeks since the St. Patrick's Day attack. I still had a constant dull headache, and bright lights gave me problems, but I was making steady improvement. It was also nice to get my driving privileges back, which happened last week.

I never returned to the hospital after my escape, but I did agree to see my local physician, Dr. MacDougal, and get a complete checkup from the neck up. This was strongly urged by Gwen, and I was doing all I could to remain on her good side. Sure, things had been good with us since my second injury-related return to Rockfield in less than a year. And *really good* the night of my return, when Gwen threw me a welcome home party that included just her, a white doctor's coat, and a stethoscope around her neck. But I was well aware I had violated the three strikes rule—1) dinner with my ex, who insulted Gwen in the process 2) almost getting her gunned down on a New York street for my sins 3) the Jovana shoulder rub—and I knew the bill would arrive at some point.

I hadn't seen or heard from Nurse Jovana since she left to "discourage" Lauren and Cliff from using any sensitive material on the air, after discovering their listening device in the bulletproof vest. She must have been convincing, since there hadn't been a peep from either of them on the subject since. Part of me wanted to join her in helping to solve the case, but the CIA had plenty of resources to find the killers without incorporating a retired reporter nursing a head injury.

The only person I discussed the case with was Gwen. Although, I left out a few parts that Jovana had filled me in on, such as the connection between Huddled Masses and Al Muttahedah. I rationalized that it was classified information, and it was my duty as an American citizen not to discuss it. But the real reason was it was so insane that, combined with my recent head injury, revealing it might get me sent back to the hospital.

Gwen's final analysis of the case came down on the side of pragmatism—that we should let the "proper" authorities take care of it. And by proper, she meant not me. She acted strangely detached from the whole thing, considering they tried to kill her. I tended to take these things more personally than my better half.

Not to be undone, I also showed off some pragmatic chops—contracting to have a top-of-the-line security system installed at the homes of my parents and Gwen's father. If these guys were willing to come after us in the middle of New York City, I figured they'd have no qualms finishing the job in woodsy, remote Rockfield. So far so good, but things had almost been too quiet since my return.

But I was determined that none of this would spoil this splendid morning. I'd finished my interviews for my hard-hitting, investigative report that would appear in this Sunday's *Rockfield Gazette*—about the preparations for the upcoming Easter egg hunt at Lefebvre Park—and my next stop was Dello's outdoor grill on Main Street to grab a juicy cheeseburger and curly fries. Living the dream.

A beep from my phone interrupted my thoughts. I glanced at the phone and saw that it was a text from Gwen—*Get back to the office ASAP!!*

My mind filled with possibilities. Some good, like Murray had left for the day and she planned to show me all the news that wasn't fit to print. But there was something about the urgency in the words, and the fact that Gwen Delaney never uses multiple exclamation points, which left me concerned. It goes against all the rules of grammar she holds dear.

As I sorted through possibilities, I heard the sirens behind me. *The police?* And my bubble was officially burst.

I pulled over, and watched Rich Tolland exit his vehicle and walk briskly toward me.

"No coffee this time?" I said when he reached the Jeep.

He pointed at the phone in my hand. "So you did get the message."

I looked at the phone, and then up at Rich—his look was deathly serious. "Oh, come on, I wasn't texting and driving. You know I'm the biggest proponent of tougher laws on it … and even did that public service announcement for you."

He shook his head. "I didn't pull you over for texting, JP. I wanted to know if you got the message from Gwen."

"What's going on, Rich?"

"You need to follow me."

CHAPTER 41

Just like our high school football days, I followed the Toll Booth's blocks until reaching the end zone. In this case, it was a weathered house on Main Street that the *Rockfield Gazette* shares with a local realtor. Rich dropped me off, and sped away without explanation.

Gwen met me at the front door with the grimmest of looks. "What's going on?" I asked, the pit in my stomach growing by the second.

What she told me next made my head spin. "Her husband was murdered?"

"That's what the FBI believes. They found him in the lake at Central Park this morning, made to look like a mugging gone badly. The building security camera captured him leaving after midnight, and getting into an unidentifiable vehicle."

"Any idea why he was headed out at that hour?"

"He called an FBI tip line just before he did, and had an interesting theory about who was behind Huddled Masses. If he was right, it answers the 'how.'"

The 'how' had been a roadblock we'd hit every time we'd discussed the case.

"She was met by two men claiming to be FBI, who said they'd met with Marty that morning, and they were investigating one of his clients. They told her that they were looking for a folder that Marty had left behind in their apartment. But according to the real FBI, Marty's time of death occurred sometime before sunrise. They also found the phones in their apartment were bugged, which is why someone knew he called the tip line. And oh by the way, these fake FBI agents met the description of the men who attacked us in New York."

"And Allison has this folder?"

"Yes, but she's obviously a mess right now, so please don't get all JP on her."

When I stepped inside the office, Allison was sitting behind Gwen's desk with Murray consoling her. My insides began to boil. It was one thing to drag me into this—I signed up for this life—but to go after Allison and her family, who were innocent bystanders, they had crossed the line.

"I'm sorry," was all I could think to say, and she nodded her thanks, mechanically, as if in a daze. She appeared more numb than anything. The really bad emotions would attack her later. At least that was my experience from Noah's murder.

Gwen led me behind the desk, rubbing her hand across Allison's shoulder as she passed her by. A laptop computer had been set up, and I noticed two familiar faces on the screen.

"I called Byron and Carter—I thought they could help us sort this all out. And they agreed to Skype in," Gwen said.

They were in Charleston, preparing for Byron's induction into the Charleston Hall of Fame—a ceremony I was supposed to attend, before a blow to the head curbed my travel plans. I took note that Christina hadn't joined them, predictably still holding a grudge from Syria.

With some encouragement from Gwen, Allison walked us through the events of the last couple of days. The painful path eventually led us to this morning, which included her rendezvous with agents Nunez and Lillibridge, better known as the "West Palm Pirates." They were in hot pursuit of a folder, which Allison unknowingly handed off to her daughter. And because Gwen had passed along her distrust of Agent Hawkins, she chose not to inform him of this. One person she loved had already died over the contents of that folder, and she was determined that there wouldn't be another, so she followed her instincts.

When she informed Hawkins that she was going to pick up her children from school, he didn't appear to be overly concerned about her safety. He'd already searched her apartment and interrogated her, so she was no longer of any use, or so he thought. Clarisse Johnson did offer to accompany her, but Allison declined, claiming she didn't want the FBI presence to scare her children. But instead of returning to the apartment with the folder, she went to a nearby parking garage where Marty paid an absurd amount of money to house a car they barely used. She then drove directly to Rockfield.

I was reminded that whenever people get in trouble, their first instinct is to return home. And if I was those after them, Rockfield would be the first place that I'd search. This worried me.

"Where are your kids now?" I asked.

"At my house," Gwen spoke for her. "Rich Tolland is on guard. He doesn't know all the details, but is aware that Allison and the kids could be in danger. He promised not to include or inform anyone else without speaking to us first."

So that's why he was in such a hurry. It made me feel better that he was there, but I knew we'd need to get him help if he was to have any chance of warding off Huddled Masses.

Gwen handed me the folder, and I read through its contents. Allison mentioned that she'd only seen the innocuous top page in her morning hurry, and didn't realize that Marty had written out his theory in the pages that followed. Not that she would have believed it. On the surface, it seemed like it was the work of a child's imagination.

It centered on his client, General Washington Carpet Cleaning, and its owner, David Tully. When I finished reading, I looked up. "Yellow Pages? That's the Good Book?"

I'd been expecting satellite phones and encrypted messages, or at least some clandestine meeting in a dark alley. Dan Brown would not be cool with the Yellow Pages being the 'how.'

"As we become more complex as a society, some of our simple has turned exotic," Murray observed.

"It's about the codes," Allison said. "Tully provided me a customized discount code to be placed in the ads for each test market, Phoenix, Atlanta, etc. To the normal consumer, it looked like a random number that would need to be provided to get their 15% off. But Marty recognized the numbers—which were only placed in directories where there was an attack—as geocoded addresses from a mapping software that he uses in his business."

"So they're addresses?" I asked.

"I used the same software to help plot some of our courses in my GNZ days," Byron's voice came through the screen. As the resident techno-geek on our journeys, his knowledge base saved our behinds more often than Carter or I would ever admit. "It's not an easy system to use, so you really need to know what you're doing. But it can map down to the sewer on your street. I just plugged the 'discount codes' in, and they're all addresses ... all leading to the same place."

"The place where the killings took place? That wouldn't make sense to me. A yacht wouldn't have an address, would it?"

"Not the location of the killings, JP. The codes all lead to phone booths in the respective cities."

"Phone booths? I thought they'd gone the way of the dodo," Carter remarked.

"Believe it or not, Big Ugly, there's actually about 300,000 of them left in the US ... mostly in major metropolitan areas," Byron said.

"So the number listed in the ad goes to the phone booth? I'm confused," I said.

The look on Gwen's face reminded me of when she tried to help me with my homework back in our school days, and I just wasn't getting it. "The phone booth is the trigger. When a Huddled Masses follower views the ad in their area, and it contains the geocode, they go live. The code leads them to the phone booth, where they call the listed number, and provide their discount code. This checks them in—the caller ID informs the powers-that-be that the call came from the designated phone booth—and sets them up to receive further instructions. To everyone else, the ad acts as it looks—a carpet cleaner with a discount code."

Murray added, "The phone number itself is immaterial—it could be routed anywhere."

"Each directory has a unique phone number, which was provided to us by Tully, so he could track the effectiveness of the ad," Allison added. "I believe they went to a call center, but I don't know where … it wasn't our responsibility."

I wasn't so much concerned about where the phone call was routed, but what was said during the call. "So a Huddled Masses follower views a coded message in an ad, which leads him to a phone booth, and he makes a call to Peggy, who is in a cave in Tora Bora or wherever. Okay, now what?"

"What do you mean?"

"He still needs instructions on how he's going to murder innocent people, before taking his own life, and I doubt they do that over the phone. And they don't operate like your typical sleeper cell, with plans plotted out ten years in advance, so they need real-time communication."

"My guess is that they're receiving another address during their initial phone call—perhaps another code that only means something to the caller. I'd bet this meeting spot is where they receive detailed instructions," Gwen said.

"That might be *how* they do it, but how did these clowns *know that's how* they do it?" Carter asked. I could tell he was in deep thought, which was always a little scary, and often flammable.

"I'm not following," Gwen said.

"How did they know they were supposed to look at an ad, and then go to some phone booth and call? They had to get instructions on how to get their instructions. If we could figure out how they do that, then we could smoke the crazies out at the starting line."

I knew how they did it. "That's what the hostage situation in Samawah was about. Jovana was right—it was a Huddled Masses convention. It was a big risk to take, so something real important must have been on the agenda … like laying out the operating procedures. And by having a firsthand, face-to-face account, they limited the probability of communication issues and gaps. Then when the 'hostages' were 'released' they scattered, waiting for the fingers to do the walking."

Gwen looked confounded. "What are you talking about, JP? Hostages? And who is Jovana?"

CHAPTER 42

"I think I need to sit down ... I feel dizzy," I said.

"What is going on, JP?" Gwen's voice grew firm.

"I don't know what I was saying—I think I confused it with a story I once worked on. My mind is all jumbled from the concussion. I really need to sit down."

Gwen intensified her glare, which broke me. "Fine—Huddled Masses is Al Muttahedah in disguise. They were created to bring unrest, fear, and eventually a civil war between social classes in America. And not just economic, they are dividing socially and culturally. That's why the Huddled Masses shirts say things like *Immigrant, Gay, Homeless, Addict.*"

"Looks like the new boss is the same as the old boss," Carter observed.

I walked behind the desk so I could view him onscreen. "It's what he meant when he said the revolution had already begun, and there was nothing we could do about it this time."

Gwen had her hands on her hips, which really wasn't a good sign. "Who's *he?* And how would you know this?"

"I recently had a meeting with a member of the CIA."

"How recently?"

"Do you remember my nurse, the one who helped me escape the hospital?"

"Miss Shoulder Rub ... vaguely."

"Well, her real name is Jovana, and she's a CIA operative who's working the Huddled Masses case."

Carter butted in, "Whoa ... Jovana is CIA?"

"And how would Carter know your nurse?" Gwen asked.

Carter spoke for himself, "She was our guide in Syria. She was my contact who set up the operation. Can't believe she's a spook—didn't see that one coming."

Gwen turned to me, her face lined with anger. "You went to Syria?"

"You said you didn't care where we went, as long as it helped me figure things out."

"I thought you went on some grown-up ... and I use that term loosely ... version of spring break with Carter. Not parachuting into the bloodiest place on the planet."

"We actually used smugglers to sneak us in—parachuting would have gotten our asses shot down," Carter continued to be less than helpful.

Gwen ignored him. "If you think I'm going to be like your mother, sitting on pins and needles, waiting for you to finally get yourself killed, you're sadly mistaken, JP."

"We had some unfinished business to take care of, and it's over now," I said. Maybe not exactly over, but I wasn't planning on going back any time soon.

Gwen was about to return fire, but caught herself. It was as if a light bulb had gone on. "Isn't Syria where those terrorists were killed—the ones who'd taken you hostage last summer?" Her face remained deathly serious. "Tell me you had nothing to do with that, JP."

Carter again spoke on my behalf, "I'd love to take credit, but it was all Jovana."

Still not helping. I needed to get me a new legal representative.

"So did you enjoy your time 'thinking' about things with Miss Shoulder Rub by your side, JP? What turned you on more—her killer body, or that she's actually a killer?"

I knew this bill would eventually arrive, and I was prepared. "You were there, Gwen—you know nothing happened. So what's your problem?"

"My problem is that you gave her the wrong answer."

"I should have rubbed her shoulders?"

"No—you should have told her that you didn't *want* to … not make me out to be some ball-and-chain that was keeping you from it."

"I was just trying to be polite. Trust me, you don't want to piss her off."

"Just remember the next time you're declaring yourself to be the great truth teller, that withholding information is the same thing as lying."

Having made her point, she backed off. But Byron picked up the slack, "This Syria trip better not have been on my account."

"It was all about Jovana—she used us to get revenge," Carter said.

"Why would she want revenge? I thought she was CIA," Byron said.

"She was also Milos' sister."

Byron mulled over the latest bombshell, before asking, "And what were you two … her cheerleaders?"

"I have no regrets," Carter said. "You mess with my friends, you mess with me … she just beat us to it."

"Nobody gave you the right to be judge and jury. That's what Officer Jones did, and look how that turned out for him."

"Don't compare what we did to that psychopath—these ass-clowns were going to kill more innocent people. We saved lives."

"Truth is, you didn't do it for me, or to save lives. You did it for yourselves, and your fragile egos."

"I'll bet your chin is more fragile than my ego."

"Why don't we find out?"

"Children! Stop!" a voice stopped everyone in their tracks, from Connecticut to Charleston.

I had never heard Murray's voice so angered. But he found his calm, and said, "We need to quit focusing on the indiscretions of the past, and look to the future. That is our only chance to stop this Huddled Masses."

CHAPTER 43

I started with our trip to Serbia last summer, and told everything I knew right up to the present.

Murray absorbed my words, before turning to Allison. He took her hand in his, and softly said, "Please tell us about this David Tully you work with."

I interjected, "Aren't we wasting time going down that road? Tully was an actor playing a role. He was Tully to Allison, New Colossus to Nora. What can we learn about someone who wasn't real?"

Murray looked annoyed by my interruption. "Identities might change, John Pierpont, but what makes us tick remains, and it can help to predict behavior."

He returned his attention to Allison, and this time she was allowed to answer.

"There was nothing special about him that I can think of. He loved soccer—he grew up in England, and was a big Liverpool fan. Marty ..." she began to tear up, but fought through it. "Marty was a fan of Manchester United, one of their rivals, so we would often joust about that. It was a good conversation piece, even though I didn't know soccer from tiddlywinks."

She thought some more. "I just thought it was strange for a CEO to be so hands-on. He would get into the details of billings and directory closings that would seem more fit for lower level staff."

"I'll bet he was quite meticulous about those discount codes he placed in the ads."

She nodded through tears.

"He named his company after George Washington, did he ever say why?" Murray asked.

"No, but he was always providing me useless facts about him. And his business started in Valley Forge, before expanding nationally, so I figured that geography might have something to do with it. But I didn't really give it much thought."

"Do you remember any of these facts … perhaps they aren't as useless as we think. He does seem to enjoy talking in code."

"It was trivia like Washington's second inaugural address was the shortest ever."

"It was 135 words. Quite refreshing, compared to the modern politician," Murray stated.

"And I remember another one, just due to how repulsive it was—that Washington's false teeth actually weren't wood, as the story goes, and he had bought human teeth off his slaves."

"That is correct, and not an uncommon practice during that time. But I don't see any potential clue off hand … how about you, John Pierpont?"

"I'm not really good at the clue thing."

I expected Gwen to confirm my lack of a clue, but she remained quiet.

Murray nodded, "I may be reading too much into it, but this Tully clearly has a sense of American history, and naming his company after the man who was the top general in the American Revolution is not coincidental, and neither is the Valley Forge location. Is there anything else from your communications that stands out?"

"We discussed his children on occasion. For whatever it's worth, it didn't seem like he was acting when he talked about them. His oldest son had recently dropped out of school, and his daughter was marrying a guy he didn't like. But his youngest, David Jr., had joined the business not too long ago."

Byron was now typing away on his computer. "Tully is a ghost—no driver's license, no credit rating, no photos, no social media."

This didn't surprise me—not only was it an alias, but he probably was stationed in some mountain retreat in East Nowhere, and spoke to her on a satellite phone. I would bet the house that no employee of GWCC ever laid eyes on David Tully.

But what Byron said next did surprise. "I got a couple hits on David Jr. A few articles at GWCC stores that recently opened, which he attended. And he's listed on the website with a photo. Bio says he attended Wharton School of Business, but I'm guessing when we check, there will be no such person who attended."

We pulled up the website on Gwen's desktop computer. David Tully Jr. was thirty-something with heavy eyebrows that hung over mysterious eyes. He was a generally good-looking guy, but nothing really stood out about him, and his ethnicity appeared generic. He looked like your typical American businessman, again showing Al Muttahedah's ability to assimilate into Western culture.

This was an interesting development, but I felt like we were going around in circles, which brought me back to my earlier question—okay, now what?

CHAPTER 44

"I think our best bet is to review next month's Yellow Pages directories, and cut them off at the pass ... or at the phone booth," Gwen said.

Allison began reading next month's closings off her list, "Chicago ... Gaithersburg, Maryland ... Cary, North Carolina ... Columbus, Georgia ..."

"That would have been an effective strategy a few days ago," Murray said. "But with their system being exposed, they will adjust ... just as they already have."

"What do you mean they've adjusted?" I inquired.

"I guess escalated would be a better word. That's what Whiskey Tax is about—the next phase, which is to create an opponent for Huddled Masses. The clearer the picture gets, the more the Pittsburgh location makes sense, as does the name Tully."

We looked back at him blankly, so Murray explained. I felt like I was back in his class ... if I ever left.

"When the Whiskey Tax group came on the scene, I was intrigued by the origin of their name, and sought out Rockfield's resident historian, Sandra Warner. She refreshed my memory about the whiskey tax that was levied by the federal government in 1791. The impoverished frontiersmen of western Pennsylvania, especially farmers who used whiskey as an exchange currency, rebelled against it. This led to uprisings, and mob violence, often against wealthy property owners of the Pittsburgh area, who had nothing to do with the tax. It became known as the Whiskey Rebellion.

"President Washington took a pacifist approach to the rebellion, but eventually succumbed to public outcry, and led troops to western Pennsylvania to quash it. Much like this group's attempt to crush a modern day attack on the elite. Except this time it's Huddled Masses, not Pennsylvania farmers."

"Now that I think about it, I do remember Tully bringing up the Whiskey Rebellion—it was one of his George Washington trivia facts. He said it was the only time that a sitting president has led troops into battle," Allison recalled.

"I'm impressed. Presidents these days can't even drive their own car," Carter said. "But what does this have to do with Tully's name?"

Murray raised a finger, to say he was getting to that. "When it comes to journalistic history, I didn't need a refresher course. Tully was the pen name Alexander Hamilton used when he wrote editorials for a Philadelphia newspaper—an attempt to drum up support for the federal government using force against the rebellion, and back Washington into a corner. *Authority of laws, or force,* he wrote. This modern day Tully is also trying to spark a confrontation, operating behind the scenes. But what he wants is an extended battle between the two groups, continuing to divide the country. Two sides that he both created and is controlling, like a puppeteer."

"So what you're saying, is both these groups—Whiskey Tax and Huddled Masses—are under the control of Al Muttahedah?" Gwen asked.

Murray nodded. "And now that the competing forces have been launched, these violent events will escalate, their responses playing off each other. And my guess is that something large will happen very soon. Their plans have been sped up."

"If they want to up the ante, then I say we match. Time to push the chips to the center," I said.

The group eyed me apprehensively, awaiting my latest installment of whack-job-ery. So I indulged them.

"I'll take everything we know and go on TV—get it all out in the open. Al Muttahedah, CIA, phone booths, carpet cleaning, the works. If you think they're desperate now, they'll be tap dancing on the hot tin roof when I'm done with them."

Carter was always a supporter of "scorched earth" strategies. "Go for the jugular, I like it. And getting outed by JP Warner will drive them so nuts, they'll do something irrational, and walk right into the trap."

"All well and good, unless that irrational act is to blow up a city block with a dirty bomb," Murray added a sobering thought.

"I've got an idea," Gwen said. "It might be a little off-the-wall, but how about we turn what we know over to the authorities … you know, the people who are trained to do this sort of thing … and let them handle it. Too crazy, right?"

Byron backed her up, "I've always admired your guts, JP, but this isn't the Jones case. He was one dude—granted, one crazed, cunning serial killer—but this is a shadow army we're dealing with. Gwen's right."

As she often is. I think I surprised everyone by agreeing without even a whimper, much less a fight. I asked Carter, "Do you know how to get hold of Jovana? She's the only 'authorities' I'd trust with this."

Which was saying something, since she'd basically lied to us every step of the way. That, and I'll be hearing about the 'shoulder rub that wasn't' for the rest of my life.

He shook his head. "She contacts me—it's the only way she works."

Same here. But it led me to a thought, "She's probably listening right now. You know how the CIA likes to play with their bugs."

I began pacing the room and shouting like a crazy man, "Jovana, come out and play! We have what you want. I know you're listening!"

My voice began to quiver, and each step was like I was trudging in mud. The room began to spin. Then once again, everything went black.

CHAPTER 45

"Go fish," Gwen said.

Gracie reached into the pond of cards on the floor of the tree fort and pulled one out. They were going old school—and not just the card game, but all electricity was off, and the only lighting came via lantern.

A long silence ensued, and Gwen turned to the boy who was restricting the flow. "It's your turn, Chase."

He didn't appear enthused. "Why can't we play a game?" he whined.

"This is a game," his sister informed him.

"If it's a game, then how come there isn't a screen?"

"Back in history, not all games were electronic. Like when Mom was a kid," Gracie said.

Gwen made eye contact with Allison, who was sitting on the edge of the lower bunk, and had been staring off into space most of the night. But Gracie's comment brought her a brief smile. *Back in history?*

The topic of modern technology reminded Gwen to check the baby monitor. It was actually an app that she'd added to her phone following JP's fainting spell this afternoon.

After being revived, he predictably refused to go to the hospital. Luckily, Dr. MacDougal, who'd been treating them since *back in history,* still made house calls. But since every Dr. MacDougal diagnosis Gwen could remember consisted of a vague reference to a virus and a prescription for an antibiotic, she wasn't confident that a head injury would be his specialty. But their luck continued to trend upward, when he brought along his son, who had recently left the trauma unit at Columbia Presbyterian Hospital to move home and work in his father's practice.

The younger Dr. MacDougal described concussions as snowflakes, in that two are never alike, and the path to a cure is often bumpy and unpredictable. So he wasn't surprised that JP's symptoms had returned, which included headache, blackouts and nausea. The only recommendation was bed rest, with curtains drawn to counter his light sensitivity. He provided him a "seasickness wristband" to help with the nausea, and suggested Advil for the headache.

The phone app showed JP sleeping soundly inside the colonial. The app probably would have made a better security system than the one JP paid a fortune to have put in—it had audio, night vision, alerts for noise or movement, and even a few pre-loaded lullabies if her baby couldn't sleep.

Gwen returned her attention to the game—a way to pass the time as it slowly crept toward morning. The meeting at *Gazette* headquarters concluded with the agreement that they were over their heads and needed to turn what they knew over to the professionals. But they didn't trust Hawkins, who was heading up the Huddled Masses case for the FBI. And if they went to the local police, they would just be transferred to him. And after what happened to Marty Cooper, using the anonymous tip line didn't seem like a good option. That left the CIA, but they had no idea how to get hold of their contact.

So they decided to sleep on their next move, with the main priority keeping Allison and her kids hidden safely away. For that purpose, the tree fort came in very handy.

"Do you have any twos?" Gracie asked, but Gwen was focused on the girl's mother, who continued to stare at the wall.

"Miss Delaney," Gracie said again, snapping her to attention.

She looked at the girl, dressed in her pajamas, concerned about an insignificant card game, unaware that her whole future had been altered. Her heart broke her.

"I'm sorry, Gracie … my mind is getting sleepy. How about we rest up and play again in the morning?"

Gracie and Chase looked disappointed at first, but recovered quickly, as kids often do. "I got the top bunk," Chase exclaimed, and practically ran up the ladder.

But once reaching the top, his expression turned from excitement to unsure. Gwen thought he might have miscalculated how high up he was, and was rethinking his decision. But his true focus was the tree branches along the roof. They were actually plastic, as JP wanted to provide the "full tree house effect" when they designed it.

"What if a bird makes a nest in them, and then poops on me in the night?" the boy asked.

Gwen stifled a laugh, and was about to explain that the branches were fake, when Gracie made her way up to the top bunk. "I'll protect you from the birds, little brother."

The act grabbed Gwen's heart. She had been an only-child growing up—Tommy came along after she was already an adult—and she thought it would be nice to have someone around who would protect you when the bird crap of life started coming down on you. They would need each other now more than ever.

CHAPTER 46

Gwen reached the bottom of the ladder. She folded it back up and pushed it closed, safely enclosing the children inside.

She took a seat next to Allison at the base of the tree. She zipped up her jacket—the day had started out like spring, but the night had turned cold. And the woods were as dark as Gwen could ever remember. The only light came from her phone, reminding her to check the baby monitor app once more—it's not like he hadn't escaped before.

A second light appeared. This one was a small orange dot coming from beside her. "I didn't know you smoked?" Gwen said in a soft voice.

"Picked up a pack on the way here, when we stopped for gas—first cigarette I've had since I was fourteen."

A long pause hung over them, before Allison spoke, "What am I going to tell them? How can I possibly look at their little faces and say those words … your father is never coming home."

Gwen put her arm around her—she was out of words, and doubted that anything would help, anyway.

"And I have to tell Marty's family. They don't even know … we're supposed to go down there to visit next weekend. Agent Hawkins said his name wouldn't be revealed for a few days, until they complete their investigation, but I can't let them hear it from the news. Oh God …"

Gwen was about to tell her that it was going to be all right, but she caught herself—it wasn't going to be.

"And Gracie knows something's up—you can't fool her for long. Chase is more wrapped in the moment, but he follows his sister's lead."

"Kids are resilient—they bounce back quicker than we do. And they have each other—just look how Gracie protected him in there. The important thing right now is that they're safe. Let's just get through tonight, then we'll take what you know to this CIA agent—if JP and Carter trust her, then I trust that we're in good hands."

"If they can even get in touch with her. And what then—we live in witness protection or something? I have to pull Gracie and Chase out of a school they love, and the only home they ever knew, and move to Seattle or Albuquerque?"

Allison glanced up at the tree house. "They're great kids ... they don't deserve this."

Gwen pulled her closer. "I know."

"And why did they choose us? I just don't understand."

Gwen had been thinking about that. It wasn't random, because every move this group made was plotted. The only connecting link was JP, but he hadn't even returned to Rockfield when Tully hired Marty Cooper's new consulting business. Not to mention, he had no relationship with Marty, and hadn't seen Allison is fifteen years. There was some other reason, she just wasn't sure what.

"I wish I knew," Gwen said, the cold beginning to overtake her senses. "What do you say we go back inside?"

Allison put her cigarette out, and Gwen helped her to her feet. Gwen pulled the stairs down, and began to climb. Allison followed her.

In the distance, Gwen could hear a rustling sound. She wondered if it was the fisher cats—more reason to get inside.

The sound grew louder, and was headed their way. It happened so fast that they couldn't react.

It was a motorcycle. But that was all Gwen could make out as it whipped by them. When she glanced down, Allison was gone.

The driver had grabbed her as he sped by, and she was now in his clutches as he skidded the bike to a stop. Gwen shone her phone in the direction, and saw that the driver was wearing night-vision goggles. *Uh-oh.*

Another motorcycle followed, coming to a stop right in front of the stairs. Gwen's first thought was: *the kids!* She needed to get inside and lock them safely in. She scrambled up the ladder and into the tree house, but she didn't have time to close it behind her. Her assailant was in right after her, and tackled her to the ground.

"We meet again," he said, smirking. The goggles and motorcycle helmet didn't hide his identity, nor did he try to conceal it. It was the British accent guy who said that it always ends badly for JP's girlfriends. He was starting to look like Nostradamus.

He got to his feet and headed for the children, who were now awake and screaming.

Gwen lunged after him. She wrapped her arms around his waist and held on for dear life. "You leave them alone—they have nothing to do with this!"

He tossed her to the ground. "You have a big mouth, just like your boyfriend."

His attention went to her, which was what she wanted—it delayed his march to the children. He flipped her over on her stomach, and pulled out a rope. He tied her hands behind her back, and then placed a gag over her mouth.

He might have silenced her "big mouth," but there were other ways to communicate. She looked Gracie deep in her eyes, pleading with her to run as fast as she could. The girl read the signal, grabbed her brother, and jumped off the top bunk—their loud thud alarming the attacker. But when he reached to grab them, they were already past him, and down the stairs.

The attacker just smiled, as if he were impressed by the escape. He made his way after them at a measured pace, and disappeared down the ladder.

Gwen slithered like a snake on her belly to get a view out the opening. Her eyes had adjusted to the dark, and she was able to see the children attempt to get away. But his long strides made up ground fast, and he collared them by the back of their pajamas.

They demanded, "let us go!" And surprisingly, he obliged. He then instructed them to run as fast as they could toward the Warner home, and inform JP that there was an emergency at the tree house. He pointed them in the right direction. "Don't stop until you get there," he shouted.

They looked frozen for a moment, unsure, until their mother yelled at the top of her lungs, "Run! Run as fast as you can!"

They took off immediately. Chase first, Gracie leading from behind.

Allison remained in the clutches of her captor. He set her on the bike, and handed her a helmet.

"Trust me, I'm not going to hurt you. I was told that if you don't arrive in one piece, I'd better not show up, so put the helmet on," he said.

When she refused, he forcefully put it on her. He then straddled the bike behind her, and in a flash, they were whizzing through the woods.

British had returned inside the tree house. Gwen noticed that both his hands were full, and she knew this wasn't good for her. He set the items down long enough to toss her onto the bed.

He reached down and reclaimed the items he'd brought with him. In one hand was the pack of cigarettes, a gas can in the other.

"You need to be very careful of smoking ... especially in such a woodsy terrain. One little ash could set the entire forest on fire."

She yelled at him, explaining where he could shove his cigarettes, but the gag made it inaudible.

"I know what you're thinking—that they'll eventually figure out that it wasn't an accident. But by that time, I'll be long gone. So the point is moot, love, and not worth your final thoughts."

She looked to her phone, which had fallen near the bed. It was torturing her—close enough to see JP, but too far to reach.

"There are others amongst my group, who thought we should just have shot you when we had the chance, or I should just strangle the life out of you right now ... but I'm a romantic. And what can be more romantic than JP Warner running to save his damsel, death be damned, before they both succumb to the fire. Willy Shakespeare would approve."

He picked up the can and began soaking the insides of the tree house with gasoline, saving a good douse for Gwen.

When the can was empty, he headed for the entrance. "Ta-ta, love."

Gwen rolled off the bed and slithered across the floor once more until she could see out the entrance. She saw him coating the tree bark in gas. He lit a match and started the fire in a circle around the tree. It immediately began to climb up the trunk, and smoke began to pour inside.

He shut the door of the fort ... like an oven. Gwen's view had been cut off, but she could still hear his motorcycle speeding away.

She could already feel the intense heat below her as she made her way across the floor, until she reached her phone. She took one last look at JP on the baby monitor, who was still sleeping soundly, and said into her gag, "Sweet dreams, baby. I hope you know I'll always love you."

CHAPTER 47

I woke up to the sound of the doorbell.

And it wouldn't stop. *Ding, ding, ding, ding ...*

I picked myself out of the bed, and the dizziness returned. I walked hesitantly, trying to get my bearings—"I'm coming!" I shouted.

As I made my way to the bedroom door, I noticed the powerful sun shining through the pulled shade, turning it an orange-ish color. But unless I'd pulled a Rip Van Winkle, it should be the middle of night—there was no sun. I pulled the shade to see that the woods behind the house were ablaze!

Light was not a friend in my condition, and I turned away. When I did, things began to click.

The woods are on fire.

The tree house is in the woods.

Gwen is in the tree house!

I gritted my teeth and ran as fast as I could down the stairs, hoping like hell that Gwen was the ringer.

But she wasn't.

It was Chase and Gracie. The boy was sobbing, while the girl remained surprisingly composed.

"Mr. Warner—they told us to get you. There's an emergency. They said not to stop until we got to you," the girl spoke fast.

"Who told you this?"

"The men on the motorcycles who took my Mom."

"Hold on ... slow down ... someone *took* your Mom?"

"We weren't supposed to look back, but I did, and saw him drive off with her."

"That was brave of you, Gracie. What about Gwen ... Miss Delaney?"

"The other guy tied her up in the tree house."

Son of a ... There was no time to waste. I was about to instruct the kids to run to my parents' house, but I didn't need to, as they were walking toward us, dressed in bathrobes.

"JP—thank God you're alright," my mother said.

"I called the fire department, they should be here any second," my father added, always calm in a crisis. He shielded his eyes, as he looked to the burning woods.

"Mom, Dad, this is Gracie and Chase. Hide them away in your house, and don't tell anyone but Rich Tolland about them," I said and began to run toward the blaze.

"JP—no!" I heard my mother call out as I raced into the woods, but I wouldn't be stopped.

I immediately felt the heat. It acted like a brick wall that I was unable to break through. But I kept hammering deeper into the forest. I could feel sharp rocks cutting into my bare feet, but I couldn't stop. I knew this was the work of Huddled Masses, and that they'd sent the kids to lure me. If they were counting on me to make an irrational decision in the name of Gwen, they'd done their homework.

"Gwen!" I shouted out, but no answer came. Nor could I hear her at all, yelling for help, anything.

As I got closer to the tree house the smoke grew thicker, and breathing became near impossible. It felt like the heat was searing the skin off my body. My head felt so light I was positive it would fall off my neck, and the spinning returned. I crashed to the ground, and was on the verge of the lights going out once again.

This time I wouldn't allow it. I rolled to my side, and propped myself up.

But my comeback would be brief. I took two steps, and grabbed my throat—it felt like it was burning inside. I fell once again, struggling to maintain consciousness. I recalled a fire safety movie from elementary school that instructed us to stay low and crawl. I could hear the sirens in the distance, but they would be too late.

I tried to drag myself over the ground. I could physically feel the life being sucked out of me, and with all my remaining strength attempted one final call to Gwen. But nothing came out.

CHAPTER 48

I woke up to find my brother, Ethan, looking down on me. I was obviously dead, but my final destination was less evident. Ethan would definitely make it to heaven, so I had that working for me, but I was concerned that he was looking *down* on me.

After a violent coughing fit, I spoke, "Is this heaven?"

"Despite your best efforts to get yourself killed, you're still alive."

"I think that's what I'm going to title my memoir," I said, before coughing up another lung.

"It wouldn't be so funny if someone ended up dead, while trying to save you," he continued.

"Are you the one who saved me? Because if I owe you my life, that's really going to suck for me."

"No—you can thank the firefighters who pulled you out of the woods."

"Gwen ... where is she? I need to get to her," I began to sit up.

Ethan lightly pushed me back to the ground. "Slow down ... the only place you're going is the hospital."

"I'm not going anywhere until I get to Gwen."

Just as Ethan was about to answer me, he was replaced by Rich Tolland, who said, "I need to talk to JP for a moment ... alone."

Rich always had a commanding presence, but standing over me in my current state, he looked downright intimidating. "Here's the story, JP. The reason you can barely talk is that you're suffering from smoke inhalation. We won't know the full extent of it until we get you to the hospital, which is going to happen whether you like it or not."

I nodded that I understood, but the only thing I could think of at the moment was Gwen. If she was alright, she would be nearby, getting the same type of medical treatment, right?

Rich continued talking at me, but his words were swallowed up by the vast commotion around us—firemen, police, neighbors trying to help out. I noticed that I'd been dragged back near the colonial, safely away from the blaze, but I could still feel its heat on my face.

"The fire is under control, but I've already heard the A-word—arson—so unless Casey Leeds recently came back to life, there is going to be a lot of explaining to do ... mainly by you.

"Allison's kids are hidden away in your parents' house. I talked to them, and they told an interesting story of motorcycles and their mother being abducted. Nobody knows they're here, except us, and I will keep it that way as long as possible—I promised Allison I would protect them, so consider them in protective custody. I didn't go into detail with your folks, but they trust that I wouldn't ask this of them if it wasn't important.

"Finally, I don't know the particulars of what's going on, or what went on in that meeting at the *Gazette,* but you better know what the hell you're doing ... because if anything happens to Allison Cooper, and you didn't go to the authorities with what you know, there will be hell to pay for you ... starting with me."

He had a point—actually a lot of points—but I only had one thing on my mind at the moment. I somehow was able to climb to my feet and took a step toward the charcoal-ed woods. "I'm not going anywhere until I talk to Gwen."

"She's gone, JP."

I heard his words, but they didn't process. "She's in the tree house, and I'm going to get her and bring her back here."

"There is no more tree house. Half an acre was burned to the ground—trees, bushes, and anything in its way. Sit back down and let the firemen do their job."

"If they didn't save Gwen, then they aren't doing their job ... so I'm going to do it for them."

Rich grabbed me by the shirt to hold me back. "When I said Gwen is gone, I meant that she's not here anymore. I passed her on my way. She was speeding in the other direction in the *Gazette* van."

CHAPTER 49

Gwen wasn't sure where the motorcycle men were headed, but based on their inability to tie a square knot, she doubted it was to a Boy Scout meeting.

They also didn't have a good handle on the territory they'd invaded. If they did, they would have known about the escape hatch built into the roof, hidden behind the fake branches. Ironically, her father had insisted on the second exit be included, in case of fire.

So once she'd wriggled out of the ropes, she climbed to the top bunk, and made her way out the hatch. She took the rope-swing to the ground and ran like hell.

She thought to first stop and warn JP, but she saw his parents come out of the house, and figured they had a better shot of talking sense into him than she did. And besides, Allison was the one in imminent danger.

She sprinted to the *Gazette* van and tore out of the Warner's driveway. She could already hear the fire trucks heading in the opposite direction.

The motorcycles had a head start, and while she couldn't match their speed, she had a better grasp of the local geography. The only way out of town was via Main Street, and she could cut off their path by using Zycko Hill.

As she pounded the gas pedal, she realized this was the same strategy JP had used to stop Grady Benson last fall. But a similar collision wouldn't work in this case, since the much bigger van would kill Allison in the process.

The van struggled with the hairpin turns of the hill, and she had no choice but to slow down before she flipped over the guardrail. She passed over the Samerauk Bridge, where the lives of Noah Warner and Lisa Spargo came to an abrupt end, before hitting a brief straightaway where she could power ahead.

The van practically bounced onto Main Street. The motorcycles were nowhere in sight, but she followed their roar. Traffic wouldn't be a problem—the streets of Rockfield were normally silent this time of night, but even more deserted than usual tonight, with half the town rushing to the Warner's.

She continued to pin the accelerator to the floor, until she was able to spot the bike's taillights in the far distance, and follow them out of Rockfield. She crossed a bridge over Lake Lillinonah. Her family used to take her father's boat out on the lake on summer days, but that stopped after her parents' divorce. Only recently did her father start taking the boat out again, with Tommy. It reminded her of how glad she was that he'd taken Tommy up to Rhode Island this week during his April vacation from school.

They dashed through the neighboring town of Bridgewater, which was as sleepy and deserted as Rockfield. When the motorcycles reached Route-67, a jagged diagonal path that stretched from New Milford to New Haven, they headed east.

Gwen continued to track them along the rural road—scenic during daylight, but treacherous at night—and at one point she got close enough to see Allison. At that moment the thought crossed her mind—*what will I do if I actually catch them?* Bump them off the road? Order them to pull over? What she really needed to do was to call the police, but her phone was nothing but melted plastic from the fire.

It turned out not to matter. After toying with her for a few more winding miles, the motorcycles took off like the Millennium Falcon entering hyperspace. The taillights got smaller and smaller, until they disappeared, and the roar of the motors faded into the distance. She made one last push, but the van just didn't have the horses to compete.

She pulled over at Hodge Park, a small strip of grass and picnic tables beside the Shepaug River. JP's mom used to bring them here when they were kids, and they'd spend the day catching salamanders, skimming rocks, and eating hot dogs. It was one of those obscure yet magical places that it seemed only Mrs. Warner knew about. "I know a place," she would simply say, and pile them into their station wagon on those long August days when JP, Gwen, and the other neighborhood kids would claim boredom.

Now Gwen needed to find a place—where they took Allison—but she didn't even know where to start. It seemed like an impossible task.

She stared out into the dark, lonely night, listening to the river rush by, and trying to channel Mrs. Warner. Then the answer came—she needed to find a person, not a place. She started the van, and was off again.

CHAPTER 50

I awoke at another stop on my medical world tour, this time in New Milford Hospital.

My first thought was Gwen. My best guess as to why she was driving away from the scene, was that she was in pursuit of Allison's captors. I must be rubbing off on her, I thought, and that wasn't a good thing.

As the sun peeked through the window, stinging my senses, I received my first visitor. It was my father.

My hope was that he'd come to spring me free, just as Carter had done in Landstuhl, and Jovana did in New York. Use his political influence to get me released—grease palms, slip bills, make an offer they couldn't refuse. The usual 'how a bill becomes a law' stuff.

"How are you feeling, JP?" he asked with fatherly concern.

"My doctor tells me I have the lung capacity of a two-hundred-year-old smoker."

"Is that the message you'd like me to relay to your mother?"

"Just tell her I'm going to be fine."

And according to my doctor, I would be. The firefighters got to me in time, before any major damage could occur, and I avoided any severe burns. Like my head, the lungs would require a couple weeks of rest. Problem was, I didn't have that type of time.

"Have you heard from Gwen?" I got right to the heart of the matter.

"I haven't, but I've been busy all night with insurance adjusters, police, fire marshals, you name it. And your mother has been engrossed in taking care of the grandchildren she never knew she had."

"How are they doing?"

"The children or your mother?" he asked with a chuckle. "The kids are fine, and while she won't admit it, looking after little ones always puts a pep in Sandra's step—I think she misses those days when you and your brothers were young."

"I'm so sorry about all of this. It's all my fault, and I will rebuild it with my own hands if need be, until every piece of the property is exactly as it was before the fire."

"I don't care about blame, JP—but I am worried about you. The shooting in New York, this fire ... hiding out children. And don't think I don't know about the security system you put in without my consent. I know I struggled with retirement, but you're taking it to a whole new level."

"It's like in *Godfather III*—just when I thought I was out, they pull me back in. I didn't mean to put people in danger, but I did, because this stuff will always follow me."

"We can only control what we can control, son."

"I agree. Which is why I'm going to move as far away from here as possible. Go to some island, where, if they want to come after the people I care about, Gwen won't be in the cross-hairs."

He got a good laugh out of that one. "You and Gwen could move to opposite sides of the universe, and surround yourselves with moats and alligators, and you would still find your way back to each other."

"My presence has done nothing but put her in danger since I returned."

"My guess is she's chasing danger right now all on her own, JP. You seem to have forgotten that she can climb a tree without you."

A reminiscing grin came over his face, as he took a seat on the edge of my bed. "You were five years old when the Delaneys moved into our neighborhood. And when they came over to introduce themselves, and bring a pie, as people often did in those days, I remember how you just stared at that little girl. I can see it like it was yesterday—she was in this flowered dress, her hair in pigtails, while you were grass-stained from head to toe after wrestling with Ethan in the backyard.

"The next week, we had the Delaneys over for dinner. It was Labor Day, the day before you went off to school for the first time. After the meal, you and Gwen went outside to play, and you two decided to climb that old oak tree along the driveway. She scooted right to the top, and you ended up stuck halfway up, which drove you crazy. You'd come home every day after school for weeks and practice climbing that tree until you could get to the top. Your mother thought you were going to end up breaking your arm, or worse, but I knew what was driving you, or more specifically, who was, and I understood that you were willing to take any risk to get to the top ... because that's where she was going to be."

"Isn't that the tree Mom claims is dead, and has been trying to get you to cut down for years?"

He smiled. "Your mother, of all people, should understand that history goes beyond the sturdiness of a structure. And believe me, son ... that tree is far from dead."

I smiled, and asked the question once more—okay, now what?

"I think you know exactly where you need to go, JP," he replied.

Having made his point, and after making me agree to stop by and see my mother after my release, as she can't bring herself to visit me in the hospital, he made his way out of my room, stopping briefly to greet my next visitor. I couldn't believe the man who figured out the important role Gwen would play in my life when we were just five years old, didn't grasp what a total jackass Bobby Maloney was.

He shut the door behind him. "So, you must have a reason for calling me down here this morning, Warner. You always have an agenda."

"I do, and I do."

"Then let's hear it, I don't have all day." Maloney looked at his watch, as if he had scheduled somebody else to haunt this morning.

"Last night, as my life flashed before my eyes, I started to rethink a few things, Bobby. And I decided that I might have been too hard on you, holding your past over your head, and not allowing you to pursue your destiny, which is to be Rockfield's first selectman. I just couldn't handle someone replacing my father."

And what I was holding over his head was the fact that he used false testimony in a drunk driving death back in college, which sent an innocent man, Lamar Thompson, to jail. It also almost got Maloney killed last year, when Officer Jones wanted to invoke his own style of justice over the incident.

"What's the catch, Warner?"

"I will not stop you from running in the election this November, after my father's interim role is up. I won't lie if asked directly, but I won't bring up the subject on my own. In exchange, I want you to switch places with me."

"Switch places?"

"Your suit for this hospital gown. You snuggle under the covers, while I walk out of here, pretending to be you."

"Isn't that medical fraud?"

"I have no idea—you're the lawyer. But I imagine it's a lesser crime than lying under oath to send an innocent man to prison."

He looked resigned, but also confused. "You're going to give up all your leverage to get out of the hospital a couple days early? It doesn't make sense—why wouldn't you hold on to it until you really needed something big?"

"This is as big as it gets for me, Bobby. Do we have a deal?"

"No."

"No? You're turning down the offer to get your life back, basically for nothing?"

"I know how you blackmailers work—this won't be the end of it, you'll always keep coming back wanting more, another favor, new conditions to the deal."

I've been called a lot of things throughout the years, but blackmailer was a new one. Like I was the guy who ruined another man's life with his lies.

"I'll give you one last chance to accept, Bobby—and you might also want to consider that Lamar Thompson is thinking about writing a book about the incident ... with all the new information that's come to his attention. I think he's still undecided whether or not to do it. I know Lamar pretty well, and I can talk to him, maybe sway him one way or another."

"Fine," he grumbled, and began undoing his tie. A few minutes later, I was Bobby Maloney, from the slicked-back hairstyle all the way down to the Italian loafers, which were about a size too small.

"Just cough a lot, and if a woman named Jovana comes looking for you, do whatever she says," was my last advice as I headed out the door.

CHAPTER 51

I drove Maloney's Mercedes S-Class Sedan directly home. The good news was that there were no investigators and fire officials hanging around. The bad news was the damage looked even worse in the morning. The magical woods where so many memories lived had been wiped away, leaving just charred remains, and a strong stench, which sent me into another fit of coughing.

There was no sign that Gwen had returned here since the fire. I didn't think she would, but I had to cover all bases. My next stop was her father's place. Once again, no sign of life—Mr. Delaney and Tommy were in Rhode Island for the week. I peeked in the garage window, and I noticed that Allison's car, a silver Audi, was no longer parked there. I wasn't sure what to make of that.

I drove to the *Gazette* building, and filled with relief when I saw the van parked out front. But my enthusiasm dissipated when I learned that Gwen wasn't there. In fact, nobody was—the place was dark when I went inside. It was sort of the newspaper business in a nutshell.

I walked next door to the Rockfield Village Store. That's where Murray, the paper's founder, spent his so-called retirement as the most overqualified cashier in history. As usual, the store looked exactly as it did when my mother first took me there over thirty years ago. The smell was the same, and the floorboards made the same squeak when stepped upon. I waited for all the customers to be served, before approaching Murray.

"Have you seen, Gwen? I'm worried about her," I led with the headline.

He looked me up and down. "After your fainting spell yesterday, and the effects of last night's fire, shouldn't she be the one worried about you?"

"She went after the lunatics who set the fire, and I haven't heard from her since."

"She didn't mention anything about that when I saw her first thing this morning. She acted as if it were any old day."

"You saw her? This morning?"

"We had our weekly meeting to go over the paper's business. She then took care of some issues regarding the morning delivery, and we were both on our way."

"Did she say where she was going?"

"She did not, nor did I pry, but I understand your concern, John Pierpont. My sources tell me that the fire was very much related to yesterday's meeting. As I mentioned, this group is very desperate, which makes them quite dangerous."

I nodded my solemn agreement, thanked Murray, and returned to the Mercedes. I made the short trip up Main Street until I came to the Rockfield Historical Society, which was located within a manicured campus made up of the library, police station, and town hall.

I found my mother in the main room, dusting old books. "Are we alone?" I asked.

"Just a couple of helpers going through some boxes in the back room."

"And everything is okay ... with these helpers?"

"Aren't you supposed to be in the hospital?"

"Dad wanted me to drop by and let you know I'm going to live."

"Are you ... going to live? If not, I see you've selected a suit for your funeral."

I attempted a smile. "All these years you bug me for grandchildren, I finally deliver, and this is the thanks I get?"

"Hiding out children, arson, shootings—it's time you came clean with me, JP."

"People who have gotten those answers have ended up hurt ... or worse. It's better that you don't know."

"I assume you're referring to the parents of these children. You know, Gwen said something interesting when she came by to check on them this morning ... she told them she was going to get their mother back."

"You saw Gwen? Did she say where she was going?"

"I wouldn't know—nobody tells me anything. I presume she went to get the mother of these children back, like she said, from wherever that might be."

"Just please keep them hidden until we return. And don't hand them over to anyone, except Rich Tolland, under any circumstances. Especially if a couple FBI agents named Nunez and Lillibridge come looking for them."

She looked away. "I was foolish to think you'd left your reckless ways behind."

"It's not the same, I swear. They're coming after me this time."

"That doesn't mean you have to return fire."

She pointed to a painting on the wall—it was of George Washington mounted upon a horse. It was painted by Charles Zycko back in the late 1700s, when General Washington and his ragtag army was passing through Rockfield, then known as Ancient Woodbury.

"Do you know who that is?"

"I think he was a carpet cleaner or something like that. May or may not have lied about chopping a cherry tree down," I said and braced for a history lesson I didn't have time for.

"The Revolutionary War didn't begin in Boston, as most believe—that was a siege, which led to the declaration of war. The first true battle took place in New York, with the Continental Army being led by General George Washington."

I nodded—too late.

"His British counterpart, General William Howe, showed up with a fleet of four hundred ships, and over thirty-thousand troops, taking control of the entrance of New York Harbor. And New Yorkers, as they're known to do, went into a panic. The temptation for Washington was to build on the momentum of the Boston siege, show no fear, and march forward without wavering. But facing an overwhelming force, he swallowed his pride, and chose to retreat. So to make a long story short, General Washington has his face on currency, while General Howe does not."

I'd bet if the British had tried to burn Washington's true love—Sally Fairfax—at the stake ... or in a tree house ... the General might have had a different response.

I told her that I understood her point—discretion over valor—but we both knew that history said I wasn't going to retreat.

CHAPTER 52

I began walking to the Rockfield police station, seeking an update from Rich Tolland. I had a feeling he might be my best shot to get a beat on Gwen's location.

But I saw something that made me stop in my tracks. Walking into the police station were agents Scott Hawkins and Clarisse Johnson of the FBI. I started having an Officer Jones flashback, so I did a slow turn and began walking in the opposite direction. I didn't think being interrogated by Hawkins for the next couple hours was going to get me to Gwen any faster.

By mid-afternoon there was still no sign of her, and my stomach was demanding food. So to avoid another blackout, this one from lack of nourishment, I drove to Dello's.

I always thought better while consuming grilled meat and salty side dishes, so I ordered a "triple decker" burger and curly fries. I took a seat at one of the outdoor picnic tables, and began plotting my new course on a ketchup-stained napkin.

I needed to re-calibrate my search, re-focus, re-strategize, and any other 're' I could come up with. But my strategy session didn't last long, as I was joined by Herbie and Cervino, who were on their lunch break. They smelled of freshly cut grass, and their clothing was stained with white chalk. They worked for the Rockfield Parks Department, and had been getting the Little League fields at Lefebvre Park prepared for tonight's first game.

"Look at Mr. Hollywood in his sunglasses," Cervino said.

"For your information, I'm suffering from light sensitivity," I responded.

"That's what they all say," Herbie added with a smile.

"And what's with the slicked-back hair? For a moment I thought you were Maloney," Cervino said.

"Warner coaches one season of basketball, and he thinks he's Pat Riley," Herbie said. They got a laugh out of that, and began devouring their lunch. Cervino washed it down with a beer, which might explain why the lines are always so crooked on the Little League fields.

Then Herbie turned serious. "Sorry about the fire, man … a lot of good memories in those woods."

"Rumor on the street is that it was arson—who the hell would want to burn down that forest?" Cervino added.

"My father's been in power for decades, I'm sure he's made some enemies. We're just glad nobody got hurt." Especially Gwen. Speaking of which, "Hey, have you guys seen Gwen around town today? I haven't been able to get hold of her," I said as casually as possible, not wanting to set off any alarms.

"Ran into her like an hour ago," Cervino surprised me.

"Really? Where?"

"At Dr. MacDougal's. I had a physical … did you guys know that the higher your cholesterol number is, the worse it is? I always thought higher meant better."

When he mentioned that his total cholesterol level was over three hundred, I suggested he remove the bacon from his bacon cheeseburger. What did these guys do without me?

I was already on my feet. "Sorry that I have to run, but I really need to catch her."

"Somebody's whipped," Cervino said, and made a whipping motion with his hand, sound effects included. Mistress Kate would be proud.

I drove to Rockfield Square, which housed Dr. MacDougal's medical practice, amongst numerous small businesses. As I was walking in, I came across Mary Rothschild, and her daughter, Emmy, who was the key three-point shooter on our basketball team.

"JP—thank God you're alright," Mary greeted me. "We could see the flames all the way up on Blueberry Bush."

"Hey, Coach," Emmy said, not sounding her cheerful self.

"I'm bringing her in for tests … they think she has mono," her mother explained.

"The kissing disease," I said with a smile, and Emmy's face reddened.

"Well, hopefully we're a few years removed from that. But on the subject of someone who's going to get kissed tonight, I just saw Gwen … and you are one lucky guy."

"You're not going to get an argument from me … I'm just heading in to see her myself," I pointed at the door to Dr. MacDougal's office. "Do you think she's done with her exam?"

"Oh, I don't know. I meant I saw her at Bardella's. She bought this little black dress for your date tonight that is going to knock your socks off … among other things."

"Our date?"

She looked confused. "She said you're going into the city tonight. I hope I didn't ruin a surprise."

"No—not at all. My head is just still a little cloudy from last night."

What are you up to, Gwen?

"Chin up," I told Emmy as her mother led her into Dr. MacDougal's office—'chin up' was our rallying call every time we got down in a game this past season, and at last check, we always came back to prevail. Right now I needed to take my own coaching advice.

I strolled into Bardella's Dress Shop, and was met by Vivian Bardella. She had owned the shop seemingly since the Truman Administration, and fashioned herself as the town's resident glamour expert. Sort of the Joan Rivers of Rockfield.

"JP Warner, what a welcome surprise," she greeted me, and kissed both my cheeks, European style.

"I love the new hairstyle," she said. "And what a sharp suit."

"It's a Maloney original."

"Haven't heard of a designer named Maloney—I will have to look into him."

"He does custom work for me. I was told Gwen was in here earlier, do you know where she might have gone?"

"Can't get anything past a reporter like you, JP. And what a fabulous choice she made on that dress … she is like a vampire that never ages. What's her secret?"

Perhaps that she always pulls through unscathed, while her boyfriend gets clobbered over the head, or almost dies trying to save her.

"There's a lot of preservatives in wine, I guess."

"If that were the case, then I'd look like a teenager."

"You're not, Vivian?"

She let out a flirtatious laugh. "You do know what to say to a girl, JP Warner."

"I'm a journalist—I just state the truth," I said with a smile. "Do you happen to know where Gwen went to?"

"I believe she was going to Francine's to get her hair done."

"For our big night out in the city, of course."

Francine's was also in Rockfield Square, so Gwen didn't have to travel far to prepare for our imaginary date. And like my previous stops, I'd missed her.

When I inquired as to Gwen's next stop—*women tell their hairdresser everything, right?*—Francine said she was under the impression that Gwen was on her way to meet up with me. I didn't recall any such meeting, but I made up something about getting our signals crossed.

When I asked her if Gwen had done anything different with the hair today, grasping at straws at this point, she told me that she'd brought in a photo of Elizabeth Hurley, and wanted it done to look like that.

"The actress?"

"Loved her in *Austin Powers.* Never understood why they didn't bring her back for the remakes."

I was starting to think Gwen was the one who had the head injury. I thanked Francine, and then retraced my steps without any luck.

I decided my best bet might be to return home and wait for her to come to me. Not my style, but I was out of options, and my head and lung issues were wearing me thin. As I drove along Skyview, nearing home, I saw the flash of police lights behind me. Things just kept getting better.

I pulled over, and watched as Rich Tolland approached the vehicle.

"I didn't steal Maloney's car," I beat him to the punch. "He loaned it to me … sort of."

"That's not why I pulled you over. I thought you should know that I just got out of a meeting with the FBI, and I told them everything I know. That Allison Cooper came to me yesterday, worried for her life, along with her children's. I provided them safety, but I believed the fire last night was related to this issue, as is the fact that she's now missing. I almost lost my job the last time I lied to them, and I wasn't going to risk it. The children are now in their custody—your mother's name was never brought up.

"I also told them that Allison met with the staff of the *Rockfield Gazette* yesterday, I was not included, and don't know what was discussed. Agent Hawkins is currently on his way to the hospital to find out what you know on that subject."

I almost smiled, thinking of him finding Maloney in that bed. "You did the right thing, Rich. But at the moment, my biggest concern is finding Gwen, and I have no clue where she is."

He grinned. "Maybe I can help you with that. They never asked me about Allison Cooper's car, so I didn't tell them that I had put a GPS tracker on it, in case it was stolen, or she was carjacked by those who were after her. And since the *Gazette* van has been parked at the office all day, and Gwen has been spotted all over town, I have a pretty good idea who is driving Allison's car."

He handed me the tracker data. I saw that Gwen was serious about that night out in the city, because the Audi was parked directly across the street from my brownstone.

CHAPTER 53

I needed to get to the city. The problem was that dusk would be descending soon, and driving at night was an impossibility in my current state. I had to find a ride, but I was low on options.

Rich Tolland was on duty the rest of the night. My father was performing his first selectman duties, throwing out the ceremonial first pitch at Lefebvre Park. And since this wouldn't fit my mother's "retreat" strategy, I didn't even ask her. Ethan and Pam were at a banquet, honoring local athletes. I tried Herbie and Cervino, but I got no answer. I remembered them mentioning their plans to hit Main Street Tavern after work, which meant they were probably half-sloshed by now, anyway.

That left one person. He was a long-shot, but I preyed on his weakness, which was also my weakness—Gwen.

"Dolly and I had dinner plans, but I'll call her and let her know I'm working late on a story. It won't be the first time I've been in the doghouse, and I doubt that it will be the last," Murray said, and we headed to the *Rockfield Gazette* van.

We picked up I-84 in Danbury, and made the hour-long trip I'd made so many times, but rarely from the co-pilot seat. I worried about the elderly Murray handling the rush hour traffic, especially on the winding Saw Mill

Parkway, but truth was, he was in complete control, and my concern only seemed to annoy him.

"So what do you think she's up to?" I asked.

"I always like to start with the most obvious scenario, John Pierpont, and in this case, it would be that she is meeting a boyfriend."

Strangely, I would sign for that at this point. "But if she were having an affair, Gwen would never leave such a trail. She's too savvy for that."

"That is true—you'd be the last one to know."

"Do you have another theory?"

"It could be a number of things, or a combination of them. Perhaps Allison provided her a clue during their time spent together, prior to the fire. Gwen and Allison always had a strong bond, so it's possible she wasn't comfortable saying certain things within our group session, and would only confide in Gwen."

"And this item she told confided in her, would require Gwen to hit the town dressed to the nines?"

"Please don't take my thoughts as fact. I'm just brainstorming at this point, and as I get older, the storms are usually milder, and often blow out to sea."

I got the feeling that the storm was being tempered for my benefit. "Remember how you drilled into our heads that a journalist's first responsibility is to the truth? I'm a big boy, Murray—I can take it."

"I'm not here as a journalist tonight, but as a friend."

"Then all the more reason to give it to me straight."

He took a deep breath and slowly blew it out. "I'm very worried about our girl. While I don't have any inkling as to what her plan is, I do know she has a history of running right into the eye of the storm. And in the case of Officer Jones, she did so literally."

"Which almost got her killed."

"And is why it's important that we get to her as soon as possible."

"When we do, could you tell her what you just told me? I'm not sure I have any credibility on the subject of running toward danger."

"Despite your reputation to the contrary, you seem to prefer to use deception and misdirection to achieve results, such as your fake Grady Benson persona and breaking into his home. It's not always effective, but in this case, I think that might be the more sensible approach."

As we got off the exit for 125th Street, nearing our destination, I put on my sunglasses—darkness had arrived, and the city lights were starting to make my head spin. We idled the van, just down the street from my place. The Audi was still there, parked across the street, and the lights were on inside the brownstone. While I might not run into storms with the same voraciousness as Gwen, I did plan on running inside the building to get to the bottom of this.

Murray held up the stop sign. "Patience isn't only a virtue, it can be a key to understanding. Observation is a journalist's most effective tool."

I detected an enthusiasm in his voice. "You miss this, don't you?"

"Excuse me?"

"Chasing the big story ... the anticipation of the moment. You miss it."

He stared out the windshield as he spoke, "Do you know who my boyhood hero was, John Pierpont?"

"I would guess a famed journalist like Ernie Pyle."

"While my grownup life has been dedicated to journalism, my childhood was all about baseball. My hero was Willie Mays. And if I were to ask Willie if he would like to play one more big game, chase down another fly ball like a gazelle, or hit another home run deep into the bleachers at the Polo Grounds, his answer would be yes, yes, yes, a thousand times over. You always miss what you love, and hope for one more chance to show it how much you care."

"Then come with me tonight. Help us write this story. One more big game ... and get our girl back in the process."

He shook his head. "I also remember when Willie came to the Mets at the end of his career, forty-one years old, ancient for a ballplayer. His mind was as sharp as ever, but the legs were heavy, and the instincts no longer trustworthy. In the 1973 World Series, I watched as my hero stumbled and fell in the outfield, while chasing a fly ball the younger Willie would have made easy work of. After the game, he responded, "Growing old is just a helpless hurt.""

I nodded that I understood.

"I will take you to Gwen, but then I will return to the safe confines of Rockfield, and try to explain myself to Dolly," he said.

"Take me to Gwen? She's right inside."

"She's going somewhere tonight—nobody buys a dress to stay home."

Right on cue, Gwen stepped out of the front door, and even though I was at a distance, I could tell that Mary Rothschild was on the mark about the dress. I wouldn't normally be able to pull my stare from such a sight, but my eyes went to the person on her arm.

It was a fit-looking man in a suit, sporting a trim beard, and holding Gwen's hand. *What the hell?* They didn't go to the Audi as I suspected, but a well-timed limo pulled up in front of the brownstone, and the man helped her inside. While patience might be the key to understanding, I thought my fists could help get to the bottom of things much quicker.

Murray followed the limo, three cars back, until it stopped in front of the NoMad Hotel, and Gwen and Beard got out. The last time I was here for Byron's fundraiser I'd made a spectacle of myself, and Gwen sent me away for reflection. I would have to fight my every urge not to let history repeat itself. Murray wished me luck, and began his journey back to Connecticut.

I followed them on foot as they entered the main dining room, where they met another man. Another good-looking guy, also in an expensive suit, probably in his early thirties.

I was seated at a table across the room, where I could watch them. I was unable to eavesdrop on their conversation, but it certainly didn't appear to be strained or tense.

My jealousies switched from Beard to the other guy, as he missed no opportunity to touch Gwen—her arm, her hand, her shoulder. Gwen was so offended by this that she laughed at all his attempts at humor like he was some comedian. Drinks were served, and they turned even more festive. It looked like … gulp … a date.

Their main course hadn't even arrived when Gwen and the man rose from their seats. He clenched her hand, and they began walking away. But not toward the street entrance—they were going in the direction of the hotel rooms. My stomach dropped.

Beard threw down a wad of cash to cover the dinner they never received, and he made his way out a side exit.

I had no idea what was going on, but my patience had run out.

CHAPTER 54

Her "date" leaned against a French mahogany writing desk, which sat in front of a large bay window with a view of the Empire State Building. He removed his sports coat and tossed it on the bed. Gwen swore it sounded like a thud when it hit.

He studied her intently from head to heels, and proved her wrong—it was possible to be more creeped out. "As you know, Hugo Whitley YPA will be picking up the bill for my services," she said, referring to her thousand dollar an hour fee, which was actually quite flattering.

He nodded knowingly. "And what exactly will those services include?"

"BBFS and BBBJ," she replied, feeling sick when she said it. She had a general understanding of escort lingo from a story she did back when she wrote for the *Globe*. She hoped that the language hadn't changed.

His look of anticipation told her that it hadn't. "Why are you so far away from me ... do I smell?"

"I'm sorry—I'm just a little nervous."

"That doesn't sound like the girl I heard about. Why is that?"

"Him—why is he here?" she pointed at the bodyguard, a Middle Eastern-looking man holding a large gun. There were two more of them stationed outside the door of the suite.

"I thought you liked to perform in front of an audience."

"Not a heavily armed one."

He ordered the bodyguard into the bathroom. The guard followed his boss's orders, shutting the door behind him. What a gentleman.

Gwen was relieved he was out of sight, but now she was out of excuses. Unlike when she'd pretended to be Kyle Jones' girlfriend—she always knew he would back down in intimate situations—this man expected action. And if she didn't do something quick, the bodyguard would make a return visit.

She walked up to him, feeling like her stilettos were weighted down by cement. She ran her hand through his hair and went to kiss him.

He pushed her away.

"I thought I made it clear that I'm not interested in the girlfriend experience," he said, and grabbed her by the chin and squished her mouth into a fish face. "If you try to kiss me again, I'll rip your lips off, understand?"

He wouldn't have to worry about that. The fact that she got that close made her want to amputate her lips. She hoped Allison could appreciate the lengths she was going.

Just to make sure there were no hard feelings, he presented her with a gift. "It's an outfit I want you to put on," he said, handing her the decorated box.

"But I thought you specifically requested this dress?"

"That was for dinner ... this is for dessert."

She made her way to the bathroom, where she was reunited with the bodyguard. She asked him if he'd step outside so she could change, but he made it clear he had no plans to leave her alone.

It was a large European-style bathroom with a walk-in shower, which she wanted to use to wash the stench off. The bodyguard was perched on the edge of a clawfoot bathtub, probably to let her know that's where they planned to drown her when the deed was done.

She could feel his beady eyes on her as she opened the box. But when she saw what was inside, she almost laughed out loud.

It was the metallic foil, halter mini dress that Elizabeth Hurley wore in the first *Austin Powers* movie, playing the role of Vanessa Kensington. It also came with a gun, but unlike the bodyguard's, this one was a prop.

Instead of returning to Rockfield last night, Gwen made a detour to Manhattan. More specifically, she went to Cliff Sutcliffe's Midtown apartment. He seemed surprised to see her on his doorstep at that hour, as did the blonde woman who strolled into the room, in only a towel, and said, "Clifford—who is knocking at this hour? How rude of them."

Lauren tried to play off her presence as a business meeting. And if that were the case, then it was like the business meeting Gwen was about to partake in. But she had much more important issues to discuss with Clifford.

Gwen implored him to immediately start promoting a Lauren Bowden exclusive, which included inside information on her own shooting, and the aftermath, courtesy of the recorder she hid in her bulletproof vest. Basically, the story that Jovana had nipped in the bud. In return, Gwen offered to convince JP to turn over the details of his Nora Reign interview.

Lauren was all for it, and Cliff wasn't in the best negotiating position, so within a half hour, the promos were up and running. *Who says a 24-hour news cycle is a waste of airtime?*

Whether Jovana was still stationed in New York, or she arrived via spaceship, she was at Cliff's apartment within minutes, threatening to remove his head from his neck. Mission accomplished—there was no need to find Jovana if Gwen could get her to come to her.

After filling her in on the most recent developments, they worked into the early morning hours on their plan of attack. Stopping an international terrorist sure did make for strange partners, she thought.

Gwen returned to Rockfield first thing in the morning, where she and Murray had their usual weekly meeting. She then stopped by to visit with JP's mother, and check on Gracie and Chase. Once she knew they were safe, she went to Dr. MacDougal's office. As JP's primary care physician, he could call into the hospital and get an update on his condition. They reported that he was being treated for smoke inhalation, was expected to make a full recovery, but would have to stay in the hospital for the next few days. Gwen had her doubts about the last part.

At the same time Jovana arrived at Hugo Whitley YPA, and informed Dennis Whitley that she was taking over for Allison Cooper, who would be on an extended leave of absence. And that she would now be heading up the General Washington Carpet Cleaning account, whether he liked it or not. Her first order of business was to put a call into David Tully to introduce herself—under her assumed name of Joey Draznok—and suggest a meeting.

No surprise, she was told that Tully wasn't available. So Joey asked to talk to David Tully Jr., and this time she was surprised, when Junior took the call. Joey explained what services would now be made available to clients, ones that Allison didn't offer, and he was suddenly willing to make the trek from Valley Forge to New York to meet with them that evening.

The CIA was able to research Tully Jr., and create a profile—meaning, they hacked the phone he took the call on. The one he'd switched to so that they could "keep things private."

There were no grand Al Muttahedah secrets on the phone, but they were able to gather evidence of Junior's extensive use of a certain escort service during his travels. Since the service was headquartered in New York, Joey paid them a visit, and set up a date for him tonight with a "new girl" who met his criteria—it seemed Junior had an Elizabeth Hurley fetish. When Gwen finished her makeover, her photo and stage name was added to the database for the escort service, along with a "top rating" and made-up customer reviews.

She could feel the bodyguard peering right through her as she removed the dress. With Jovana's help, it had been altered to look like the plunging Versace dress, held together by oversized gold safety pins, which helped rocket Hurley to fame. Gwen changed into the metallic mini dress with matching boots. She felt like she'd just arrived from outer space.

Before returning to the bedroom, she noticed that a bottle of champagne had been left for her. She opened it, swigged right from the bottle, and then exited the bathroom with the bottle in one hand, and two champagne flutes in the other.

She stood in the bathroom doorway, striking her sexiest pose. "Are you horny, baby," she said in a bad Austin Powers imitation.

"Nobody is paying you for comedy," he said, his eyes drawn to the silver dress. She walked to him, mumbling to herself, *"C'mon, Jovana ... where are you?"*

When she reached him, he tried to push her to her knees, but she resisted. She held up the champagne bottle. "I like to have a drink first to celebrate ... and then the party starts," she purred. She poured a glass and handed it to him.

His eyes bulged with anger. "Nobody's interested in what you like!" He grabbed the bottle out of her hand and began to swing it at her like a tennis racket. She closed her eyes and recoiled, but he stopped, thinking better of it—a dead whore would cause big headaches. He tossed the bottle on the floor and it began to spill out. He then threw his glass against the wall, shattering it. "You're going to lick this room clean when we're done, glass and all."

He pushed her down again, and unzipped. She then surprised him with a different kind of head than he was hoping for—sending a head butt into his crotch area.

The pain transformed him into a raging bull, and pulled her to her feet by her hair. "You like to play rough ... I play rougher," he said, and jammed her up against the bay window face first, so hard she thought he would shove her right through.

Gwen screamed as loud as she could.

And like a magic genie, Jovana appeared. "Put it away, Junior, or I'll shoot it right off."

Gwen felt relief.

Until another man burst into the room and tackled Jovana from behind.

CHAPTER 55

"JP—what are you doing?" Gwen shouted out.

"I could ask you the same."

"You shouldn't be here."

Having just saved her life, and being completely willing to overlook her "other life" as a prostitute, you would think I would have received a more appreciative greeting. But then I started to understand what was going down.

A Middle Eastern-looking goon came out of the bathroom with weapon in hand. And to add to his arsenal, he picked up the gun dropped by the bearded man I'd just tackled.

This annoyed Beard, who spit at the goon, before turning his anger to me. And in a much more feminine voice than I expected, said, "Way to go, Warner. Bravo."

The goon ripped off Beard's beard, and then pulled the wig from his head, revealing dark hair pinned up underneath. "Jovana?"

I had to hand it to the CIA makeup artists—she really did look like a dude. But now she just looked angry. "What the hell were you thinking?"

"I thought you were coming to kill Gwen."

I'd followed Beard out of the hotel, and then back inside through a freight entrance. He, or rather, she, made her way up a back stairwell to this suite on the fifth floor, which wasn't easy for me with my numerous maladies. I watched as she overwhelmed the armed guards who were manning the hallway in front of the suite. When she pulled her gun and entered, all I could think of was that Gwen was in that room, and I needed to save her from this crazed gunman. So I did what came natural ... which was to screw up a perfectly good plan.

Gwen's "date" clutched around her neck from behind, like he was imitating one of Carter's wrestling moves. He didn't look like a killer to me—I got the feeling he didn't get his hands dirty that often—but he also looked scared, and scared people can do irrational things.

With his free hand, he grabbed a glass of champagne and smashed it against a writing desk. He then held the jagged edge to Gwen's neck. "One false move and she dies!" He didn't sound convincing, but that wouldn't make Gwen any less dead if he decided to dig that sharp edge into her carotid artery.

"Who are you?" I demanded.

"It's David Tully Jr.," Jovana spoke for him.

With closer examination, I recognized him from the website. And since we were making introductions, I informed him that I was JP Warner, he had his hands around my girlfriend's neck, and it would be in his best interest to step away.

He seemed less than impressed, and ordered Jovana and me to our feet. It was starting to remind me of Syria.

"The only one here who's going to kill anyone is me ... unless you let the woman go," Jovana stated.

"You don't seem to be in a position to be making those threats."

"That's what Qwaui said, just before I shot six holes in his chest. Do you want to be next, Junior? It's your decision."

All her bravado did was back him further into a corner. I needed to do something before she got Gwen killed.

"You won't hurt her," I called out.

He looked confused. "And who's going to stop me?"

"The universe. It won't let you do it ... it brought us together for a reason, and it wasn't so that it would end like this."

"In that case, the universe better get here really fast."

Jovana removed her jacket, and tossed it on the bed. She then undid her tie and began unbuttoning her dress shirt. "If she's worth a thousand an hour, then I must be worth risking your life," she said.

"Do you think I'm stupid? Stop whatever you're doing!"

"What's wrong, Junior? Are you disappointed I'm not wearing that dress with the gold safety pins? It's in the bathroom, I can slip it on for you if you'd like."

Her eyes subtly shifted to Gwen, who returned a look of understanding. It was quick and brilliant, and you'd have to be looking for it to notice. Junior and his goons weren't.

Gwen's arm thrust toward her attacker's neck, jamming one of the safety pins into it as hard as she could. They had planned for all possibilities.

When Junior screamed out, Jovana made her move, successfully knocking away the gun from the guard. But he was able to recover, and pulled the spare on them.

The window crashed in, startling everyone—Jovana tackled me to the ground. Another Middle Eastern-looking goon swung in like a one-man SWAT team. He covered Junior, and fired off an erratic round in our direction with a sub-machine gun.

The bodyguard didn't get down fast enough. He was riddled with bullets and slumped to the floor, as did his gun. Jovana reached for it, and was ready to return fire. But the mission was to get his boss out of danger, not get into a shootout in a New York hotel. The round in our direction was about clearing the way for a clean escape. He loaded Junior onto his rope, and they swung out the window, disappearing into the night.

I ran to the window, just in time to see them reach the ground. They whisked him into a black SUV, and took off.

"They're getting away," I shouted to Jovana.

"No they're not," she said, seemingly disinterested.

"Shouldn't we go after them?" Gwen asked with urgency.

"Not yet. First we need to find out where they're going."

PART FOUR –

CARPET BAGGERS

CHAPTER 56

Charleston, South Carolina

April 12

The ferry docked, and members of the party were assisted to dry land by a group of park rangers. They led the guests through the sally-port entrance and into Fort Sumter.

Byron Jasper, the man of the hour, led the way, being pushed in his wheelchair by his assistant, Lamar Thompson. Right behind him was his fiancée, Tonya, followed by Mama Jasper.

The next wave was made up of esteemed guests and dignitaries, including the mayor of Charleston, the head of the Charleston Hall of Fame, Rex Denson, along with numerous others who had shaped Byron's life. This included his third grade teacher, his college football coach, his doctors, and the key members of his foundation.

Carter took up the rear, with his two best girls on his arms—Christina, who appeared uncomfortable in her fancy dress, and Kate, who seemed strangely comfortable in the June Cleaver number she was wearing. Carter wore his usual sleeveless denim jacket and wraparound sunglasses, even though nightfall had arrived.

The day began with a luncheon at Mama Jasper's restaurant, followed by a ceremony on the battery, in which the mayor gave Byron the key to the city. Carter hoped it worked at Frankly My Dear's, his favorite strip club in town.

After watching a beautiful sunset sink into Charleston Harbor—at least that's how Kate described it—they were loaded onto ferries, and made the three-mile watery trek to Fort Sumter, where the official introduction would take place. The sea fort was where the first shots of the Civil War were fired on this day, April 12, back in 1861.

Carter wiped a pound of sweat from his newly-shaved dome as he stepped inside the walls of the fort—the humidity was stifling. The fort was really just an outside park with a wall around it, sitting on a man-made island in Charleston Harbor. He would have preferred a venue with air conditioning, but he did enjoy the smell of the sea air, reminding him of trips he took here with his father when he was a young boy.

They were greeted by a group of cadets from the nearby Citadel military college, on hand for the ceremony. Carter saluted the uniformed men and women.

Prior to the festivities, they were provided a quick tour of the place by the federal park rangers. When a female ranger laid out the ground rules, such as nobody was to touch any of the artifacts, and not to play on the cannons, she held her gaze on Carter. He was too hot and bored to be offended.

The tour began at the parade route, which was a grassy, park-like area. The first stop was the artillery exhibit in front of the left-flank casemate. At each stop along the tour, the ranger told a little more of the story of April 12, 1861, beginning with the first shot, which was fired upon the fort at 4:30 a.m., while many in Charleston's battery sat on their balconies and toasted the start of the hostilities. Carter had never been an active participant in combat, but he'd been in the middle of enough of them to know that war was nothing to ever celebrate.

The tour arrived at Battery Huger, a massive concrete monstrosity that took up most of the fort's interior. It was built in 1898, in preparation for the looming Spanish American War. Today, a small museum and gift shop were inside it, and the top had been made into an observation deck with an impressive array of flags, which could be seen for miles.

Carter loved the view from the observation deck, and part of him was intrigued by the prospect of seeing it for the first time at night. But he was overtaken by the urge to explore other areas of the fort, which he'd been dying to do all day.

He grabbed Kate's hand, and pulled her away. She looked surprised by the sudden detour, but he calmed her with a grin. "What do you say we go play on a cannon?"

CHAPTER 57

Christina took her seat in one of the folding chairs, facing the makeshift stage. She couldn't decide whether her uncomfortable feeling was due to the dress, the dreadful humidity, or both.

The stage had been decorated with red, white, and blue bunting, and Charleston Harbor would have served as a spectacular backdrop, if not for the massive pile of concrete called Battery Huger, which the stage was backed up against, blocking the view.

The Jasper family was seated on the stage, along with the mayor, and the head of the Charleston Hall of Fame.

Christina wiped the sweat from her brow, and leaned back in her seat. The area around her had filled up with guests, and for the first time she noticed that Carter and Kate were missing. She smiled to herself, remembering Carter telling her that his goal was, to use his words, "bump uglies," in all 108 national monuments across America, which he believed to be his patriotic duty. Christina got the idea that he would now be able to cross Fort Sumter off his list.

The mayor got things underway, picking up where he left off back in the battery—his long-windedness was the only breeze blowing through this place at the moment. He was followed by a stream of Byron's friends and admirers coming up to the podium to share some brief thoughts about him—everyone from his football coaches to Major Ellison, who was the doctor who saved his life at Landstuhl. And of course there was typical JP—he couldn't find the time to show up, but still needed to make his presence felt, by taping a congratulatory video.

Each speaker, no matter how different their relationship to Byron, touched on similar themes. All talked about his determination and loyalty. That he'd be the one they'd want in a foxhole with them, and if anyone could overcome something as daunting as paralysis, it was Byron.

For Christina, it felt strange not taking notes, asking questions, and seeking an angle for the story. After a dizzying six months as an international correspondent, hopping from one story, and country, to the next, it was hard to decompress and actually enjoy a night out.

Rex Denson, the head of the Hall of Fame, took to the podium to introduce Byron. He was a man in his sixties, who looked like a combination of Colonel Sanders and Mark Twain, with a shock of white hair, and a fluffy mustache.

He spoke in a slow but steady drawl, "We are proud tonight to add Byron Jasper to an impressive list of Charlestonians who have entered this hallowed hall, including his mother and grandmother.

"Many have asked why we've chosen to have this ceremony on this day, in this place. Fort Sumter represents the beginning of a war that was truly America's darkest hour, pitting brother against brother, and covering this great nation with the stain of American blood.

"But as we look back all these years later, we now see that those men did not die in vain. The Civil War created a reunification of the covenant— that we truly were a country based on freedom for *all* men. A freedom that has allowed Byron Jasper, a descendant of slaves, to achieve such great feats … and we here in Charleston know that he will continue to do so."

After a long ovation, Denson pointed to a line of men in the blue dress-uniforms of the South Carolina militia.

"I want to thank the cadets from the Citadel for being here tonight, and they will now provide a 21-gun salute in honor of enduring freedom."

They raised their guns in unison, a commander barked an order, and they fired.

Christina had been present for these salutes before, and always came away regretting that she wasn't wearing earplugs. But that wasn't the case this time. It was as if some of the guns failed to fire.

She viewed the cadets, most of them wearing confused looks. But when she looked back to the stage, there was nothing confusing about what had happened there. Rex Denson was lying on the stage floor, his white suit stained with blood.

Christina returned her attention to the cadets, and noticed that the one in the center was still pointing his gun in the direction of the stage. He had shot Denson.

The crowd began to scream out. But they were in a fort, three miles from shore, so nobody would hear them. And if they thought they would receive help from the park rangers, they wouldn't—a couple of imposters stepped forward and ordered everyone to get on the ground.

The fake rangers secured all in attendance, including those members of the rangers and cadets who weren't involved in the plot. They forced all parties to lay face down on the ground, and collected their cell phones and personal items.

The shooter made his way to the podium, where Major Ellison was furiously trying to save Rex Denson's life. He stepped to the microphone, and announced, "Lieutenant Henry S. Farley was the man who fired the first shot of the American Civil War, here at Fort Sumter. And I am honored to be the one to have fired the shot that will begin the next civil war—one that will end the tyranny of the United States once and for all. This fort is now under the control of Whiskey Tax."

He paused for a moment, as if waiting for questions, and then went into full speech-mode, "Despite the fiction Mr. Denson's provided here tonight, soldiers *did* die in vain. They fought valiantly to maintain the greatness of this country, which had courageously sought its freedom from the rule of the British and King George. Only to have their descendants be forced to watch as the great men who built this country were mocked, marginalized, and now attacked—the wealthy, white landowners, who risked everything to invest in this land and its freedom. This has led to a broken economy, broken families, and broken values. But we members of Whiskey Tax will no longer stand by with passive resistance while Huddled Masses declares war on us."

Christina thought it came off prepared, lacking the passion of someone who truly believed the words. She also thought it sounded a little strange coming from someone with a British accent. And while on the topic of strange, she realized that she was the only one of the guests who hadn't been forced to the ground.

"Is everyone accounted for?" British asked one of the fake park rangers.

"All are accounted for except Jeff Carter and his female companion," the ranger shouted back.

His look turned annoyed. "Find him, and bring him here."

He turned his attention to Christina, giving her the chills, even on this humid night. "In the meantime, it looks like your lucky night, Ms. Wilkins. You are about to break the story of a lifetime."

CHAPTER 58

New York City

A beautiful woman in a metallic, space-age dress interrupted my thoughts. She handed me a glass of water and a couple of aspirin.

"Thanks," I said meekly. I stuffed the pills in my mouth, and washed them down with a swig.

She took a seat next to me on the couch. We were in the Great Room of my brownstone, where we had come to regroup following the debacle at the hotel.

"You look tired," Gwen said, and rubbed the back of her hand softly over my cheek.

"You look like you just leaped out of an Austin Powers movie."

She smiled. "Should we shag now, or shag later?"

I raised the glass of water as if toasting her. "I have a headache."

"That's what guys always say. And speaking of costumes, what's with the Maloney look?"

I ran my hand over the slicked-back hair—it felt as if it had been soaked in cement. "Francine thought I should have a new look for my big date tonight in the city, and then I stopped in at Bardella's and picked up the suit.

I'm surprised I didn't run into you in there," I said, just to let her know that she couldn't get anything past me ... even though we both knew she could.

"I was just following the old philosophy—don't dress for the job you have ... dress for the one you want."

"So you're like a hooker or something?"

"Your girlfriend happens to be a thousand-dollar-an-hour escort, not a hooker."

"I think you undercharge," I said, and she actually appeared flattered by the statement.

"Because you're so sweet, I'll give you half price."

"It's not funny, Gwen ... you could have gotten yourself killed."

"Can't believe you're talking."

I just shook my head, which wasn't as simple of a task as it used to be. "I guess we reversed roles this time."

"You normally wear the shiny dress?"

"It's just something Murray told me—that you're programmed to run toward the storm to solve a problem, while I'm inclined to take the road of trickery and deception. But in this case, you were the deceiver, and I was the one barging in on the eye of the storm."

"Based on the effectiveness of the mission, I think I best return to my old ways."

"That's the thing—you will default to your DNA. And with me around, there's always going to be plenty of storm clouds to run toward. Eventually they'll win, and I can't let that happen ... it's too risky having me in your life."

"That must be the concussion speaking, because I recall you telling my 'date' that we were being protected by the universe, and that it had big plans for us ... which by the way, was super sweet."

"I meant it, but I also believe in a good contingency plan. So I was glad we had a gun-toting Serb on our side."

"I think you are greatly underestimating how skilled I am with a safety pin," she said with another smile, but I still wasn't seeing the humor.

"What if I didn't come when I did?"

She gave me a crooked look.

"Okay, what if Jovana didn't barge in when she did?"

"The only reason there was any shooting was because you two stormed in. Guys like that don't hire escorts to create scenes and leave dead bodies strewn around hotel rooms. They hire escorts because they quietly go away when they're done."

I guess her scream was just part of the act then. "And you know this how?"

"We all go through some weird phases ... it doesn't mean I love you any less."

"Still not funny."

She heaved a sigh. "I did an exposé on high-end call girls for the *Globe*. It was all the rage after the Spitzer thing. Happy now?"

"When we get this bastard who's behind this I will be."

Her eyes filled with resolve. "And we get Allison back."

CHAPTER 59

Jovana stepped into the room. She was wearing a tank top and jeans that I recognized.

"I apologize for stealing your clothes again," she said to Gwen—more contrite than the last time we were all here.

"They're actually Christina's—she left them behind when she moved out," I said.

Jovana just shook her head. "You sure do have a lot of women in your life, Warner. You'd think you'd have a better handle on the female mind."

It was going to take a lot more than a couple of aspirin to get me through tonight.

She turned to Gwen. "I overheard your conversation—I think you were being too modest. Going in, I'd hoped we could get a hair sample, or a fingerprint, which you were able to get on that champagne bottle. But the blood you extracted sure made our job a lot easier. If you're ever looking to make a career change, I think you'd make a good agent."

Suddenly that hosting job with Lauren seemed a lot more appealing to me. Jovana casually strolled into the small kitchen and opened the refrigerator door.

"Jeez, Warner—we had more food in that shithole in Syria."

Every time she mentioned the 'S' word, Gwen's brow furrowed. And I got the idea that our friendly neighborhood CIA agent was doing it on purpose.

She removed a bottled water, which was the only thing in there, and slammed the refrigerator door in frustration.

"Any word on the DNA test?" I asked.

"We've got a match."

I sat up through the pain; surprised she'd gotten the results that quickly. "I'm going to go out on a limb, and take a guess that his name wasn't David."

"Oh, it's David alright, and he's the son of the man we're looking for."

"He really is David Tully Jr.?"

"Actually it's David Claiborne, but his birth name was David Franklin Jr. He took his mother's surname after denouncing his father, David Franklin Sr."

She reveled in the surprised look on my face—David Franklin was Hakim's birth name. "He met Evelyn Claiborne while she was studying abroad in London. They fell in love, and eventually Franklin returned with Evelyn to her home in the Philadelphia suburbs, and they were married. Franklin's best friend from school, Mathew Bannon, served as his best man at the wedding.

"They had three children, two boys and a girl, with David Jr. being the youngest. The elder Franklin had converted to Islam in the 1970s, but it wasn't until the events of the first Gulf War that there's any record of him becoming radicalized. He left his family to become a Jihad warrior everywhere from Somalia to Afghanistan, along with his friend Bannon, who had left his professorship, and was now known as Qwaui. They made their mark in that world, with reputations as brutal fighters who spared no sympathy for the non-believers.

"They worked as individual contractors until America's hyper-focus on Al Qaeda created opportunity. That was how Al Muttahedah came about—as an acquisition of many of the frayed assets that were the result of the 'War on Terror.' They operated with a different mentality from the previous groups, in that they focused solely on the death and destruction of their enemy, rather than the glory and publicity that others sought by seeking grandiose events like 9/11. They understood that a collection of small acts could paralyze communities."

"I thought you said that Hakim was nothing but a ghost?" I challenged.

"Sometimes ghosts come back to life."

"Hold on," Gwen said, trying to wrap her mind around this. "This guy David, the one from tonight, is the son of Hakim, the world's most wanted man?"

"Not to mention, the owner of General Washington Carpet Cleaning."

"If that's the case, why did we let him get away? He could have led us to his father," Gwen said.

"For all we know, he could already be on a plane to Saudi Arabia by now," I added. "It might have been our only chance."

"He's not on a plane," Jovana stated.

"How can you be sure?"

"Because he went directly back to Valley Forge. He's currently holed up inside the headquarters for General Washington Carpet Cleaning."

"And how would you know that?"

"Let's just say, when we met in the restaurant, a GPS tracker might have slipped into his drink. Wherever he goes, it goes with him."

I nodded, impressed. "So when he got in trouble, his first instinct was to run home to Daddy."

"You really think Hakim is in Pennsylvania?" Gwen asked. "It's just too absurd."

She was right—it was. So much so that it made perfect sense. While searches for this man stretched from Serbia to Syria to Pakistan, he was right under our noses. America's biggest enemy running a small business ... and the ultimate sleeper cell ... from inside our borders. When we grew frustrated chasing false Bin Laden sightings, the inside joke among reporters was that while we were searching for him in some obscure mountain range on the other side of the globe, he was probably rollerblading through Central Park and having a good laugh at us. It wasn't so funny anymore.

It was unprecedented, preposterous, and yes, crazy. But as someone who'd flirted with crazy on occasion, I realized it was just crazy enough to work. At least until his horny son just blew his cover.

"I find it strange that a son who would so vehemently oppose his father, suddenly got the urge to join the family business. Something doesn't add up," Gwen said.

Jovana received a beep, and pulled a phone from her pocket. I got the idea that it wasn't your average phone, and it's what she was using to track Junior's movements.

She studied it, and her face scrunched with dread. "Turn on the television, Warner."

CHAPTER 60

Lauren Bowden appeared in her usual role as the Angel of Death. On the bottom of the screen read the words, *America's Most Courageous News Anchor.*

Seriously, it said that. I understand she was held at gunpoint, and later took a bullet to the chest on 42nd Street, *but c'mon, really?*

"If you're just joining us, we have breaking news to report," she said with a twinkle in her eye.

I began to run through possible scenarios in my head. The one thing I was sure of, was that it wasn't related to what happened at the NoMad Hotel. The CIA had completely cleaned that one up the moment we vacated the premises, or so Jovana claimed.

"On this April 12, the anniversary of the first shots of the Civil War, Fort Sumter is once again under attack," Lauren announced.

I got the feeling this wasn't a case of a Confederate sympathizer getting liquored up and deciding to "take back the fort!" This was the quick escalation that Murray predicted.

Lauren began wiping away tears. "I'm sorry for my unprofessional behavior," she said, but not specifying if she meant the crying, or her entire career. "But as a proud South Carolinian, and the former Miss Beaufort County, this is personal for me."

America's most courageous anchor found the fortitude to trudge on, "Here's what we know so far. Tonight, during a ceremony held at Fort Sumter, all those present were taken hostage. The estimate is that thirty to forty souls are being held inside. There have been reports of a shooting, but that is unconfirmed at this time. And to make matters worse, the captors have claimed to have surrounded the fort with mines in the harbor, making a rescue a risky event, and one that will have to be approached with caution."

Lauren briefly paused, before stating, "As always, GNZ goes right to the heart of the story, and we have reporter Christina Wilkins on the phone with us now—she is currently stowed away inside the fort. Christina, are you there?"

"Yes, Lauren, I am," she replied in a soft voice, as if she feared being discovered. Her picture was plastered on the screen as she spoke. It looked like a high school yearbook photo, reminding me of just how young she was. "Please don't get yourself killed, Christina," I muttered to myself.

"First off, what is your situation? Are you in need of medical attention?"

"I am currently unharmed. I apologize for the low volume of my voice, but I don't want to give away my location. These people are very dangerous."

"Please tell us what you observed tonight."

"I was present for a ceremony to honor former GNZ cameraman, Byron Jasper."

It felt like an anvil had hit me square in the jaw. With all that had gone down in the last twenty-four hours, the ceremony had slipped my mind—Byron and his family, along with Carter, were among those taken hostage.

Gwen read my sick look and put her arm around me, as we continued to stare at the screen in disbelief.

"Just as the ceremony was about to begin, a couple of cadets from the Citadel, who were here as part of the festivities, were overheard making comments to the effect that, if the South had been as pro-active as the

Whiskey Tax group, there would have been no need for a ceremony, and America would be a better place.

"This set off the Jasper family, who declared themselves as unabashed supporters of Huddled Masses. They exchanged words with the cadets, and things quickly escalated. At one point, Byron Jasper's mother, a prominent restaurant owner in Charleston, began screaming, "You're not my master, and I ain't your slave!" This set off an ugly chain of events—the Jasper group began chanting 'Huddled Masses!' and 'No New Taxes!' at the Whiskey Tax supporters, who were greatly outnumbered. They rushed the cadets, who appeared overwhelmed, and disarmed them. They were then forced to the ground at gunpoint.

"The head of the Charleston Hall of Fame, which ironically, Jasper was being honored by, tried to be diplomatic. But the Jasper clan shouted him down, telling him he was either with them or with their enemy. When he refused to concede to their threats, he was shot with one of the guns taken from the cadets. The man who did the shooting was an employee of Jasper named Lamar Thompson."

"I know Lamar Thompson all too well," Lauren cut in, as Lamar's photo replaced Christina's on the screen. It was shaded dark, making him appear sinister. "He is a felon and drug abuser ... and worse than that, he is rude and uncouth. So where do things stand, Christina?"

"The captors said they planned to kill a hostage each hour, unless their demands are met." Suddenly Christina's voice filled with fear. "I must go ... they're coming my way."

"There she is ... get her," I heard Byron's unmistakable voice.

"Byron—no!" Christina said, right before her connection was cut off.

"That was staged ... there's no way," I stated the obvious.

Lauren looked into the camera with a look of determination. I'd seen that look before—hold on to your hats.

"And tonight I ask what many of you at home are thinking—what's wrong with this country? What is the point of me being an American hero if I can't recognize the country I'm a heroic symbol of? People have always made it to the top in America by either being born into it, or those like myself, who are willing to do whatever it takes to make it. The fact is, not everyone is going to be successful in this country, and when Huddled Masses starts to get that through their thick skulls, then we'll all be better off. And for all of you out there who would argue that all men are created equal, I would tell you that I've been with many men throughout the course of my life, and they certainly aren't all created equal."

"She never lacks for a unique perspective," I said.

"All I'll say, is it's a good thing she's sleeping with her boss." Gwen commented.

I looked quizzically at her.

"Long story," she said, and pulled me closer. "Look, JP—Carter is in there, and Byron and Christina are obviously up to something. They have a plan."

That's what worried me.

"Nothing we can do about it," Jovana cut in coldly. "But we can head directly to the source and cut off the head of the snake."

"You think we should go after Hakim?" I asked.

"I was thinking Lauren Bowden," she said with a confident smile. "But come to think of it, Hakim might be a better idea."

CHAPTER 61

Gwen came out of the bedroom wearing a baggy sweater and a pair of jeans twice her size. Besides a few stragglers that Christina left behind, the only choice of clothing was from my wardrobe. Not ideal, but still a better option than her Austin Powers dress. The "safety pin" one might have proven useful, but it was left behind in the hotel, now likely property of the CIA.

I changed into an all-black ensemble, similar to what I wore during my last showdown with a mass murderer—Grady Benson—and since that worked out well enough, I figured it was good luck. Just because my superstitions fail to fit my quest for truth and logic, doesn't make them any less real … knock on wood.

Jovana jammed a handgun into the back waistband of her jeans, reminding me of Carter. She then draped a holster over her tank top, and slipped a denim jacket over it.

As I watched her prepare for battle, I thought of the words of a more docile warrior named Murray, who had stressed our enemy's use of historical connections as part of its arsenal.

"Seizing Fort Sumter on April 12, wasn't exactly subtle. Maybe we should focus on historical events for April 13, to try to beat them to the punch."

"It's going to be a historic day when I put a bullet through Hakim's skull, I know that," Jovana said, checking her gun, before placing it in the holster. "Now do you want to make history, Warner, or do you want to wait to see it next year when the movie comes out?"

"April 13 is Thomas Jefferson's birthday … and also the day they dedicated the Jefferson Memorial on his 200th birthday. Maybe we should watch it closely tomorrow."

Jovana flashed me a look to kill, and I don't think she was bluffing.

"Sorry, my mother is a historian, and my brother is a history teacher … it comes with the territory."

"Back here in the present, we need to get a move on, while we still have the element of surprise on our side," Jovana countered, and fit the last of her weapons into the holster.

I didn't have any guns or holsters, so I jammed my phone and a pack of breath mints into my pockets, and asked, "Do we need bulletproof vests?"

Jovana shook her head. "A waste of time—guns aren't really Hakim's thing. He's more of a beheading kinda guy."

On that note …

The only vehicle we had access to was Allison Cooper's Audi. Jovana removed the tracking device that Rich Tolland had placed on it, and we were off to go meet Hakim, David Franklin Sr., David Tully, New Colossus, or whatever he was calling himself these days. I was starting to long for the days of Kyle Jones and Grady Benson, when I only had to keep two aliases straight.

Gwen drove, while Jovana sat shotgun. I was placed in the back like a child. I put on my sunglasses to block out the night lights, but they didn't keep the thoughts out. "I'm surprised you weren't able to get us one of those limos that brought you two to the hotel tonight."

"We didn't have time to arrange it."

"Don't you think we should call for backup, or at least let them know where we're going?"

"I work alone ... and if you don't want to be here, we can drop you off," she said tersely. That was the end of the conversation. I sat silently as Gwen drove over the George Washington Bridge, and onto the Jersey Turnpike.

Gwen ended the torturous silence by turning on the radio. She found the all-news station, searching for an update on Sumter. The Coast Guard had surrounded the place, and the outskirts were being checked for mines, before any rescue attempt could commence. I had a bad feeling that the Huddled Masses plan was for no hostages to leave the fort alive. That way nobody could dispute Christina's claims about what occurred, and the road to civil war would continue to be paved.

We drove over the Delaware River Bridge, and onto the Pennsylvania Turnpike, facing little traffic in the wee morning hours. When Gwen clicked off the radio, the only remaining sound was the monotonous drone of the tires grinding against the pavement of the highway.

I really didn't handle silence well, so I broke it, "I hate to be Debbie Downer here, but do we actually have a plan?"

"I'll know it when I see it," Jovana said.

"In that case, I apologize for asking. Isn't that the same strategy they used on D-Day?"

"Don't worry your pretty little head, Warner. We've been in tighter spots than this and made it through just fine, right?"

Now I was sure she was bringing up Syria on purpose, just to get a reaction from Gwen. It was like she knew this might not end well, and was detaching herself from us emotionally. Not a good sign.

Although, I couldn't blame her for not wanting to get too close with her history. Losing her parents and brother like she did, and who knows how many others.

But there was another side of this. One that the reporter in me was pushing me to explore, but I refused to heed the call. What if she was detaching herself because of what she planned to do to *us?* She had a relationship with Qwaui, which allowed her to set up that meeting in Syria—

so could we rule out that she had one with his longtime friend, Hakim? We never saw that DNA test that confirmed it was Hakim's son, or the tracking that showed he was in Valley Forge. Hell, I hadn't even seen a badge that proved she was CIA.

But we'd come this far, and we had no choice but to dance with the devil.

The exits began to fly by—Delaware Valley, Philadelphia, Willow Grove, Norristown. And finally we arrived at *Exit-326 Valley Forge/King of Prussia*. As Gwen eased down the exit ramp toward the tollbooth, I noticed a couple of General Washington Carpet Cleaning trucks ahead of us, probably going to the same place we were, but for very different reasons.

My first thought was that these poor guys are probably just scraping by, trying to make a living, and had no idea the company they worked for was involved in things that went far beyond shampooing carpets.

My second thought was, "Look out!"

CHAPTER 62

Valley Forge, Pennsylvania

His face lit up when he saw her.

She didn't reciprocate.

"I'm sure Dennis will be elated that you finally got your meeting," he said, maintaining his grin.

She didn't reply.

Allison had pictured David Tully in her mind on many occasions. She always imagined an aging James Bond, the Sean Connery version. But the man before her was quite the opposite.

"I assume you know my true identity at this point," he said.

"Yeah—you're the man who had my husband killed."

She stepped toward him with the intent of wrapping her hands around his neck. But his armed guards took issue, pointing their guns directly at her.

He motioned for them to stand down. "Just please give us a moment."

They stepped outside the room, without a word. He then urged her to come close to him—*be careful what you wish for, old man!*

But when he whispered in her ear, things changed—this was much bigger than her. And she believed every word he said.

Once they had an understanding, his smile returned. "I've missed our conversations, Allison. It's only been a few days, but it seems as if it was forever since our last talk. You're what has kept me going these last few months."

She said nothing.

"If you'd feel more comfortable, I could set up a phone, and we could speak that way ... like we've always done."

"My mother always taught me that if I have nothing nice to say, don't say anything at all."

"As my account rep, I believe you're contractually obligated to talk to me about my advertising. So how about we discuss that? Did you receive my sign-offs on the Columbus book, and for the Chicago test market?"

"I'm taking time away from the agency to deal with the death of my husband, so I'm not currently your representative."

"If you're not running my account, then I might have to take my business elsewhere ... I've been very clear about that."

"Why did you choose my family?"

"It was all part of Allah's plan."

"Spare me! I worked with you for six months, and the only person you worship is yourself."

He began laughing.

"What's so funny?"

"It's just that you remind me of my late wife, Evelyn. She always brought me comfort. It's one of the reasons I brought you here."

"You kidnapped me because I remind you of your dead wife? You're one sick puppy."

"No reason to be upset—death will part us very soon. I just thought it would be nice that the final voice we hear is a soothing one."

"So did you kill your wife, too?"

"Of course not—I loved Evelyn with all my heart. When I was called to fight for Allah, she didn't understand that I didn't have a choice in the matter. She died three years ago of breast cancer. Returning to Valley Forge allowed me to feel close to her once again. When I first came back I'd make trips to visit her in the cemetery near Philadelphia, but obviously that's an impossibility now."

"So that's where we are—Valley Forge?"

"Welcome to the world headquarters of General Washington Carpet Cleaning. Thanks to the help of you and your husband, we're one of the fastest growing businesses in all the land."

Allison burned. "You never answered my question—why us?"

"Why—the question people always ask, yet it's so inconsequential. And all it does is lead to more questions."

"You took my husband away from me, left my children fatherless, and dragged me to this dungeon ... I think the least you owe me is an explanation."

He nodded, as if the request was acceptable. "My son, David Jr., attended school with your husband at Wharton. It was important for a man in my position to keep tabs on those who got close to my children. Unfortunately, not everyone's intentions are noble in this world. But I came away very impressed with Marty Cooper. His smarts, his loyalty, his inventiveness. So when the time came to begin my masterpiece, I knew Marty was the kind of man who could help me. But I was completely unaware of what an asset his wife would become in the process."

Allison used every muscle in her body to restrain herself, thinking of those poor unsuspecting people. "So what did my husband die for? And please don't give me the 'doing it for your deity' line ... no god, or anyone, would put so much thought into creating something, just so people like you can tear it down."

"The world will find out soon enough what I have in store for them."

"No—not what is *going to* happen. I'm sure that will be predictably perverse. I want to know why you're doing it. Why was it worth it for my children to grow up without a father?"

For the first time he looked irritated. Like she'd hit a nerve. "You ask too many questions—if you remember, you work for me."

"You said you brought me here to talk, I'm just trying to make conversation. So what happened, did you get dumped by a girl? Did your parents not hug you enough?"

"Hug me?" he chuckled sardonically. "My father used to beat me unmercifully. When I was eleven, he beat me so bad that I was in a coma for six weeks."

"Maybe he realized what his son was going to become."

"It was because he caught me with his wife, my mother."

"With? As in you were *with* your mother?"

"My mother loved me. She protected me from the monster."

"No—it sounds like she raped you."

"She knew what I'd done to those girls. If I didn't make her happy, she was going to tell the police." His voice had turned emotional, and in a weird way, it gave Allison hope—he was actually human. Albeit just slightly.

She didn't know what girls he was talking about, but she was sure it didn't end well for them. He was nothing but a common serial killer using religion as a shield. "Just like you have no choice here? You always have a choice, David."

He stared right through her. "My mother got my father drunk, and drowned him in the lake. I found him when I came home from the university—she said if I didn't do whatever she wanted, she would blame me for his death … and the others. So I took her down to the lake and had her join my father. When she took her final breath, I felt such relief."

It was as if he had brought her here to confess his sins to his mother, his wife, or some combination that she represented to him in his delusional mind. Whatever the case, she thought this was the opportunity to try to get him to stop the madness.

"Nobody killed your parents, David. They are alive and well inside you. Your father taught you about ruling with fear, and your mother showed you the dark effects power and seduction can have. You have combined that into the monster you became, and used this Al Muttahedah group to rationalize it. You might have killed my husband, but he's going to live on in my children. His laugh, his loyalty, how smart he was. That's how someone leaves a legacy in this world ... not doing whatever you're doing."

He pulled his stare away. Allison was hopeful she'd reached him. It wouldn't bring Marty back, but maybe, just maybe, he might rethink what he was about to set off, and other children wouldn't have to grow up without their parents.

But that thought was short-lived. "Guards—take her away," he called out.

As they dragged her out of the room, he said, "I've grown very disappointed with the service from your agency, Allison. I regret to inform you that you are fired."

CHAPTER 63

Fort Sumter

Christina looked on as Mistress Kate was led through the "parade route" and up onto the stage by one of the bogus park rangers.

"I found her hiding in the abandoned barracks on the left flank," he informed the leader, the one with the British accent.

"Where's Carter?"

"She told us that the coward made a run for it—tried to use the docked ferry to head for land."

"And you believe this?"

"Of course not. But when we checked, we found that the ferry did leave the dock. It didn't make it very far—about a quarter of a mile before it tipped over. It's too dangerous to organize a search with the Coast Guard surrounding the fort."

British scoffed, "It would be a complete waste of time. He's in the fort—that was nothing but a diversion. Get the word out that if he doesn't surrender within the next five minutes, I'm going to gut his girlfriend and toss her into the harbor to feed the fish."

Park Ranger nodded subserviently, and resumed his search for Carter. Christina wasn't sure it would be in his best interest to find him.

British turned to Kate. "So this is the world famous dominatrix Mistress Kate? You look more like a Plain Katherine to me."

She stood proudly in her conservative, floral print dress, her red hair tied up, and wearing studious-looking glasses. "I will be addressed as Mistress Kate," a powerful voice erupted from the petite woman, surprising Christina.

"You're not exactly in a position to make demands, *Katherine.*"

"You disobeyed me, and now you will be punished."

"I'm not one of those perverted souls who enters your dungeon—now tell me where your boyfriend is."

The words were strong, but his tone was unsure.

"I think behind your tough talk you are just a perverted little boy who wants to be punished. What do you want me to do to you?"

He didn't reply.

"Answer me!"

"I do have this foot fetish that maybe you can help me with," he replied, and followed it with a roundhouse kick to Kate's head, which dropped her to the ground.

"More specifically, I would really enjoy putting my foot through your face," he said, as he peered down at her.

He looked out at his audience. "Take a good look at what society has become. The achievers being held hostage by a morally bankrupt underclass, where those like Katherine here—who cater to their sickness—are celebrated. The addicted, the sexually perverse, and the minorities who have attempted to steal this land from its white settlers. But after they and their Huddled Masses are held responsible for what took place here tonight, even their lapdog media will no longer be able to defend them!"

"Well, it's a good thing I'm a rich white dude then," a voice echoed from above.

By the time British looked up, Carter had already leaped off the top rope, or in this case, a deck of Battery Huger that stood behind the stage.

It was like a belly flop from a high-dive, and he landed on British, crashing right through the wooden stage. Christina ran up to the stage, and when she peered down into the newly formed crater, she saw Carter adding insult to injury, slamming his opponent's head into the ground.

But when she turned around, she noticed a gun aiming right at her. The Whiskey Tax soldier was about to pull the trigger, when he was hit by a freight train.

Mama Jasper sent him to the ground with a perfect form tackle, and Lamar Thompson scooped up his high-powered rifle. The other members of the Jasper party, along with the cadets, pounced on the remainder of the "park rangers" and disarmed them.

Fort Sumter was secure once again.

Christina took in every detail, knowing that she would have the responsibility of accurately recording the second Battle of Fort Sumter for history. As she did, she began laughing to herself—what was the point, who would believe it?

CHAPTER 64

The sun began to rise over Charleston Harbor, as Christina took the steps to the observation deck. She hoped to find a moment of peace, following the craziest story she would likely ever cover—on her night off!

But when she reached the top step, she cringed at the sight before her. "Dude, what are you doing? Gross!"

"Just draining my dragon," Carter replied.

"You do know they have bathrooms on the fort, right?"

"I put the flag back up," he casually said as he continued to do his business.

She looked up to see that he'd returned the American flag to its usual post, after their captors had replaced it the previous night with a Huddled Masses flag, whom the Whiskey Tax wanted outsiders to believe had taken over the fort.

She looked back at Carter, and realized what he was doing. He was soiling the simple black and white flag with Huddled Masses logo on it.

"I thought I'd give it the respect it deserved," he said with a broad grin.

Christina looked away. She stepped to the wall, and viewed the Charleston waterfront in the distance. It was a spectacular morning, as the sun shimmied off the Ravenel Bridge. She even spotted a pod of dolphins swimming in the harbor. But she wasn't feeling the joy.

Carter finished relieving himself, scrubbed his hands with the baby wipes he never traveled without, and joined her at the wall. He pointed out the retired aircraft carrier in the distance, docked near land. "The Yorktown—used to tour it all the time with my dad. He loved military history. We would pack up the car every summer and journey to some historic battlefield or monument. I think he'd be proud that I fought in the Second Battle of Fort Sumter."

"I always forget you came from actual parents. It just seems like you appeared out of a swamp or something."

He smiled. "That sounds like something JP Warner would say."

"Is that a compliment?"

"The highest. So you wanna know how I did it?"

"Not really."

"I was under the impression that you journalists can't function until you get to the bottom of the story. Me personally, I always thought there were much better bottoms to get to—bottom of the bottle, that cute bottom on ..."

"I get your point. But journalists also believe in having solid, believable sources, and I doubt you're a very good source on this subject."

"You sure that's the real reason?"

She sighed. "It doesn't matter anymore. After what I did last night, my career is over ... if it even had started. It would be like a reporter coming on and defending Bin Laden after 9/11."

"I think you're being a little dramatic ... and that's coming from a former professional wrestler. The truth always comes out in the end."

"It does? Like with what really happened to Qwaui and Az Zahir in Syria?"

"Well, maybe not always. But don't sweat it, if the news thing doesn't work out, Kate's looking to hire a few girls to work in her dungeon. You're kinda bossy, so it might be a good fit," he said with a smile.

"Leather doesn't really work on me, but thanks for the offer." She took in a deep breath of sea air and blew it out. "I hate to say it, but JP was right."

"He usually is—just don't let him know, or you'll never hear the end of it."

"He told me I'd have to do things I wasn't proud of in this business, like he had to do when you guys were held hostage last summer."

"Welcome to the big leagues, kid ... now, getting back to my heroic tale. During the tour, Kate and I snuck off to the old barracks on the left face. To make a long story a little shorter, I was about to fire my cannon, when I heard the shots. So I climbed over the exterior fort wall, and made my way to the Salient, where the ferry was docked. The driver had been knocked out, so I took over for him. When I got about a few hundred feet out into the harbor, I dove off and swam back—the ferry did a 'ghost rider' for about a quarter mile and flipped on its side.

"While I was doing that, Kate did what she does best—making people's fantasies come true. And that British guy's fantasy was to be large and in-charge, which she led him to quite brilliantly. People think it's about whips and chains, but that really has nothing to do with it. And most importantly, it bought us the time we needed."

"After all that, I'll bet an old man like you needs a nap."

"It's going to be comments like that I miss the most."

"What do you mean miss?"

His face turned stone cold serious. "You're right, I do need a nap ... a long one. So I'm going to be taking a break."

"You're leaving me?" Christina blurted, her shock quickly turning to anger. "Let me guess, JP's ego couldn't handle us working together, and having success. I hate that jerk."

"This might be news to JP, but not everything revolves around him. I just need some time away, and it's a good opportunity for me and Kate to spend some time together. She's going to be on tour this summer, and I'm going to follow her around the country."

"She goes on tour?"

"Every date is already sold out."

Christina shook her head. "Wow—you are totally whipped."

"We never bring our work home. She leaves the whips out of our bedroom, and I never enter wearing a cape."

"You know what I meant. And you'll be back—just like JP ran to Sticksville to be with his girlfriend, and he's already so bored that he's taking vacations to Syria."

"My situation is totally different from JP's."

"It is?"

He thought for a moment. His always-expressive face said he didn't like the answer, so he changed the subject—Christina was convinced that all men were born with that trait.

"Besides, it will be good for you to be out on your own, and not have everyone thinking you got to where you are because you're sleeping with JP."

Her mouth dropped. "People think I'm sleeping with JP!? Where would they get that idea?"

"Let me see—you went straight from college to international correspondent at a major station ... even if it is cable news. You used to live with him. And look at his history with the women he's worked with—Nora Reign ... Lauren Bowden ... should I go on?"

"People are really saying that?"

"I have no idea—I stopped listening to what people are saying back in 1978. The point is, you've got a lot of potential, and as long as you don't burn yourself out you're gonna be great."

He looked at his watch. "I gotta bolt—Kate's got a show in Atlanta tonight, and we need to hit the road. If I ever get an address, you can send me a 'Thank You' note for saving your life."

They didn't do hugs, so Carter gave her a powerful pat on the back and headed for the stairs, leaving her with her thoughts and a urine-stained flag. But then something hit her. "You can't leave," she called out.

"I can't?"

"No—the FBI isn't letting anyone off the premises until they debrief us."

Carter began laughing. "FBI ... that's a good one. You're easily the funniest journalist I've worked with ... although, that's not really saying much, is it?"

He laughed some more and kept walking.

"Enjoy your break ... or retirement ... or whatever you're calling it," she shouted to him.

He looked back at her with a grin. "If it's anything like JP's retirement, then I'm sure I'll be running for my life any minute now."

CHAPTER 65

Valley Forge

The back doors of the van swung open and the guns pointed at us. Gwen screamed, and Jovana shouted, Get down!" Here we go again.

Gwen hit the brakes and the Audi skidded to a stop before reaching the tollbooth.

I couldn't believe we were so naïve as to think that Hakim would just let us stroll into his terror headquarters. But I was done "getting down," so I sat and watched the men leap out of the van and dash toward our vehicle.

We were ordered out of the car, and when we did, the surprises continued. The men announced themselves as CIA, and chastised Jovana for going it alone, without communicating with Langley. They also confirmed that Hakim and his son were indeed trapped in the General Washington building, and they were under orders to demolish it. They didn't say it, but there were those at the highest level of government who would never allow it to be known that Hakim had set up shop inside American borders.

Jovana seemed resigned, but not Gwen. "My friend Allison is inside."

"I'm sorry, miss. I really am. But this is bigger than one life … and we have orders."

Gwen started back toward the car. "Then you're going to have to blow it up with me inside, because I'm going to get Allison out of there."

That's my girl.

I think the CIA guy sensed that she wasn't going to back down—and the cynic in me thought they saw a chance to get rid of a mouthy journalist who knew too much, along with Hakim. Kill two crazy birds with one explosion.

CIA guy looked at his watch, and blew out a frustrated breath. "I'll give you a half hour, then the place is going down whether you're out or not."

With no time to lose, we piled into one of the vans, and headed for the world headquarters of General Washington's Carpet Cleaning, located not far off the exit in an industrial park.

The gate booth was open, allowing us to drive right in without resistance. I got the idea we were expected guests.

The building was a two-story office without much fanfare—no signage or logo, and no life-sized photo of George Washington standing in his boat as he crossed the Delaware. *Like he wouldn't have capsized the boat doing that...please.*

We dropped the CIA operatives off at the front of the building. "Thirty minutes," were the leader's final words to us. More like a warning.

Gwen pulled the van around to the back of the building. It was attached to an airport-hanger-sized warehouse, in which a garage-style door had been conveniently left open. For a guy who supposedly didn't like meetings, Hakim sure had rolled out the red carpet for us.

We drove inside and parked in the first empty space we found, amongst a sea of similar-looking white vans. We hopped out, and made our way through the musty warehouse, before entering through the unlocked door of the building.

The inside wasn't exactly decorated as the devil's lair. In fact, it looked like a typical office. A reception desk, copiers and fax machines. A farm of cubicles for the peons, and office space for the higher-ups on the food chain.

But little did they know the guy who was atop that food chain, and numerous Most Wanted lists, was barricaded below in the Pennsylvania version of an Afghan cave. This was one company where you didn't want to be called into the boss's office.

While I was busy checking out the office setup, Jovana spotted something more important. Blood. A trail of it, and it looked pretty fresh.

I read the horror on Gwen's face, and tried to comfort her. "He didn't go through all that trouble to get her here safely, just to use her as a human GPS. It's not her blood."

She nodded, but didn't look convinced.

Jovana was already following the trail, which led us to, and then down, a staircase. The blood led to another door with a sign that read: *OFF LIMITS*. But it wasn't today. We pushed the unlocked door open and entered. When we heard it lock behind us we knew there was no going back. We bounded down more stairs, the only sound being the echoes of our shoes.

The good news was my knee was hurting so bad at this point that I almost forgot about my head and lung issues. The bad, was that the stairwell was pitch-black. But the always-prepared Gwen Delaney had a flashlight that lit the way.

When we reached the bottom, a piece of paper was waiting for us. Jovana picked it up and read: *Therefore strike off their heads and strike off every fingertip of them ... 8:12.*

Jovana turned visibly angry, as she crumpled the paper and tossed it unceremoniously to the floor. "These psychos are so bad with interpretation and context, that the only other job they'd be qualified for is cable news."

In another time and place I would have laughed.

"On the wall," Gwen said, holding her flashlight at an arrow drawn in blood. She then pointed her flashlight down the empty hallway. I looked to Jovana, and hoped she was starting to "feel" her plan.

At the end of the hallway was what I was expecting, but never would be prepared for. "Oh God," Gwen said, and held her hand over her mouth. She looked like she was about to puke.

Jovana went right to the severed head, and picked it up like it was a basketball lying in the driveway. "It's Junior ... Hakim's son," she informed.

She held it up, and I felt he was looking at me—not much different than when we were in that stare-down last night in New York. I don't normally put much stock in the expressions of the dead, but it didn't look like this ending came as a total surprise to him.

Gwen began to recover—as gruesome as it was, it wasn't Allison. She shone the light ahead, and we saw that the hallway split.

"Take the one to the right," Jovana said.

"How do you know that?" I asked.

"Because that's where the head was looking. It was put there to point us where he wants us to go."

I'd seen some horrible things on my journeys, but decapitating your own kid to use as a directional marker was seriously cold. Even for someone as deranged as Hakim. And for some reason, this didn't discourage us.

Jovana gave the head a final once-over, searching for further clues it might possess. But it must have been just a run-of-the-mill severed head, because she set it back down on the ground, and led us down the hallway.

This is where Carter would've gone with "we're over our heads here," but I chose, "We're getting in pretty deep. Shouldn't we go back and share this with your CIA buddies?"

Without missing a stride, Jovana said, "Those guys aren't CIA."

"Excuse me?"

"I've never seen them before—that doesn't mean they aren't, but there was something off with them. I'm certain they work for Hakim, and their job was to deliver us here."

"Why didn't you say something? Or here's a thought ... maybe not go along with the plot to bury us under this building."

"If I'd exposed their cover, we'd be dead."

I wasn't so sure. It seemed that Hakim was pretty determined to meet with us.

We arrived at the end of the hallway, and were staring at an elevator. In front of it was another gift from our host. It was a hand, which I assume also belonged to Junior. And I knew why it was left here.

So did Jovana, who picked it up and fitted it in the electronic molding, where the up and down buttons are usually located. It was a hand recognition identification system. The hand triggered a loud beep, followed by the elevator doors sliding open.

For better, or more likely worse, we stepped inside. Jovana attempted to wipe the blood off her hand, but it was the kind of stain that will stick with you forever.

There was only one button to push. It wasn't labeled *non-stop trip to the depths of hell,* but it might as well have been.

When we stopped our descent, and the doors opened, we were greeted by another trail of blood. But no sign of human life ... or death. No bodyguards, terrorist assassins, or body appendages. This corridor was well lit, and was stainless steel. It struck me as clinical, like a science lab or a medical center. Ironically, there was no carpet.

We walked cautiously down the hallway, which led us into a cavernous room filled with modern-looking machines. It reminded me of Walter White's meth-lab on *Breaking Bad.* The back wall was lined with metal canisters wrapped in plastic. I got the idea they weren't filled with carpet-cleaning soaps.

"It's a chemical weapons factory," Jovana confirmed my worst fears as we hurried through the hazardous area.

The room was attached to a warehouse-type room that was full of more canisters, and who knows what else. *Rocket launchers? Missiles?* There was no sense in slowing down to take inventory—we knew our only chance was to get to Hakim. Since he'd just cut his youngest son into pieces, and spent most of his adult life plotting whatever sick event he had planned, the odds of swaying his mind weren't exactly in our favor. But at least we had Jovana, and her "when it comes to me" plan.

The blood trail stopped at an open door. Jovana had us stand back, and took guns into both her hands. She entered, weapons pointed. But no shots were fired.

Gwen and I followed her in.

Before us was the man we were looking for, but he was a lot different than I'd expected.

CHAPTER 66

I'd spent enough time in hospitals this past year to recognize that sound. The incessant beeping. There was some music playing in the background, but it couldn't block it out. Removal of heads didn't seem to phase Hakim, but this sound unnerved him.

Hakim was famously reclusive, unlike some of his contemporaries, who made Lauren Bowden seem camera shy. So the last photo of him I could recall—the one used by all the news agencies—was taken about ten years ago. In it, he appeared both vibrant and intimidating.

But the man before me was gaunt and sickly—likely dying. He'd recently turned sixty, but he resembled a man in his eighties or nineties. He was a hundred pounds, tops, and his once black beard had turned Santa Claus white.

I just stared at him, as the beeps droned on.

He smiled back at us from the bed. "It's ESRD," he said, matter-of-fact—end stage renal disease. "Don't look so sad—we all die at some point, it's what we accomplish while we're here that counts."

His voice was low, but the passion was still evident. His accent was mostly British, mixed with a little eastern Pennsylvania, and a lot of crazy.

I pulled my eyes away momentarily, and scanned what looked like your typical hospital room. There were no bodyguards present, at least out in the open. Hakim appeared defenseless, and at our mercy, but I got the idea that he still had the upper hand.

His red eyes—likely due to his disease, and not because he was the devil, although I wasn't ruling it out—latched on to Jovana. "I see my angel has arrived. You have a knack for appearing when you're most needed."

Gwen and I both shot an angry glance at her.

"I've never seen this man in my life ... other than in photos," she defended.

"She's right, we have not had the pleasure of meeting before today. But without her work in Syria, and then in New York, I'm not sure we'd be on the doorstep of immortality."

"I don't know what you're talking about, but unless you want your oxygen cut off, you better watch your mouth," she shot back.

Hakim ignored her threat, shifting his attention to me. "And you, Mr. Warner, I must both thank and apologize to you."

"Is that why you went through all this trouble to bring us here? Because a card or an email would have sufficed."

He released a small laugh, which appeared to take much effort. "I respect a man who can find humor so close to his death. Just as I respect your accomplishments as a journalist—being the first to expose Al Muttahedah, as you did. It was an impressive feat, and it really forced us to raise our level, for which I am indebted—but you must have known that it would eventually cost you your life."

"Is that the thank you or the apology?"

"I do apologize for the treatment you received from some in my organization. It all goes back to when the Americans captured Az Zahir. As you know, he cut a deal to deliver me to my enemies, in return for his freedom. Most think he tipped me off, double-crossing the CIA, but the truth was, Qwaui *wanted* to hand me over, so he could take control. I had no choice but to flee.

"I told them that I'd gotten word of an impending attack on my life and went into hiding, but never revealed my knowledge of their role in it. So business continued as usual, except that I was forced to keep my location a secret, apart from a trusted few, which didn't include Qwaui or Az Zahir. And America was the last place anyone would believe I was. It bought me time, but being isolated, with health failing, my power was being challenged more regularly, and my ability to communicate strained. Which brings me to the debacle in Serbia last summer, which is where my apology comes in.

"I refused to give my blessing to Qwaui's plan to capture and kill you. He was acting out of revenge, related to your exposing of our organization, but I knew all it would do was bring more unwelcome attention, especially at a time when Huddled Masses was about to launch in the US.

"But he defied me, claiming it was necessary to force Nora Reign back in line. This was rubbish, of course—Nora could have been dealt with without causing an international incident. So I apologize to you for any harm that was done to you and Mr. Jasper." He looked to Jovana. "And for your brother. I just hope you can find some solace in that Qwaui and Az Zahir were brought to justice."

"What do you mean brought to justice?" I said.

His focus intensified upon Jovana. "I leaked information to you through contacts and intermediaries. Their job was to make sure that you had access to Qwaui, and provide you safety within Syria. And I knew if you could deliver JP Warner to them, you would be able to gain the type of access you needed to deliver the justice we all sought."

"You should have had me killed in the process," Jovana said, aiming her gun at his beard. "But lucky for you, you will not live long enough to regret it."

"I gave you what you wanted," Hakim shot back. "Plus, it was mutually beneficial. Huddled Masses had just begun in December, and was about to enter its most important stage. The last thing that could be afforded was an internal power struggle, and by removing the enemy within, the path to revolution had been cleared."

He left out the part about how, if Qwaui gained control of Al Muttahedah, he would have received the credit for Hakim's masterpiece. This was as much about ego as it was about war strategy, and had nothing to do with Allah.

I was getting jumpy. We needed to find Allison and get the hell out of here, before the building was demolished with us inside. But we were at Hakim's mercy. This was his show.

"The idea that Mathew would ever lead this organization was ludicrous," he continued, using Qwaui's birth name of Mathew Bannon. "He should have been grateful. I took that shy kid from Oxford and turned him into an international legend. But he knew I planned to pass the torch to my blood. That's why I recently brought my son David into the fold."

"And by blood, are you referring to that trail you used to lead us here?" I asked.

It also got me thinking—there was no way Hakim was capable of killing Junior in his current condition, which meant somebody else did the honors. I took a peek out the open door. Still no sign of anyone. Maybe they heard the place was going to be imploding soon and made a run for it. Which is what we should have been doing.

Gwen interjected, "It doesn't surprise me that you'd do something as sick as kill your own son, but I am surprised that he chose to join a man he spoke out so adamantly against. My guess is that he didn't have a choice."

"The man you weep for, Ms. Delaney, was a rapist. He was facing twenty years in prison for what he did to a prostitute—as he would have done to you if I hadn't intervened. I offered him a chance to join our organization in exchange for the charges disappearing. I saw much of myself in David, and had hoped he would be the one to carry on my work.

"But he squandered numerous opportunities. His first task was to clean up the damage from the Nora Reign incident, but he worked directly against my instructions, resulting in that spectacle in New York. And when I forbade him to return there, he instead followed his perverted urges tonight, bringing us more unwanted attention. It was as if he was purposely disobeying me, but when I confronted him following his return, I still offered him a final chance—*if they repent, and keep prayer, leave their way free to them.* But he chose a different path."

"Now that he's gone, who are you going to blame your failures on?" Gwen remained defiant.

"I am ultimately accountable for the actions of my organization. That is why, after my son's initial failures, I reasserted my authority. If not for that, I don't believe your friend Allison would have arrived unharmed, as she did."

Gwen's antennae shot up. "Where is she?"

"Today is about the big picture, Ms. Delaney. No need to concern yourself with such small details."

The look on Gwen's face ... it was like a combination of every time I'd annoyed, irritated, or pissed her off, all wrapped into one, times a thousand. I know Hakim had his terrorist cred to protect, and was trapped in that bed, but if I was him, I'd still try to make a run for it.

She stepped toward him. "You want to talk about big picture things—how about your breathing, is that big enough for you?"

CHAPTER 67

Jovana grabbed Gwen by the shoulder, stopping her in her tracks. "Not a good idea."

"Very astute," Hakim said. "You are as adept at saving lives as taking them—a rare trait."

The question was, *what lives were saved?* He wasn't referring to his own—he knew we could end it at any moment, and I got the feeling that's what he wanted us to do.

"When this machine is cut off, it will signal the final battle. And the men outside—the ones who made sure you arrived safely—will level this place," he said.

"What is it rigged with?" I asked.

"A diligent reporter like yourself, Mr. Warner, surely noticed the arsenal down the hall. The explosion will launch the gasses into the air like an aerosol. Philadelphia will be hit with devastation, and death will reach far into New Jersey and Delaware. Some will call it the worst chemical attack on American soil, but I would call it a cleansing."

"So you plan to go out in style," I said.

"I might be leaving this planet, but our work is just beginning. A pre-dated letter has been sent to GNZ, giving Huddled Masses credit for the attack. It will be the moment in which the line has been crossed, and America will be at war with itself—chemical attacks can be particularly unappealing, especially when the photos of the dying children come to light. Sides will be taken, Whiskey Tax will retaliate, and after today's events, the US government and military will be forced to intercede."

The revolution can't be stopped, I thought. And while I didn't doubt this place was a big poison-gas booby trap, or that other atrocities were in the pipeline, I knew his "revolution" would fail. History told me so. And I thought I should relay the message.

"It was a nice touch re-launching the Civil War on April 12. You're very clever with the history—Fort Sumter, George Washington, Whiskey Rebellion. But doesn't this really go back to September 11th?"

His face grew irritated. "9/11 was nothing but a glamour shot by an egomaniac—a lot of collateral damage, but no real objective met! Hard to believe that such small thinking toppled such a large building."

I couldn't believe that at the most defining moment in my life, the Sandra Warner history lessons were actually taking effect.

"I'm not referring to September 11, 2001. I meant September 11, 1777—the Battle of Brandywine Creek, which took place not far from this very spot. It was a crushing defeat for George Washington's army, but in retrospect, it turned out to be the key turning point in the war.

"The loss at Brandywine cleared a path for the British to take Philadelphia, the then-capital. It also forced General Washington to begin the groundwork for a winter retreat, here to Valley Forge. The conditions were horrendous, and the stay was most remembered for starvation and the bloody footprints in the snow, since most soldiers didn't have shoes. But it was these tough times at Valley Forge that galvanized them, and transformed the unit into a fighting force to be reckoned with when spring arrived. And they didn't stop fighting until their homeland had earned its independence. Do you know what made them stick together in such horrid conditions? It's that they believed in the cause ... so much so that they were willing to die for it.

"Huddled Masses was a good plan in theory. You understood that the US is dysfunctional internally, but the one thing that will bond us together is being attacked by an outside force. So it was tactically smart to fight from the inside, and recruit Western-type soldiers who would fit in, look like us, act like us.

"But what they're lacking is belief in the cause. They might have joined forces because of hatreds they hold toward the United States government, or what we stand for, but you can't win a revolution fighting *against*, you have to be fighting *for* something.

"Huddled Masses and Whiskey Tax are nothing but mercenaries. And when it came time to sacrifice, there was hesitation. That's why you had to send the pirates to West Palm to babysit the captain, and make sure he went through with it. And then Nora tossed a wrench into your plan. She'd been specifically recruited by Tino Fernandez to get you that all-important time slot on worldwide television. It would be the catalyst that transformed you from a series of domestic terror events, to a threat for the future of the nation.

"And speaking of mercenaries, it took me a while to figure out what Tino's role was in all this. The only cause Tino ever believed in was the career of Tino Fernandez, which made him much like you. And you understood the importance, for better or worse, that media plays in the thinking of Americans. So who better to be your media sock puppet than the hottest name in the industry? This Huddled Masses/Whiskey Tax showdown you created would be the top story every night for the foreseeable future, as the violence and division continued to escalate toward your desired civil war. And Tino would have been scooping everyone on these stories ... because he was working for the group that was plotting the events. Just another mercenary pushing his or her own agenda, who didn't have the will or fight that a revolution requires.

"So in the end, all you'll have to show for your efforts is a few months of terror, and a chemical attack on a major city. Horrific, sure, but certainly not revolutionary. In fact, it's been done before ... in 2001, exactly 224 years to the day that the Battle of Brandywine took place. Turns out you're nothing but a bad sequel, Hakim."

I knew my speech would set him off, but there needed to be a call to action. If we were going to die in this tomb, we might as well do it on our schedule.

His body was limp, but his face was ablaze. He held his fist triumphantly in the air and found a final shout in his voice, "I for one have the will to give my life for the cause!"

He pulled a large knife from beneath his sheets. For a moment, I thought he was going to rise out of the bed like a horror movie and stab us all. But that just wasn't realistic in his condition, and if there was ever a lesson in the harsh realities of the world, this was it. What was within his reach was the cord to his dialysis machine, which he sliced in half.

The final battle had been launched.

CHAPTER 68

I've known Gwen Delaney for over thirty years. So when I grabbed her hand to pull her in the direction of the exit, I knew she'd pull away.

She was not leaving without her friend. And it wasn't even worth my breath to explain that Allison was probably already dead. The fact that Hakim didn't even assure us that she was alive, to use as leverage, whether she was or not, didn't make me feel any more confident.

Gwen was in charge now—moving from door to door all the way down the hallway, screaming, "Allison!" at the top of her lungs. Problem was, they were all locked and soundproof.

I'd almost expected Jovana to declare us liabilities and shoot us on the spot, but she was too busy running in the other direction. We could commit suicide if we wanted; she was getting out of here.

But she surprised me with her return. And she didn't come empty handed. She was carrying the bloody hand of an older man, and by process of elimination, I determined it came from Hakim.

Gory as it was, it was also practical. We would need it to enter these rooms. So we hurried one by one, using the hand to unlock the security code. The fifth door opened to find a weary looking, but very alive Allison Cooper. She was wearing Gwen's Columbia sweatshirt, which she's convinced is good luck, and I was starting to come around to her thinking.

Gwen and Allison hugged. When they broke the embrace the first thing Allison asked was about her children. I thought if she wanted to see them again, we best be moving. Jovana actually said it.

We ran down the hallway until we reached the elevator. Jovana pressed Hakim's hand against the control board, and it opened. She pushed us on, but didn't follow. She then gave me the hand, literally.

"Use it to get through security … and get out of here as fast as you can," she urged.

I was confused. "What are you doing?"

"I'm going to try to stop the chemicals from being released. It's a long shot, but I have to try."

"Are you nuts? Let's get out of here!"

"I guess I'm also willing to die for the cause."

"Then I'm coming with you," I said, and began to step off the elevator.

"Not a chance, Warner," she said, and held up her gun.

Before I could counter, the elevator doors shut in my face, and we were upward bound. *What just happened?*

Gwen tried to comfort me, "She'll be okay, JP—you've been in tighter spots than this, right?"

I faked a smile back at her, but I didn't see how there was a way out.

The elevator took us to the only floor it stopped at. We then re-traced our steps, using the flashlight to maneuver through the dark corridors. The one thing we had going for us was what I had told Hakim—these mercenaries were not willing to go down with the ship. They were likely using a timing mechanism, to make sure they were long gone when the bombs went off, buying us some time.

We found our way up the many staircases, my knee throbbing, my head dizzy, and used the hand ID to exit back through the *OFF LIMITS* door. Once through, we ran as fast as we could through the dark showroom, then the office, *and what the hell?*

The office was full of employees. I guess you don't get weekends off in the carpet cleaning business. I thought this was a good time to dump the hand … in the first garbage can I found, and began yelling, "Bomb! Get out now!" Gwen and Allison followed my lead, and began shouting the same, while never slowing down.

A couple guys looked at us like we were kidding, as if it was some office prank. Their laughter ceased when Allison grabbed them by the shirt collar and practically dragged them out. You could tell which of us was experienced with children.

It wouldn't be enough to do the heroic leap out of the building just before the explosion, like in the movies. The remnants of this blast might spread for hundreds of miles. The best bet was to take one of the vans and drive as fast, and as far away from here as possible. As we reached the exit leading into the warehouse, I looked back and implored the workers to follow us.

We ran to the same van we'd arrived in, and sped away, doing what General Washington did best—retreating. Behind us was a line of vans, filled with GWCC employees, trying to avoid being the longest funeral procession in history.

We were about a mile away when the ground began to shake.

CHAPTER 69

Homeland Security had set up a command center in the parking lot of the nearby King of Prussia Mall.

Balloon-like tents were used to shield us from any poison or radiation that had been released in the air. Alerts were sent from Boston to Washington DC, warning citizens to stay inside and close all windows and vents. The report mentioned the explosion in Valley Forge, and the possible release of "dangerous chemicals." It didn't use words like terrorism, sarin, and Huddled Masses, but that didn't stop the collective freak-out from a country already on edge.

I remained barricaded—not by choice—in one of the tents, stripped down to my boxers. I looked to Gwen and Allison, and said, "Well, I guess if I had to live through Armageddon, I would want to do it with two hot babes in their underwear."

Gwen turned to me. "Seriously?"

"Bad timing?"

"Just bad."

Agent Hauck of Homeland Security entered, still wearing his Hazmat suit, but carrying the headgear. I took this as either a good sign, or that we're totally screwed so what's the point?

"The good news is our initial tests showed no signs of sarin, cyclosarin, mustard gas, or any other chemical agent in the air. Or on your clothing or belongings," he said.

Gwen and I traded a disbelieving glance.

"Just to be safe, we will continue to hold your items, and the alert will remain in force for the next eighteen hours."

He handed us a shopping bag. "Here are some clothes I picked up in the mall. I didn't know sizes, but these looked one-size-fits-all. Consider it a gift from Homeland Security."

We quickly put on the assorted clothing. But instead of saying thank you, I asked, "Are you sure there's no chemicals?"

"No—I just made it up to make you feel better. We'll all be dead by nightfall."

"In the cold, still air, similar to this morning, a plume of gas can get above the boundary level, and with the right wind pattern can travel long distances. In a similar situation during the Gulf War, the sarin gas traveled 300-miles from Iraq to the US base in Saudi Arabia. They also thought it was a false alarm."

"Thanks for the history lesson, but the Gulf War was a long time ago, and we have much more sophisticated tracking methods these days."

"Did you look at the satellite photos? Often you can see a yellow patch if the gas gets above the boundary level."

"I work for Homeland Security ... we occasionally train for things like this. But we appreciate you offering your expertise."

"You're very welcome. And if you need anything else, I'll be here."

"What I need, is for you to start telling me the truth about what happened."

"I thought I already did."

"So your official story is that you were doing a report for GNZ on the growth of small businesses in America?"

"I'm technically retired, but still contracted to do four features a year."

"I'll be sure to set my DVR. And this 'feature' focused on General Washington's Carpet Cleaning, because of its unprecedented growth this past year. So you drove to Valley Forge this morning to meet with founder and CEO, David Tully. And to use your words, you 'stumbled' upon something, which led you to believe there was an impending chemical weapons attack by Huddled Masses. You evacuated all employees, just before the building imploded, and saved the day."

"That sounds about right."

"And you were assisted by a CIA agent named Jovana, who either didn't have a last name, or you didn't know it."

"Have you been able to locate her? She separated from us, hoping to stop the chemicals from releasing," my voice strained with concern.

"If she actually exists, which according to the CIA, no agent by that name does, and she was inside that building, there was no way to survive that."

My stomach sank. But deep down, I knew she was a goner the moment that elevator door shut. "She gave her life to try to stop this attack."

"Someone must have. Or another possibility—no such attack existed."

"So you're saying that we're lying?"

"And not very well. I think there are three possibilities to explain what's going on—one, you could have created a hoax to bring attention to yourself, for which you will receive a long prison sentence, and repay all costs associated with the explosion. Two, you're holding out on us, which would be lying to a federal agent, which again, will result in a long prison sentence. Or three, we determine that you are working with Huddled Masses like your buddy Nora Reign was, making you an enemy combatant, and that way we can hold you indefinitely without a trial."

"You should talk to Agent Hawkins at the FBI—he'll vouch for my character."

"I don't think you understand how serious this is, Warner. Either you start telling me the truth, or I'm going to start booking your itinerary for Guantanamo."

"You want the truth?"

"If you do a Jack Nicholson imitation, I'm going to send you directly to prison."

"The truth is, General Washington Carpet Cleaners was a front for Al Muttahedah and their leader Hakim. They created both Huddled Masses and Whiskey Tax with the intent of dividing America, and the long-term goal of starting a civil war. Like all criminal masterminds, Hakim brought us to his lair to explain his evil genius, before launching his final attack. It was your typical B-movie."

Hauck turned and began to walk away. "I'll be back whenever you want to get serious. I'll get that itinerary started."

I guess he really didn't want the truth after all. And I could add Homeland Security to the long list of law enforcement agencies I've annoyed at one time or another. The reporter seeks truth, while law enforcement seeks to catch the "bad guys," and I've learned that the two don't always mix.

CHAPTER 70

"Do you think Hakim was bluffing?" Gwen asked me.

"No."

"Do you think Jovana was able to stop it?"

I shook my head. "There just wasn't enough time."

"I'll bet his son swapped the chemicals out," Allison said. "Marty used to talk about a David Franklin, from back when they went to Wharton together. They used to call him Benjamin Franklin because he would always be doing these crazy science experiments in his spare time. He would know about chemicals."

"He denounced his father, and was forced to join the family business, so it's not out of the realm of possibility that he tried to sabotage his father's plans," Gwen said.

"It's possible," I said. "I did a story on chemical weapons a few years ago. The only way to break down a chemical agent like that is either incineration or neutralization. To neutralize it, he would have to use some sort of water and caustic compound, like sodium hydroxide. But the more likely scenario is nobody stopped it—that it just didn't work. That's the thing about dispersing chemicals into the air to use as a weapon—it's risky and inefficient."

My own words grabbed me, and sent me into thought.

"What is it?" Gwen asked.

"When it comes to mass murder, Hakim has always believed in efficiency over style. Remember how crazy he got when he thought I compared his work to 9/11? He would never use such a risky method for his 'final battle.'"

"But didn't he say this was just the beginning of the war? *I might be leaving this planet, but our work is just beginning.*"

"You're right, he did say that. But he also claimed that when his dialysis machine stopped, it would trigger the 'final battle.'"

"The two statements are contradictory."

"Only if 'final battle' was referring to his life, or an attack by Huddled Masses. But not if it was one of his historical references."

"I'm not following."

"If Fort Sumter was the first battle of the Civil War, what was the final battle?"

Gwen nodded, now seeing where I was going with this. "Wasn't it that courthouse in Virginia?"

"The Appomattox Court House," Allison assisted.

I shook my head. "I think that's where Lee surrendered to Grant, but I'm not sure it was the final battle."

I knew someone who would be sure. I pulled out my phone, which received a strange look from Gwen, who mentioned, "We were supposed to have all our items checked for contamination."

"You heard Agent Hauck—it was just a big hoax. No harm, no foul, right?"

She rolled her eyes as I made the call.

"JP—thank God you're alright," my mother answered. "I just realized that you hadn't returned home last night, and I became concerned that my loyal but foolhardy son had gone to Charleston to try to help his friends."

"Charleston? No, I would have just gotten in the way," I said.

"I'm just so glad it ended without further violence," she continued. "I was up all night, hanging on every perilous moment. It reminded me so much of last summer, when you were hostage, and finally I couldn't take it anymore. I felt so horrible for Byron and his mother, they are such wonderful people, they didn't deserve such a thing. And for Christina, who was obviously forced to say those horrible things about the Jaspers."

"All that's really important is that nobody got hurt." And that she would stop talking long enough so I could get to the reason I called.

"It sounds like the head of the museum is going to make it. There are a lot of conflicting reports, but it seems as if the captors saw the light and surrendered. It's being reported that everyone is being detained for questioning—we'll probably learn more when that's over."

My guess was that a super-sized former wrestler helped them to see that light.

"Then just when my faith in humanity had been restored, I woke up this morning to learn of this horrible explosion in Pennsylvania, and possible poisonous chemicals released in the air. The world was a much more simple place when we didn't own a television!"

"I heard about that. I guess it's not as bad as they expected though, so that's a positive."

"Until the next disaster hits ... probably this afternoon, the way things are going. I'm just glad you're nowhere near there. Speaking of which, where are you, JP?"

"That's sort of why I called. Gwen and I decided to take a trip this weekend to check out some historical sights from the Civil War and ..."

She began laughing. "You are such a terrible liar, JP ... where are you really?"

I chuckled nervously. "You got me. We're actually at the mall. But we're in a debate about what was the final battle of the Civil War. Gwen said it was the Appomattox Courthouse, but I thought it was Gettysburg."

"Now that sounds more like you two. And for the record, you're both wrong. Appomattox wasn't really a battle, but a surrender."

"That's what I told her."

"But it was much closer to the final battle, chronologically speaking. Gettysburg took place two years prior, in the summer of 1863 ... I can't believe you didn't remember that, JP."

"You know I've never been good with dates. So what was the final battle then?"

"It was the Battle of Columbus."

"As in the guy with the boats? The one who thought he landed in India, but still got a holiday in his honor?"

"Now you're just being silly, JP—Columbus, Georgia. It took place a week after Lee's surrender, and the day after Lincoln died. Some people believe the Battle of Palmito Ranch was the last battle, but by that time Johnston had already surrendered to Sherman, and the Confederacy had been dissolved, so history considers Columbus to be the final battle."

Why did Columbus, Georgia seem so familiar to me? "I think I did a story there once, but I can't remember what it was about."

"Was it military related?"

"I'm not sure ... why do you ask that?"

"Because Columbus is where Fort Benning is located."

CHAPTER 71

Columbus, Georgia

He drove along the Chattahoochee River approaching his destination. He passed through the gates, and numerous security checks without a hitch, as he was confident he would. He pulled the van into the two-story, single family home in the Upatoi area, located near the main post entrance. The home looked straight out of Main Street USA, giving no indication that it was inside one of America's largest military bases.

He paused momentarily to reflect on the day's events. He knew the end was coming ... he'd known for years ... but the finality of the moment was still overwhelming. When he received the signal, his whole world had changed, just as they'd planned. His emotions were mixed—on one hand he'd lost a mentor and father figure, but he was also honored to have been trusted with such a key responsibility.

Each event had been building to this moment. The Huddled Masses killings, the response by Whiskey Tax, the symbolism of Sumter, the diversion created by the explosion at Valley Forge, all had cleared the path, but this would be a direct hit on the United States military. One in which the president would be left with no choice but to declare war on citizens of the United States.

He stepped out of the van, and walked to the front door. He ignored the American flag, hanging limply in the sweltering Georgia afternoon. He knocked on the door, and announced, "General Washington Carpet Cleaning."

When there was no answer, he knocked again. The third time he called out Jared's name. When he did, the door swung open, and a giant of a man stood before him. But it wasn't Jared. The man grabbed him by the shirt and pulled him into the house.

***

He clenched the bomber's arm, and swung him against the ropes. He waited for him to rebound in his direction, so he could drop the hammer elbow on him—the crowd would cheer wildly, and he would reward them with a flexed bicep.

But this wasn't a professional wrestling ring, and the bomber just crashed into the hard wall and crumbled to the ground. Disappointing, but it would have to do.

Coldblooded Carter pounced on his prey. He grabbed the man by his ponytail, and lifted him to his feet. He released two right-hand punches to his face, sending him meekly back to the floor.

He shouted for the bomber to get up, but he remained motionless. "You're bleeding on the carpet—I thought you were here to clean it, not color it!?"

"How did you ..."

"How did I figure out that the devil went down to Georgia, and he planned to blow up Fort Benning? I got a call from my friend JP, and he let me know that he thought there might be some carpet bombing going on in the area. I was tired after driving all morning, and coming off a long night, but since I was only an hour away in Atlanta, I figured what the hell. How many times in life do you get to beat the crap out of a terrorist?"

"Where is Jared?"

"You mean the enlisted traitor, who conspired with you in your attempt to blow up the base, and the innocent men and women he claimed to serve with?"

"Where is he?"

"He's upstairs with my girlfriend. Trust me, you got the better end of that deal."

"I have a bomb. You can kill me if you want, but you're too late."

Carter took a seat on the couch, not feeling the urgency. "So I heard. I'm told it's a dirty bomb, powerful enough to take out a ten-mile radius."

"If I was you, I'd make a run for it. This isn't your fight."

Carter put his feet up on the coffee table. "If you were me, you'd be all sorts of awesome, and wouldn't be lying like a beaten lump on the floor. And this is very much my fight, which is now going to be yours."

"Do you have some sort of death wish?"

Carter laughed. "Every time I wish someone dead, it never comes true, so I don't waste my time with that anymore. Wishing and hoping isn't a strategy ... but having the 789th Explosive Ordinance Disposal Company on your side is. I don't know if you've heard of these guys, but they're the best bomb disposal unit in the army, and luckily they're located right here at Benning."

"This isn't just some roadside IED. This device was years in the making."

"I've come to the conclusion that there are two types of people in this world—those who break things, and those who put them back together. I'm a breaker, as in, I break skulls. But those guys outside who are risking their lives, they're fixers, just like you used to be, Kevin."

"That's not my name."

Carter pointed to the seat across from him. "Why don't you take a load off?"

The bomber didn't move, but his emotionless expression had cracked. They were making progress.

"I don't know why you look so worried—if that bomb is as good as you say, then we're gonna get blown to pieces in a few minutes. What could I do to you that's worse than that?"

The bomber cautiously moved to the seat. Carter stared at him—he looked a little different with the longer hair and goatee, but he never forgot a face.

"What was that like, 2004 when you went missing?"

He didn't respond, but he would have been as bad a poker player as he was a terrorist.

"I spent weeks trying to track down leads in Iraq, with my boys JP and Byron. Almost got our asses killed a bunch of times. Most people thought you were nothing but dust and bone at that point, but JP never bought that theory, and forced us to keep digging."

"They tried to kill me, you know."

"Who did?"

"The United States of America."

Kevin Sturges had graduated Harvard Medical School at the top of his class, and had begun a residence at one of the most prestigious hospitals in the world when 9/11 hit. Overtaken by a combination of duty and patriotism, he left to join the military. The army made the young, good-looking doctor from a well-known Boston family the face of the American soldier. As the story went, he left the base by himself one night in 2004, seeking to help a group of soldiers that had been wounded in a firefight. That was the last time he'd been seen or heard from.

"When I was serving at Dawood Military Hospital I saw things—drug use, kickbacks to locals for our medical supplies, which were always running low, and sending soldiers with concussion symptoms and PTSD back into battle. When I brought this to my commander's attention, everything began to change.

"They liked their golden boys to be seen and not heard. And when I spoke louder, I was sent to that illegal war in Iraq as a punishment. I signed up to fight those responsible for taking my friends' lives in 9/11, not that. But to the outside world, I was still the star of their recruiting poster. And when a high-profile American soldier was killed, that football player, they wanted their star doctor to confirm their story that he died from friendly fire.

"It would have taken a first-year med student two minutes to see that there was nothing friendly about this man's death. It was obvious that he'd been executed. And since there was no enemy near his company that day, he had been executed by his own men … murdered. And I refused to go along with their lies.

"I started to receive an even colder shoulder, for doing the right thing, and I got mad. So I contacted a book publisher in the US, and planned to write a tell-all about the murdered soldier, and other horrors and lies I'd witnessed. But word must have gotten out, and the idea that their golden boy would turn on them, when the war-effort had hit its lowest point in popularity, and just in time for the elections, was unacceptable for those in charge. So I was taken out one night in a Jeep, and all I was told is there was a "situation that requires your skill-set." I guess that skill was surviving against all odds in enemy territory."

"Yet you lived to tell about it. Lucky us."

"With the controversy stemming from the previous high-profile 'friendly fire,' they couldn't risk shooting me. So they left me to die. And of course, they painted it so that I did so in the most heroic way, trying to help fallen soldiers.

"I was captured the next morning by Hakim's men, and brought to him. I was the first to diagnose his kidney disease, and over time we built a mutual trust. They treated me with respect, and even offered me a safe return to the Americans. But I chose to stay … the Americans were now my enemy. I became his personal doctor, always on call, and came with him when he returned to the United States. Not even Qwaui knew where he was, but he trusted me."

"Which makes you Dr. Samuel Abdul Mudd. And I hate to break it to ya, but the reason for the hospitality was that you were keeping him alive. Hakim always struck me as a pragmatist, unlike Qwaui, who was a true believer. He wouldn't have sent his doctor to do his dirty work for him, and then take all the credit."

"Great leaders get courageous men to follow them."

Carter shrugged. "Never met the man, but I'm familiar with his work. Specifically how he treated those he had no more use for, like my friend Byron, who ended up paralyzed, and our guide, Milos, who was killed. Or how about that mother in the shopping mall gunned down before Christmas, or that family who was tossed overboard in West Palm. And Tino Fernandez shot on national TV ... okay, Tino probably deserved it, but the others were innocent."

"I might not always agree with the methods, but when fighting the world's most powerful tyrants, it must be done in unconventional ways. The United States is broken—they have turned into all that they fought against in 1776, and Hakim is the one with the courage to bring the revolution. And there are plenty of us willing to fight behind him."

"Sounds like a plan ... at least until you help Uncle Al win the so-called revolution, and then they reward you by declaring you a non-believer, and turn you into the Headless Horseman ... except without the horse."

"He has always respected my beliefs."

"Well, lucky for you, you worship the one God that will be acceptable in this post-revolution world—Hakim."

"The revolution will continue, no matter what happens here."

"So I've been told. Then no harm in telling me who your friend upstairs is ... and your other buddy who was working the guard gate."

"I've run a free private clinic in Columbus this past year out of my apartment. I treat soldiers with PTSD, depression, and general shell shock.

They don't get the proper medical treatment they need, or the proper support. But they're afraid to say anything, thinking they'll be labeled and lose their position. I provide complete privacy."

Carter laughed, which seemed to irritate the doctor. "What's so funny?"

"People like you crack me up—you have all these fancy degrees, yet you don't know anything. I only went to the School of Hard Knocks, but I still know there is no such thing as a perfect society or country. You know why? Because societies are made up of people, and like my Pop used to say, there's more horses asses in the world than there are horses. And the only guarantee is that those in power are gonna take a dump on the peons.

"So when things break, you can either blow it up, or you can try to fix it. And that's the thing about you that's not making any sense to me ... you're a fixer, not a breaker. That's why you became a doctor, it's why you joined the military, and it's the reason you pointed out all that shady stuff that was going on. This bomb thing is just not working for me ... and certainly isn't working for you."

Carter took out his gun, and set it on the coffee table. "There's one bullet in it, so do what you wish. You can take the easy way out and kill yourself. You can kill me, but since I'm your only friend right now, that wouldn't make much sense. Or you can take option three—which is leave it right where it is. Then we can walk out of here and you can peacefully turn yourself in. It's up to you."

"Why would I want to live?"

"Revenge."

"Revenge?"

"My friends JP and Byron think it's hollow, but I believe in it. We all need a dream to get us out of bed in the morning, and sometimes man's dream is to kill the bastard who tried to kill them."

As Dr. Sturges mulled over the offer, Carter made his final pitch, "I promise you that I'll investigate your claims—and if I find you're telling the truth, I will hunt down the people who tried to kill you. I don't care how high on the food chain they are. And then maybe you'll have the pleasure of testifying at their trial. Or even better, maybe you'll win the revenge lottery and they'll end up in the same prison as you."

Sturges picked up the gun, briefly looked at it like it was a magic lantern that held the answers, and set it back down. He surrendered.

Carter raised him to his feet, pulled his arms behind his back, and secured the prisoner.

"You carry handcuffs with you?"

"They're my girlfriend's ... long story."

"They're going to kill me when we walk out there. What I know is too dangerous for them."

"Not with me by your side they won't."

They walked out into the bright afternoon sun. Carter and his prisoner, followed by Mistress Kate and hers. They handed over the prisoners, who were stuffed in the back of a military vehicle, and driven off.

"The explosive has been deactivated," said the leader of the Bomb Disposal Unit. Carter expected no less.

"Can we get a photo?" another member of the group called out.

Carter obliged, as always, before realizing they weren't talking about him. They wanted a shot with Kate.

Carter stood off to the side, enjoying the warmth of the sun beating off his face, and taking in the curious scene before him. His phone rang—he knew it would be that worrywart.

"I thought retirement was supposed to be less dangerous. What's all the commotion about?" JP said.

"Hey—that's my line."

"Role-reversal seems to be the theme of the day."

He looked at Kate, dressed for tonight's show in a leather catsuit, surrounded by happy soldiers, and playfully hitting them with her whip.

Carter smiled wide. "Tell me about it."

EPILOGUE –

REUNITED, & IT FEELS SO GOOD

CHAPTER 72

Rockfield, Connecticut

Memorial Day

I sat on the grassy slope. It was the same place Ethan and I used to sit when my father would take us to watch Little League games before we were old enough to play. It was hard to believe the participants in those games were now in their mid-forties. Time kept marching by, and there was no bigger reminder of that than attending your high school reunion.

I glanced up at the cloudless sky and sniffed the smell of barbecue. Even this reunion-cynic would have to admit that the weekend was perfect. Saturday was an informal gathering, in which the highlight was renting out a small movie theater in New Milford, where we watched old videos of our glory days, including our prom, on the big screen. We even stopped by our old stomping ground, The Natty, and had a ceremonial beer for old time's sake. I think we scared off a few teenagers who were hanging out, and hoping to avoid lame old people like us.

Sunday was the official event at Hastings Inn. It was a dress-up, grown-up night, and ended with words of wisdom from our class adviser, Murray, who toasted: *To the future of the past, as presently constituted.*

And for those who stuck around for the Memorial Day holiday, we held a family picnic today at Lefebvre Park. The park was named after a French general who assisted General Washington during the Revolutionary War, which I think means I've officially come full circle.

I viewed the festivities from my perch. There were people I hadn't seen in years, plus the regulars like Steve Lackety, Herbie, and a very liquored-up Vic Cervino. Rich Tolland was playfully tossing a football around with his cute, chubby kids.

I took special note of Allison Cooper, who had a big smile on her face as she mingled about. Gracie and Chase were at her side, looking lovably bored, as kids their age often do. But it wasn't the same smile I remember. We never fully get back to who we were before the storm hit.

I felt a presence behind me and I spun around—old paranoias die hard. My intuition proved correct, as danger was approaching.

I wasn't going to get up to greet Bobby Maloney, so he was forced to sit on the grass beside me, overdressed for the picnic in his fancy suit.

"I just wanted to thank you for putting our differences aside, and let you know that I'm going to announce my candidacy for First Selectman tomorrow," he delivered his prepared line.

I reached out my hand and we shook. "I look forward to a great competition between us, and may the best man win."

His face tensed. "What's that supposed to mean?"

"I told you I wouldn't stand in your way, Bobby, but I never said I wouldn't run against you."

He looked ill. I had my critics, but there was no way anyone was beating Peter Warner's son in this town, if I ran.

"I had no idea you were even interested in politics … are you a Democrat or a Republican?"

"What are you?"

"I'm a Republican."

"Then I'll be a Democrat. It doesn't really matter—same disease, different doctor."

Part of me felt bad that I'd ruined the remainder of Bobby Maloney's holiday weekend. But the other 99.9% thought it was pretty funny. I had no interest in politics, but I planned to let the possibility of me entering the race linger up until Election Day just to tweak him.

Although, I did have to become a politician in the time following the Valley Forge explosion. The next day, Gwen, Allison, and I were summoned to a secret meeting with some folks who were very high up on the food chain. At that meeting it was explained to us what really happened with Huddled Masses, in case we were confused, and thought we'd witnessed something else. The bottom line was, there was no way that the American citizens were to ever know that the world's most notorious terrorist leader was hiding out right under their noses, and cleaning their carpets.

As an obsessive seeker of the truth, this was a concession I thought I'd never make. But I guess making compromises that were once unfathomable was part of growing up. Besides, I had more people to worry about these days than just me, and I couldn't risk putting any of the people I care about in danger.

They did agree to my one demand, which made my silence slightly more palatable, and in return, they knew the threat of them revoking our deal ensured my silence.

The "on the record" story, for what it's worth, was that Hakim was killed in an airstrike on the Pakistani/Afghan border. They credited information discovered in the Syrian bunker in finding the elusive terrorist leader.

His key followers, Liam Scott and Manny Ontiveros—the West Palm Pirates—found their end on the bottom of Charleston Harbor. While they were being escorted back to shore from Fort Sumter, they somehow were able to go overboard, and commit suicide.

While the means might be sketchy, the ends were that Huddled Masses was no more, and America could take a deep breath of relief. And for all intents and purposes, Al Muttahedah was done. Sure, there were still many followers and sympathizers out there, but without the leadership of Hakim or Qwaui, the ship was rudderless, and was now nothing but salvage. In the end, Hakim's chemical attack turned out to be an epic fail, and his final battle was a devastating loss. He went out with a whimper, but if he really knew his history, he could have predicted such—it was the Roman generals, long before General Washington, who coined the phrase *all glory is fleeting*.

And he didn't even get any credit for the creation of Huddled Masses, and their fifteen minutes of infamy. History would record its mastermind, as it often does, as being someone who couldn't refute the claims. And in this case it was a disgruntled reporter, Nora Reign, who was declared dead the last week of April.

It was a smart attempt by her to put herself into a diabetic coma by not taking her insulin, as it forced her out of prison circulation, where her murder was a certainty, and into a situation where she was under heavy scrutiny. She was playing the odds, by limiting the number of her potential killers, but in the end she was right, she wouldn't make it to that trial. She knew too much. I hoped for Dr. Kevin Sturges' sake that he was working on similar survival plans.

I took another look at the picnic area, and I noticed the most gorgeous creature I'd ever seen heading in my direction. Now the day was officially perfect.

CHAPTER 73

The camera hanging around Gwen's neck bounced as she walked briskly toward me. It reminded me of a similar moment at the Rockfield Fair last year, but the circumstances were much different this time.

She wore her "Class of" T-shirt with shorts, and was rocking her Jackie O sunglasses. Upon reaching the bottom of the slope, she put her camera to her eye and aimed it up in my direction. "I need a shot for the reunion yearbook ... you won Class Loner."

I couldn't hold back my smile. She knew me too well—my comfort zone was observing life from a distance, and telling its story.

She climbed up next to me and took a seat. She draped her arm around my shoulders. "That wasn't so bad now, was it?"

"I actually had an enjoyable time."

"That's good to hear, because we just voted you head of the committee for twenty-five year reunion."

"Twenty-five years? I'm just trying to get through the next one unscathed."

I thought back to one year ago today, when I was stuck in traffic on the Long Island Expressway with Lauren Bowden, returning from a weekend in the Hamptons. So much had happened since then that it almost deserved its own reunion.

We stared out at the waning festivities. "We've come a long way since high school, huh?" Gwen said.

"Yeah, about twenty years."

"Thanks, Mr. Literal. I've had at least ten people tell me this weekend that I haven't changed at all. Haven't I changed?"

"This is a trick question, isn't it? I'm not answering without my lawyer present."

"I know they mean it as a compliment, but how sad would it be if I really hadn't changed at all in twenty years?"

"We have changed, we just haven't aged," I said with a grin.

"Well, for the record, I like what we've evolved into. But also that the core things I love about you have remained untouched."

It was perfectly said, and I should have just left it as is, but I couldn't, "I like touching your core things."

She smiled, but I could tell she was lost in her own thoughts. "What do you notice about everyone here but us, JP?"

"That none of them have recently stopped a potential civil war, or shut down an international terrorist organization?"

"Since Allison played as big a role in that as we did, that would be a no. The correct answer is—we're the only couple here without kids."

"We do have a very fertile class. Erica Marks has a seventeen-year-old. They just went looking at colleges last weekend. How is that even possible?"

"Can you imagine being parents when we were like twenty? We couldn't even take care of ourselves back then."

She caught herself, and began backtracking, "I didn't mean it to sound like we're ready now ... or implying ... I was just making an observation."

"I know what you meant. And if that time ever comes for us, we'll know."

"The universe will tell us, right?"

I smiled devilishly. "You know, we could go home and practice just in case the universe calls."

"I read somewhere that you have to set roots before you sprinkle seeds."

"Fortune cookie?"

"I think it means that it's about time you get serious about buying that farm. That is, if you really plan on setting some roots here."

"I don't want to buy a farm."

"So it was all talk then?"

"Not exactly—I want *us* to buy a farm."

She reached over and gave me a deep kiss. I took that as a yes, or at least a definite maybe. "How about we go say goodbye to the gang, and then go home and start practicing?"

"You mean ..."

"Exactly—we need to practice raising chickens, chopping wheat, and whatever else they do on a farm."

She stood, and pulled me to my feet. For the first time in a long time it wasn't necessary. My lungs were back to full capacity, the concussion symptoms hadn't returned, and the only thing not back to full strength was my knee, but it was on its way. Things were looking up.

Gwen took a couple of steps down the slope and her phone rang. When she answered it, her face turned serious. "We'll be right there," she said.

She looked back at me with urgency. "JP—it's your parents."

CHAPTER 74

Gwen had no answers to my many questions as she drove the *Gazette* van to my parents' house. I felt a bad case of déjà vu coming on.

The first thing I noticed upon arriving, was that there were no ambulances or any type of emergency vehicles. When we went inside, my mother and father were sitting on the couch in the living room.

"Oh, good, you're here," My father said. "Come sit down, we have something to tell you."

Here it comes. The life-changing news—my father's prostate cancer had returned, and spread. Or there was something wrong with my mother. My stomach gripped.

I wasn't going to sit down. That's what they always say in the movies— sit down for the bad news—I was going to stand.

My mother began, "As you know, when we were on vacation, we drove down to see Byron and Tonya in Charleston. Well, we stayed overnight, and decided to take a day trip to Savannah the next day, which is only about a two-hour drive. I was excited to see all the history there, but there was so much more. We absolutely fell in love with the place."

"We loved it so much we bought a house there," my father added.

"You bought a house? That's what was so urgent?" I said. "So nobody's dying or anything like that?"

"We're going to live, but where we're going to be living is what we wanted to discuss with you."

"We're in the process of selling our house here, and we are going to move to Savannah in November, after I fulfill my duties as first selectman."

I felt like I'd been hit by a rocket ship. "You can't move."

"Not only can we, but we are," my mother replied, strangely smiling at this terrible development.

"But you've lived here for over forty years. How can you just pick up and leave like that?"

My mother turned to my father. "I told you we needed to break it to him slower. I know my children, and JP does not do well with change."

"I can't believe you would just sell this place to a stranger. To move to some dangerous place," I continued. "Savannah's in the same state as Fort Benning, where that lunatic tried to blow up the base. And not that far from Fort Sumter ... it could have been you held hostage there that night."

My mother just grinned at me. "Oh, JP, your beauty is that you don't even recognize the irony of your words. And would this danger be anything like having our property burned to the ground?"

She had a point, and to be honest, any place away from me was likely safer.

"Listen, JP," my mother said, in her consoling voice. "Your return here, and all that's gone on this past year, have shown us how important it is to live life. Your father and I had gotten to the point that we were documenting history more than making it. We realized it's time for our next adventure."

"After a politician retires, there's only one more big election left, so we want to make the most of our time," my father put it more succinctly.

"We wouldn't feel good about this if things weren't in order here. But you two have each other now. And I have full confidence in Ethan and Pam taking over the historical society—Pam has been helping me there for so long, she can probably run the place better than I can, anyway."

"And it's not like we won't be back to visit the grandchildren at every opportunity," my father added.

"And as far as selling to a stranger, we're hoping it doesn't come to that, JP."

"That's why we brought you over here. We wanted to offer you the first chance to buy the place before we put it on the market."

I looked to Gwen, who was grinning like a Cheshire cat. "You knew about this, didn't you?"

"We're running an interview with your father in tomorrow's *Gazette*, in which he discusses their plans for retirement—they wanted to tell you before you learned it from the press."

I turned back to my parents. "I knew you liked her better than me."

"Regardless of our feelings about Gwen, you're the one we're offering first dibs to," my mother said.

I turned back to Gwen. "If you sell it to both of us, then we have a deal."

When Gwen gave her approval, after I agreed to her numerous conditions, hugs abounded, and a victory bottle of champagne was uncorked.

As dusk descended on the sun-soaked Memorial Day Weekend, I stepped outside, not sure what just happened. I was setting roots, while my parents were pulling theirs up? As Gwen and I walked to the colonial, arm in arm, I stopped and took a sweeping look around the yard, taking special note of that old oak tree we used to climb. It felt like it was for the last time, which was strange, since I'd just made a long-term commitment to the place.

"Are you sure about this, Gwen? Living together is a big step."

"Who said we're going to live together?"

"When two people buy a home, that's usually how it works."

"There's two houses, so I figure I'll just pick the one I like better, and then you can go live in the other one," she said as we stepped inside the colonial, and made our way up to the bedroom. "And you're the one who should have doubts, not me—living with the woman who always runs toward the storm might not be good for your health."

"I think the storm clouds are starting to subside. You'll be bored with me before you know it."

We stopped at the edge of the bed, and jaws fell open. "Why do I think that will never be the case?" Gwen commented.

On the bed was a dress. The one that Gwen wore last year on New Year's Eve, and had left at the brownstone. Until Jovana ran off with it.

There was a note attached: *I apologize for taking so long to return this, I've been traveling quite extensively this past month. Hopefully you won't need me to save your asses anytime soon.*

We just looked at each other—ghosts do come back to life. I had no idea how she got out of there before it blew, and probably never would. I was just glad the avenging angel was alive, and that she was on our side.

I went to the window and looked out over the backyard, watching as the setting sun cast its glow behind the trees. It looked different to me, and not just because of the fire damage. And when I felt Gwen's arms wrap around me, I understood why. I no longer saw the past; for the first time in a long time I was looking at the future.

ACKNOWLEDGMENTS

Thanks to another great editing job by Charlotte Brown. With Huddled Masses being a second in a series, it doubled her challenge - not just having to maintain consistency to the beginning of the book, but all the way back to the first book. And because of her work Huddled Masses was able to make a seamless transition from Officer Jones. Thanks also to Damon of Damonza for a terrific, professional cover on short notice, Curt Ciccone for again performing his formatting magic, and to all those who helped with proofreading, especially Sandra Simpson, the book is so much better because of you - it's not an easy job trying to hunt down my many mistakes. As for a couple topics in the book, O'Halloran Advertising taught me everything I know about Yellow Pages advertising - I told them I'd find a way to work it into a novel one day! And to all those brave journalists who have risked their lives to cover the civil war in Syria. By reading your courageous tales, it was the best research an author could have, without actually being there.

KEEP IN TOUCH WITH DEREK

website: www.derekciccone.com

Facebook: Derek Ciccone Book Club

Twitter: @DCicconebooks

Email: Derekbkclb@yahoo.com